MY ONCE
IN A LIFETIME

A YORK BEACH NOVEL

NICOLE VIDAL

COPYRIGHT

TABLE OF CONTENTS

KEEP IN TOUCH WITH NV

Visit me on Social Media or online to learn about my newest releases:

Facebook (http://fb.me/NicoleVidalAuthor)

Instagram (http://instragram.com/nicolevidal_author)

My website (www.nicolevidal.com)

Goodreads (https://bit.ly/NVGoodreads)

Amazon (https://amzn.to/2XCLSlR)

Pinterest (http://pinterest.com/NicoleVidal_Author)

NORAH

Lying here alone after another night of sheet-tangling, body-bending, orgasm-coma-inducing sex, I wonder if I'm wrong.

Everyone around me has found their happily ever after. The first to fall was my brother, Joseph. He and his childhood sweetheart, Genevieve, reconnected after ten years apart. Now they have a son together. Next was Gen's adopted sister, Kelsey. She met Captain Ramirez at Joseph's wedding. They got hitched almost two years ago. My sister, Kelly, also found her forever in Hollywood's Sexist Man Alive. Nicholas and Kelly got married in Aspen about six months ago. Even our beach-cottage besties and Genevieve's siblings, Maggie and Peter, have found happiness. I'm the last one standing requiring a plus-one rather than a couple invitation.

Maybe I do want a man in my bed when I wake each day. Perhaps it isn't this man. He was clear on his intentions—just sex. Incredible sex. He makes my body hum like no one else. In fact, I haven't been with anyone else since we met at Kelsey's wedding. We knew each other before that, but that was the first time we were together. I flirt with other men when the opportunity presents itself, but only the memory of his big, calloused hands caressing my skin makes my core throb. But as for a relationship, I'm not the woman to change his mind. Besides, I have a corporate partnership on the horizon. I don't need a man to get it. A mutually beneficial sexual relationship is fine with me. *Right! Right?*

Padding to the kitchen, I find a note near my coffee maker set to brew.

N,

> *Didn't want to wake you. See you soon.*
>
> *J—*

He may want just sex, but on occasion, like this note or making coffee for me when he stays, his actions scream that he's capable of building a life with. Instead of dwelling on my unsettled feelings—feelings I shouldn't acknowledge, feelings I promised myself and Jacob I wouldn't have—I start the coffee and pull out my files and get to work.

As an accountant, I crave order and predictability. Until recently, the Moretti Family Brands account has been in my boss's hands. With my partnership looming, he assigned it to me. This file has been toying with me for months. I have taken it home with me more than I care to admit. Well, I have access to the server, so I print what I need and shred it when I'm done. Fixing this error would make a vote unnecessary. I would be a shoo-in.

There's a discrepancy, but I haven't been able to find it, despite hours of searching. After a refill of my coffee, I follow the money from a different angle. The company is a conglomerate comprising of six smaller companies, each owned by a different family member. Instead of taking the balance sheets as one, I pick each company apart line by line.

The first two held by the youngest sons balance and are error free. Moving on, the daughter's statement is off by minute amounts each quarter. Overall, it could be human error. The total amount is less than ten thousand dollars a year. Considering the company is worth a few billion, it's chump change. My phone pulls me out of work mode.

Joseph: Are you free tonight?

Me: Yes. Why?

My phone rings.

"Hey. Jackson is sick, and I need a date," my brother states.

"What's wrong with my nephew?"

"He's teething and has a sky-high fever. Gen doesn't want to leave him with Mrs. Jones."

"What time and what should I wear?"

"You're the best sister ever. I'll pick you up at three. Business attire will be fine."

After hanging up, I work a few more hours before dressing in a navy sheath dress and peep-toe heels.

Joseph and I arrive at the posh hotel hosting his work event just as cocktail hour begins. He said he needed a date, but it's for show. I'll be on my own for the entire evening. Believe me, it isn't a hardship. My brother works for the regional soccer team in marketing. The guest list reads like a who's who of athletes and celebrity superfans, like Jack Nicholson is with the Lakers. It doesn't take long before someone approaches me. He's tall and thin with glasses. The glasses aren't necessarily a turnoff; they just didn't look good on him.

"Can I buy you a drink?"

"It's open bar."

He laughs. "Have a nice night," he replies before walking away.

I guess my honesty was a bit too much. Taking a sip of my pinot, I turn, catching Joseph's eye. He nods and continues schmoozing the whale he's talking to. Each year my brother works this party to gain sponsors for the club. He's exceptional at this aspect of his job. He has secured an increasing number of sponsors and money each year since he took this job.

A tall, built, blond man steps beside me. He may even be a player on the team. I'm a horrible sister; I don't have any idea who is on the team's roster. I attend maybe one game a season, and it's typically when my sister-in-law can't.

"Hello," he says. His accent is tantalizing.

"Hello. I'm Norah. Pleasure to meet you…?"

"Silvio." I could have simply checked his name tag, but asking seemed more polite.

"What do you say we get some air?"

"I don't sleep with married women," Silvio replies curtly.

"I'm not married." I flash my left hand, showing my bare ring finger.

"Didn't you arrive with him, and isn't your last name the same as his?"

"Yes, but that doesn't make me his wife. It makes me his sister."

"My apologies. You were saying?"

I know in this moment, this man has no place in my bed or my life. His first mistake was not listening. I said "air" not "out of here." His second was assuming I'm a groupie. However, I listen to him drone on about his training regime and game schedule for the upcoming season until Joseph approaches.

"Are you ready, Nor?"

I loop my arm around his. "Absolutely." *Thanks for the save, big brother.*

On the ride home, Joseph talks animatedly about the sponsors he nabbed tonight and how it'll impact his year with the club. I'm only half listening. He loves his career, and that's wonderful, but the numbers from earlier today are still ticking in my head.

As soon as I'm home, I step out of my shoes, retreat into my office, and work through the lines systematically. When I reach the oldest son and the parents' books, I find the discrepancies. I go back to the previous year and run the same line by line check.

Last year, the parents and the oldest child's companies were squeaky clean, but the youngest three were not. I keep digging into the wee hours of the morning and notate the errors that I find. The rotating cycle has been occurring for at least the last eight years. How could Stan, my boss, miss this? It took me nearly six months to crack the errors. Stan clearly hasn't been paying attention. Near ten the next morning, I wake with paper stuck to my face at my desk.

JACOB

Collapsing in my chair, I down a lukewarm cup of coffee. It was hot when I poured it earlier this morning. There are a few clients requiring attention and an assignment to mete out. Tank, my rottweiler, lazily lifts his head as I reenter my office. I've raised him from a puppy. He's a great companion and guard dog. He won't let anyone near my home or its occupants. There's a soft knock on my office door.

"Come in."

"You wanted to see me, sir?" Callen, my newest team member, enters my office.

"Morning. Have a seat."

Callen nods, sitting rigidly across from me. He just finished eight years in the marines. He's tall and thin—too thin in my opinion—but deadly with a sniper rifle. He's also an expert in hand-to-hand combat.

"I have an assignment for you." I hand him the file. "Miss Goldberg needs personal protection on the set of her newest movie in New Orleans. The assignment is longer than most, spanning two months. You can opt to stay for the entire time frame or swap out midway with Nolan. Please study, learn, and examine this file. Then create a safety plan for the client. I want it ready for review by end of day tomorrow."

"Anything else, sir?"

"No."

Callen leaves with the file under his arm. This will be his third assignment, but the longest. Quite frankly, my concern is his ability to manage a Hollywood starlet, not her security. Hollywood A-listers are notoriously difficult with following protocol. However, I would have that concern with most of my male staff. Miss Goldberg is attractive and wealthy. I wouldn't put it past her, or any actress, to fake attraction to break security parameters. With expedience, I handle the other issues before my next intake meeting.

"Mr. Blackthorne, your client has arrived."

"Thank you, Gemma. Give me five and bring her in."

"Yes, Mr. Blackthorne."

"Jacob is fine, Gemma."

"Yes, sir."

Gemma is the daughter of my former commanding officer. She's in her early twenties. Her teen years were difficult, according to her father. I hired her as my office assistant soon after I opened the doors. So far, having structure working for me has been monumental. No trouble in the last four years, except she refuses to call me anything but Mr. Blackthorne or sir.

I formed Blackthorne Security four years ago in coastal Maryland. I have over one hundred acres, which includes my home, an office, a training facility, a bunkhouse, and an indoor shooting range. Also, just a short drive away, I have an office in town.

After my meeting with Miss Forrester and her parents, I head home for the day. There really isn't a weekend for this type of work. Hurling my bag onto the kitchen island, I change and hit the gym for a few hours. Entering the facility, I find Nolan and Maia sparring in the ring. Despite her diminutive stature in comparison to Nolan's, Maia is a badass and can hold her own. If I could find two more woman like her to add to my team, I would, even considering the demons she fought to get where she is.

A grueling weight session and a long run later, I absorb the heat from my huge shower. When I found this property, it needed major rehab. As I built Blackthorne during the day, I refurbished this home at night. It took nearly two years, but I transformed this into a comfortable, modern farmhouse with a chef's kitchen and spa-worthy bathrooms.

Generally, when I'm home, it isn't abject silence. Unfortunately, this weekend it is. It's times like this that I loathe the space my home provides. I would never admit to it, but I miss having Connor living here. I don't begrudge him his decision to move out, and it was my choice to build the bunkhouse, but it wasn't so lonely here. Nolan is leaving this evening to travel to his assignment. Maia will join me tomorrow afternoon. She's returning to Kelly Barnett's detail to relieve Christoph. After a stalker and her marriage to Nicholas Ellis Barnett, Hollywood's Sexist Man Alive, my team escorts her to and from her store and special events. The remainder of the staff have assignments elsewhere.

I'm travelling to Maine to meet with the Barnetts for a quarterly review and with the Morgans for the first review of their security plan. Mr. Barnett's sister, Noelle, recently married New York's most eligible bachelor, Cash Morgan. I've been working with the Barnetts for over a year. The Morgans are a newer client. We provided personal security and handled a few events for Mrs. Morgan. Once they moved out of New York City to be near her brother, they hired Blackthorne to secure their new home.

When I first formed Blackthorne, I met each client and travelled for each job. I overextended and exhausted myself. After the first year, with three solid team members, I scaled back my travel. I only travel when necessary or requested by my client. Both the Barnetts and the Morgans are high-profile clients who request discretion, so I go to them. I also consider them friends. The Barnetts are leaving midweek to travel for a film, so the timing is ideal. Maia will stay at the house in York Beach for Mabel, their surrogate mother/housekeeper, while they're gone.

To speed time along, I flop onto my bed, hoping sleep will claim my brain. The chance of that is unlikely. I haven't slept well since I returned from my last deployment. That isn't true. I only sleep well with *her*— another fact I'll never admit out loud. I don't deserve to be happy again.

NORAH

My firm, Quinn Sterling, is a pillar of the accounting world. We have been in business for the last one hundred years. Currently, the firm is run by Robert Quinn and Stanley Sterling. I started here as in intern in college and, upon graduation, earned a job as an associate. That was almost six years ago, and I'm poised to become a partner. I have worked my ass off to get to this point in my career.

It's quiet this early in the morning. Settling into my chair, I pull together my notes and the Moretti files for my meeting with my immediate boss, Stanley Sterling. He has been my supervisor from my first day.

"Good morning, Norah. What is so urgent?"

"Stan, thank you for meeting me this morning. I'll get right to it. Over the last six months, I have been working with the Moretti file. I kept finding small discrepancies, but I couldn't pinpoint the origin of the error. Over the weekend, I finally cracked it." I continue explaining the rotating cycle the family is using to siphon money out of their business and how the malfeasance goes back at least eight years.

Stan's reaction to my words is not what I expected. He shifts in his chair, leans forward, and taps his pen on the desk calendar furiously.

"Thank you for bringing this to my attention. I'll take the file and look into it personally."

"Excuse me? You're taking the file? It was just assigned to me for the partnership review board."

"Yes. Do you have any other copies of this information elsewhere?"

"No. I follow protocol. Every copy shredded and properly disposed of both here and at home."

"I'm sorry, Norah. This is the way it has to be." Stan collects the stack on his desk, setting it on the credenza behind him.

Normally, I know how to comport myself in any situation. Right now, I'm floored. "I have worked with this firm for almost six years. You know my work is stellar. Otherwise, I wouldn't be on the cusp of getting my name on the door. What am I supposed to do now?"

"Norah, I suggest you go back to your office and work with your other clients." I rise from the chair, bile in my throat and more harsh words ready to spill off my tongue. Then I see it—a glimmer of fear in his eyes. It was brief, but it was there.

"Thank you, Mr. Sterling." I excuse myself from his office and plod down the hall to mine. I make a hearty salary and invest well. I'm accustomed to a few luxuries in life: expensive lingerie, red-soled shoes, and my luxury car. Louboutins don't make noise on carpet, but if they did, mine would be making a racket. Once in my office, I lock the door and turn on the privacy shield.

I'm at a loss. The upheaval that meeting caused pushes me to the edge. It's my job to find those types of errors. It's why Stan gave me the file in the first place. Isn't it? Maybe it was a test to gauge my ethics.

I login to my computer and select the client file area of the secured server and input my password. Access denied. I try again. Access denied. Once more and I'm in. I search the database. The Moretti file is gone from the company server. Maybe it was a test. But it was there on Saturday when I accessed it. Stumped, I shift over to my inbox. While I sift through today's drivel, my mind works on why the file is suddenly missing.

Near four, I pack up to head home. As I approach my car in the garage, there are two men leaning against it. I stop before getting too close. I'm standing in the middle of the driving lane at least five feet from them.

"Excuse me, please get off my car," I announce more confidently than I feel. My partnership may have crumbled into dust this morning and likely can't be resurrected. Now my Q60 needs a detail to buff his fingerprints off the hood. I don't feel like adding more tasks to my week.

"My apologies. We're looking for Norah Cavallaro."

I attempt and likely fail to conceal my concern. I can protect myself, but that doesn't mean I'm not scared. I can't lie about who I am at this point. "What can I help you with, sir?"

"You need to keep your nose out of our family business," the tall, lanky one in the navy suit states, walking toward me.

"Who are you?" At heart I'm an investigator, a detective. The puzzles, finding errors, and fixing them—it's like crack to me. To do it, I need as much information as I can get my hands on.

"I'm Sid, and he's my brother, Carlo. We work for Sergio Moretti."

"I see. Well, I don't have anything to do with your family business. If you'll excuse me."

As I step closer to the driver side of my car, Carlo blocks my progress. Carlo is short and burly. I could outrun him, even with these sky-high beauties on my feet.

"Miss Cavallaro, there will be no other warnings. Avoid our family business or there will be dire consequences."

"Please move out of my way. I have nothing to say to you." I step to the right as Carlo moves left. Sid moves in on my left. Once again, I ask politely and move to the right. This time Carlo grabs my left forearm. Without a second thought, I twist out of his grip and shove him. Hustling, I throw open my car door and lock myself inside. I immediately call security for the building.

"This is Norah Cavallaro of Quinn Sterling. There are two men harassing me. I'm parked on level two, spot forty-two."

"My partner headed your way about a minute ago when we saw the feed," the security officer replies. Both men stand in front of my car, daring me to accelerate. The moment security rounds the corner, they scatter.

"Miss, are you hurt?" an overweight, middle-aged security guard named Roberts asks as I roll down my window.

"No, but the shorter one is."

After a recap of the events, he hands me his card with a case number on the back. "We'll pull the footage and forward it to the police department. Please reach out to Boston PD in the morning and give them this number. They may want a statement from you, especially since you defended yourself."

"Thank you." As I roll up my window, I let out a cathartic deep breath. I consider returning to my office for more files to work from home but decide against it. Nearly two hours later due to insane traffic, I park in my garage.

You would think my run-in with Sid and Carlo would persuade me to stop digging. Not even a little. I need to prove my lack of involvement regarding the cooked books to get the partnership I earned. I strip off my work clothes, don some yoga pants and a tank, and get to work.

JACOB

Maia and I arrive in York Beach late afternoon. She's walking the beach while I prepare for my meetings on the balcony. I consider reaching out to Norah but decide against it. Normally, we get together when I handle an event she attends. Besides, I was just with her on Thursday. Connor calls her "Escape." She may be. When I'm with her, I feel free from the demons that inhabit my brain, flashbacks lessen, and I actually sleep. She also disarms me without trying. Content with my work, I change and hit the gym. More than an hour later after showering, I meander through the quaint village in search of some dinner. After a delicious dinner from the inn and an attempt at watching some television, I try to let sleep claim me. I toss and turn for a bit before settling in.

"Hurry, he doesn't have much time," echoes in my head. I can see the scene of the mortar attack as if I were still standing in the midst of it. Michelson is dragging Adams toward me, and two other unit mates are taking up defensive positions so we can load Adams into the Humvee. When I turn to motion our mates in—

I bolt up on the bed and calibrate to my surroundings. Sweat beads on my forehead, and my hands are numb from clenching them into fists. The flashbacks get worse as the anniversary nears. While almost another year has passed, Adams, Carter, and Jones will always be remembered for their actions on that fateful day. Connor and I make sure of it. We're alive because of them.

As the sun rises, I finish a long run along the beach and around the quaint village. This area is like Crescent Bay where I live. After showering, I walk next door to the Perk, a coffee shop, for breakfast. As I stand in line, I hear someone call my name. Other than my clients, I don't know that many people in this area.

"Good morning, Jacob."

"Hi, Kelsey. How are you?" I don't dare say it, but Kelsey looks about four months pregnant. The first time I was with Norah was after Kelsey and William's wedding almost two years ago. Our first time set fire to my hotel room, and I haven't looked elsewhere. No other woman will ever come close.

"I'm well, and you?"

"Pretty good too."

"What can I get for you?"

After receiving my order, I head to the Barnetts' for my first meeting of the day. When I pull into a spot near the front door, Maia is escorting Kelly to the car for work.

"Good morning, Jacob." Kelly steps off the large porch.

"Hi, Kelly. Good to see you."

"Nicholas is in the office."

"Thank you. Have a wonderful day."

Maia nods as she closes the door for Kelly. At first, Kelly was reluctant to have personal security. Nicholas hired me when mysterious packages started arriving and there were break-ins at his home in California and Colorado. With Captain Ramirez's help, we determined she had a stalker. The measures in place seem to have decreased the photographers outside her shop. Part of today's discussion is to reduce her coverage slowly and see how the press reacts. The only drawback I see is when her stalker gets out of jail, we'll need to increase it again despite the restraining orders that will likely be in place.

Like with every quarterly review with Nicholas, we cover the strengths and weaknesses in Kelly's security as well as his. We discuss the house security as well as Mabel, his surrogate mother. She has been spending less and less time at the house since Nicholas and Kelly's marriage. Rather than living here, she has an apartment just outside town. Nicholas and I decide that discontinuing her security detail, unless she's at his home, is the best course.

After wrapping up with Nicholas, I drive a few houses over to meet with the Morgans. Noelle Morgan is Nicholas's sister. She and her husband, Cash, moved into this home about five months ago. We set up the security system and will assist with a few high-profile events throughout the year.

"Cash, good to see you."

"Good morning, Jacob. Noelle will be right down. Water?"

"Thanks." I take the water and follow him onto the massive, covered deck. A moment later, Noelle joins us.

"Morning, Noelle. How are you?"

"Hi, Jacob. I'm well. Thank you."

There must be something in the water here. While I wasn't sure about Kelsey, Noelle is pregnant, which is even more apparent considering Cash's response to her entering the room. He stands, moves to her side, and guides her into the chair. As we discuss the security measures in place and the events they plan to attend, my phone vibrates in my pocket.

"Could you excuse me a moment?" I pull out my phone, and a text makes my blood run cold.

Norah: I NEED HELP

Me: Where are you?

I wait only a fraction of a second before calling Blaine, my private investigator, purveyor of information, and white-hat hacker.

"I need you to locate a phone, right now!" I rattle off her number and wait impatiently as I hear him tapping away.

"The phone is pinging at 1451 Watercliff Terrace—"

"Thanks." I hurry back to Cash and Noelle. "I'm sorry, I need to cut this short. There's an emergency with a client."

I run to my car and speed down the driveway. As I hit the road, I dial Captain Ramirez's cell phone.

"Good morning, Captain Ramirez speaking."

"Captain, Jacob Blackthorne. I just received a distressed text from Norah Cavallaro, and I'm heading to her townhouse. I wanted to keep you advised."

"I'll meet you there." Technically, I have no authority here, but Captain Ramirez and I have an understanding when I work in his city. He's aware of Blackthorne Security's presence, and we contact him if anything goes awry.

When I arrive at Norah's, the front door is breached, the wood split into pieces. Despite my urgency, I clear my way around her townhouse, calling out for her. The pillows of her couch are strewn on the floor, the cushion of her chair slashed, and the TV tipped forward. The dining room hutch doors are wide open. Every cabinet in the kitchen is open, food litters the floor, a few dishes are broken, and the door to the dishwasher is lying on the tile floor. She hasn't answered me. The last time my heart raced this fast was…. I push that thought away and climb the staircase. When I reach the top, I find Norah lying on the plush carpet. She's motionless and pale. As difficult as it is, I check her pulse. It's weak but steady. I clear her bedroom and office, both trashed more so than the main living space.

"Jacob!" Captain Ramirez calls out.

"Up here. All clear." I bend to check on Norah again. No change. I attempt to wake her but fail.

Captain crests the stairs, assessing the situation. "Take her to York Hospital. I'll call it in for you. Ask for Willa Reynolds when you arrive."

"We should keep a lid on this until we know what's going on."

He nods as I lift Norah into my arms and carry her downstairs. Despite jostling her, Norah hasn't made a sound. Regardless of the circumstances, she feels as if she belongs cradled in my arms. I secure her into the passenger seat of my rental. As I drive, I keep my fingertips on the pulse point of her delicate wrist.

I screech to a halt in the emergency bay and hurry around the car. When the sliding doors open, a tall, dark-haired woman with big blue eyes greets me.

"Mr. Blackthorne?"

I nod.

"Right this way."

NORAH

My throat is dry. My heading is pounding like a jackhammer. I feel someone rubbing circles on my hand. When I attempt to sit up, I feel dizzy.

"Easy, beautiful. Just rest. I'm staying right here."

I know that deep voice. My mind is too fuzzy to place it. Slumber takes over again.

I feel weight on my thigh. Blinking a few times, I turn my head to the right. My reward is a nondescript brown door. Moving slowly back to center, my chest tightens. Even now in sleep, he's gorgeous—chiseled jaw, cleft chin, one dimple in his right cheek, and a smile that makes my heart skip beats. I'm acutely aware of his no-relationship mantra, but that doesn't mean I wouldn't want him in my bed each morning or more if he were to change his mind.

I extend my hand as far as the IV will allow, lifting my fingers to graze his chin. After a few passes, his cobalt eyes fly open.

"Hi," I murmur.

"Hi, gorgeous. How are you feeling?" His voice cracks as he asks.

"Not great. Thank you for coming."

"Always."

"What time is it?"

"Near four," he replies after glancing at the wall clock.

"What did they give me?" I absently rub the injection point on my neck.

"Ketamine. You should call your nurse."

I push the button and wait for someone to enter my room.

"I need you to tell me everything but not until we leave here," Jacob says.

I nod as a beautiful nurse enters my room.

"Hi, I'm Willa. How are you feeling?"

"I'm thirsty, a bit dizzy, and my right hand is numb."

"Overall, those side effects are expected. We gave you naloxone to counteract the ketamine in your system. As long as you aren't alone, you can go home in the next hour or so."

"I'll take care of her," Jacob volunteers, which surprises me a bit. I know where we stand; he doesn't have to do any of this. Yet he came for me.

"I'll have the doctor check you again so you can leave," the nurse informs me before heading toward the door.

"Thank you," I sigh, resting my head on the pillow.

"Is Gen's cottage empty?" Jacob asks.

Gen is my sister-in-law who now owns her grandparents' beach cottage a few houses away from where she lives with my brother and nephews. "Probably, but she'll be worried the second I ask though. It's not far from my townhouse. How bad is it?"

"Fair point. Trashed. I didn't really examine anything. I was more worried about you." My chest constricts at his words, but I refuse to acknowledge them. "Will you be comfortable in my hotel at least for tonight?"

I nod. Jacob pulls out his phone and texts someone, presumably William.

After the doctor checks me out again, he indicates I can dress to go home. I shift my legs over the edge of the bed and push to stand. Thankfully, Jacob is right there to catch me.

"Let me help you."

"I can do it myself." I tug at the strings holding the gown together and wobble a bit. Jacob grips my hips, fingers digging into my flesh. A memory of another time and place with him flickers in my mind. *Focus!*

Lifting my chin slightly, I look into his eyes.

"Norah, I have caressed every inch of your gorgeous body with my hands and mouth. Let me help you."

I sigh deeply and turn slowly so he can untie the gown. The brush of his fingers on my back sends spikes of heat through me. When I look through the pile of clothes, I don't find my bra or tank top.

"They had to cut it off."

I nod, grab my pants, and pull them on before turning to face him again, topless.

Before I can ask, Jacob tugs one of his shirts overhead, handing it to me. Pulling it on, I knot it on the side. Wearing his shirt is a level of torture I don't deserve right now. A look must cross my features.

"I'll be fine." Jacob mumbles.

I don't plan on correcting his assumption that my thoughts are about his comfort with him.

If only that were what I was thinking about. Willa returns with my discharge instructions, paperwork, and a wheelchair.

"Thank you for your help," Jacob addresses Willa as she wheels me out.

"You're welcome. When Captain Ramirez calls, it's important."

Jacob extends his hand to me as I rise from the chair. I hesitate before sliding my hand in his.

After settling into the passenger seat of his car, I buckle up. Jacob pulls away from the curb without a word, but he takes my left hand in his. Try as I might, I can't ignore the tingles flying up my arm as I try to reconcile the disconnect between Jacob, my unmatched booty call, and this tender, caring, protector version of Jacob.

"Can I have your phone?" I request.

"Why?"

"I'm starving."

"I'll order food when we get to the hotel."

I nod and gaze out the window. "What about clothes, my phone, my laptop?"

"After we're settled and you tell me everything, I'll figure out all of that. I'm sure this is hard for you, but I know what I'm doing."

Deep down, I know he does; it's why I texted him. I sigh. "Okay."

I watch the familiar scenery pass by. The throbbing in my head decreases a bit more as I attempt to reel in my feelings. All of them. Anger at myself. Rage at Moretti's men. Loss of my partnership. Loss of my mentor. Probable unemployment. Violation of my home. Then it hits me. I claw at my neck. It's gone; my necklace is missing. Instantly the tears start to fall.

His grasp on my hand tightens. "Norah, breathe. I have it. I took it off before Willa kicked me out of your room. Breathe, gorgeous." Slowly, Jacob pulls off to the shoulder. Turing to face me, he wipes the fallen tears from my cheeks with the pad of his thumb before reaching into his pants pocket.

"How did you know?" I don't recall telling him about my necklace or its importance.

"Kelly has one too. I assumed it was equally as important to you as it is to her."

"Thank you. It was the last gift our mother gave us."

Jacob nods, curving his arms around my neck. After clasping the delicate, triple heart necklace, he cups the sides of my face before pressing his lips to my forehead.

"Are you up for a short walk?"

"Sure," I reply, wondering why we're going for a walk now.

"Do you want more layers? I have a hoodie."

"Yes, thank you." I pull it on, and I'm instantly wrapped in a warm, comfy cocoon that smells fresh and spicy like Jacob.

JACOB

Reaching for her hand, I tuck her against me. I'm sure it isn't a great idea considering she called me to protect her. The lines between friend with delicious benefits and client are already blurry. Truthfully, we didn't follow my usual client intake process but...

"Where are we?"

"We're meeting Captain Ramirez on your sister's beach." That's only partially true; it's owned by the four houses on the street. "Since I set up the security, I know it's safe." We approach the lone figure on the secluded beach. "Thank you for meeting me, Captain."

He nods. "How are you, Norah?"

"I've been better. Thanks for asking, William."

"After you left, we finished a cursory search of your townhouse. Do you have any idea what they were looking for?"

"No, I don't have hard copies at home. I have access to the office server via my laptop, but it's encrypted, has fingerprint recognition, and an access reader. You need all three to access the secured financial data. At the office, you need your personal access ID and the file ID."

"Whatever they think you have is of the utmost importance to them. Could you identify them?" William asks her.

She's holding up well so far, but William is only concerned with tonight. I'm sure there have been other incidents that didn't raise her level of concern but will after tonight.

"Probably not," Norah replies.

"Jacob, I'll get you the reports once I have them." I nod as he continues, "Norah, I will need a statement from you later about today's events. I had Officer Sanchez pack you some clothes and shoes. She did the best she could. They sliced much of your closet, but your shoe collection appears to be intact."

Norah smiles at his attempt at levity. Her shoe collection is sexy as hell, extensive, and pricey. They make her toned legs look a mile long.

"I've taken your phone and laptop into evidence to check for bugs or tracking software. " Captain Ramirez shares.

"Thank you. I'll keep you in the loop when I learn pertinent information." I reach out and take the bag of her clothes from him.

"You're welcome. I appreciate that. Take care, Norah."

She nods. I curl my arm around her waist, guiding her back to my rental. Tucking her back into the passenger seat, I hear a soft exhale. Has no one ever taken care of her?

As I settle into my seat, I hand her my phone, open to the room service menu of the Bluff. "Why don't you check out the menu and order some food? Hopefully, it'll be ready soon after we arrive."

She takes my phone and reviews the menu. "What do you want?"

"A burger, fries, vanilla milkshake, and some type of dessert. I'm not picky."

She smirks and calls the kitchen, placing our order.

Pulling into the lot, I park as close to the building as possible. Placing my hand on her forearm, I tell her, "I'll get your door."

After grabbing her bag from the rear seat, I escort her into the hotel, and up to my suite. The closer we get to being alone, the more she's shaking. I know it isn't me; she just realized the gravity of the situation she finds herself in.

Once the metal door clicks closed, I set the bag on the floor and pull her into my arms. Appropriate for a client, not at all. For Norah, necessary for my piece of mind. Initially she's tense, but slowly she relaxes against me. Her fierce independence is attractive. Right now, I need her to trust me and lean on me to figure out who wants to harm her. I'm not sure how long I stand there holding her, but it's perfection—her hands flat on my back, her head over my heart. Her lush breasts pressing into my chest make pulling away impossible, even if it's the right thing to do. Room service knocking has her releasing me. I point to the bedroom, and she retreats.

The server enters and sets up our meal. After signing the receipt, I latch the security lock and go to find Norah. She's leaning against the counter, attempting to finger comb the knots out of her long, shiny, midnight hair. A memory of threading my fingers into her hair flashes through my mind. *Focus!*

"Dinner is served."

She laughs and twists her hair up on top of her head before following me into the other room. I pull out her chair and hear another sigh. Who is she dating? They need lessons in being gentlemanly. Before I take the first bite of my burger, Norah is halfway done with hers.

In an effort to slow her down, I ask, "Tell me what happened today."

She inhales sharply. "I probably need to start yesterday or even earlier. The longer I evaluate the last six months, the more I think everything that has gone wrong is connected."

I set my food down. The worry that just overtook me is palpable. In my head, I know she can take care of herself, but the muscle in my chest is screaming to put her in a bubble and protect her with everything I have.

She isn't yours to protect.

She is for now!

"About seven months ago, I had a meeting with my immediate supervisor, Stanley Sterling. He indicated that the board was looking to add two partners this year. I'm one of the candidates—or I was, I guess."

"What do you mean?" I reach across the table and take her hand in mine.

"You'll understand when I finish telling the story. Stan gave me four client files to review at that meeting. Two were simple mom-and-pop businesses, one was a major retail chain in the northeast, and the biggest was the whale of them all—a multibillion-dollar conglomerate. The first three were impeccable, but the last just wasn't adding up."

"Not adding up how?"

"Balance sheets and profit/loss statements are like crack for me. If the numbers don't balance, it's like a puzzle I need to figure out. The company consists of six separate entities. When I started to review the file, there were small discrepancies here and there. Nothing substantial, so I went back a year. The two companies where I found discrepancies were squeaky clean, but the others had errors. It took me almost six months to find the pattern in the books."

"You worked on it for that long without giving up?"

"Yes, I'm always thorough."

Another memory crosses my mind of her thoroughly licking my…. *She's your client right now, not your… lover, booty call, friend with benefits.* I need to separate the two—*now!*

"For ease of explanation, in year one, companies one through three are clean, but companies four through six had errors. In year two, it was the reverse. In year three, the same as year two. In year four, the same as year one."

"You brought your findings to your boss?"

"Yes, and he took the file from me. I'm not sure if he knew about the errors or if it was a test."

"What do you mean 'a test'?"

"As I mentioned, I'm on the short list for partner this year. I thought it must be an ethics test or something. After today, I know that isn't the case. It makes me think that my boss is into some shady stuff and it was a different kind of test—a test where I would simply ignore the discrepancies, which usually means skimming or money laundering of some kind."

"I'm sorry, Norah. Maybe you won't lose your job."

I nod and continue. "At the end of the day yesterday, two guys were leaning on my car in the parking garage. I asked them to move, they didn't. The tall, skinny one gave me a warning from their boss. I tried to get in my car, and the short fat one, Carlo, grabbed my forearm. I twisted out of his hold and shoved him."

"That's why they drugged you. They knew you could defend yourself."

"Yes, I'm a black belt godan level."

"Impressive, is that fourth or fifth?"

"Fifth. Anyway, I worked from home today. Near noon, I heard some abnormal noise coming from the rear of my townhouse. I peeked out the blinds and saw two unfamiliar guys. I ran back to the front, checked the dead bolts on the garage and the front door. I texted you, then ran upstairs. I planned to stash my laptop because it was logged into my office server. I didn't make it to my office. One of them caught me on the stairs. The last thing I remember is feeling the needle in my neck and someone holding me down. You know the rest."

"Why didn't you call me about yesterday?"

"Jacob, we aren't a couple. We're friends who have extraordinary sex." Brutally honest. I feel that straight in my chest. It's what I said I could handle.

"What is the name of the conglomerate?"

"The Moretti Family Brands."

"The Moretti Family is after you?"

"Should that mean something to me?"

"They're allegedly a real-life Corleone family."

Her face blanches, and her hand trembles in mine. Without releasing her, I rise from my seat and move next to her. Lowering to the floor, I grip her hips and turn her to face me so I can look her straight in the eye.

"Norah, I will protect you, even if it's the last thing I do."

Her hand lifts to my jaw. "Jacob, don't say things like that."

"It's who I am. Rarely do I take assignments anymore, but I'm staying with you until you're safe." I lean forward, brushing my lips across hers, blurring the line even further.

NORAH

Refraining from taking this kiss deeper requires monumental restraint. Reluctantly, I pull back.

"Is there anything else I need to know?"

Well, that's a loaded question. If we're talking about our personal relationship, that could take some time to hash out, and now isn't the time to do it.

"Not about today. I don't know if my car trouble after girls' night out or the flat I had last month is connected. What else do you need to ask?"

"Where were you when you got the flat?"

I share the details, and he moves on. "What do you recall about the guys from the parking garage?"

"There were two. The tall one introduced himself as Sid, and the short one as Carlo. Building security arrived, and they ran off. There's security footage and a report I was supposed to call for today. I have the card in my…." I shake my head.

"It's okay. I've worked with much less. What about today?"

"They were different people. The two I saw in the back were both tall, wearing all black, but I didn't stay long enough to make out their features. The one who tackled me on the stairs was stockier and had a colorful tattoo on his forearm. He likely has a broken nose from my foot."

That elicits a small smirk. "Serves him right. How did you know I was going to be here?"

"Kelly told me Nicholas was meeting with you. She may have an idea about us that I didn't dispel her from."

"What does that mean exactly?"

"She knows we've been together, no details though." A look I can't decipher crosses his face. "Was it supposed to be a secret?"

"No, not at all. I just didn't think you and Kelly were that close. If you told me Kelsey knows, that wouldn't surprise me."

"We aren't, but she pieced it together when you were handling the issues with her stalkers. Plus, Kelly noticed how your features soften when you look at me. Kelsey knows there is a man but not who. Apparently, I'm less bitchy when I'm sexually satisfied." I don't think I've ever seen Jacob blush until this moment. Considering some of the ways he's made my body sing, it's surprising he's embarrassed. It's a devastating look. *I'm screwed.*

"Will you give me all your personal information so I can have Blaine run a check on you? I want to make sure no one is actively looking for you."

"What do you need?"

He answers, and I rattle off the info Jacob wants.

"How long until someone starts to worry about missed texts or phone calls?"

"My family and friends? A few days, probably."

"Once I know how exposed you are, I'll carefully inform your family that you're safe. Why don't you get some rest? I need to make some calls and figure out our next move."

"I need to shower first. I'll be done in a bit."

"Okay," he replies, moving to the door for my bag. Normally, it would drive me crazy for a man to take care of that for me. Not him. The door opening, pulling out of chairs, and carrying things for me doesn't bother me when he does it. It makes absolutely no sense. Then again, no man I've ever dated did it before.

"Do you feel up to showering?" Jacob asks after setting my bag on the dressing bench.

"Are you offering to help?"

"As the man with whom you share extraordinary sex, I wouldn't think twice about joining you. However, as the man you called to protect you, I shouldn't. I will if you need me to." As much as I want to scream yes and ask him to join me, it's not the best idea ever.

"I'm not dizzy anymore, and I feel better after eating. You'll hear me scream if I'm not okay."

An unreadable expression crosses his face as he takes a seat on the bed.

When I texted Jacob, I knew he would come. I didn't plan on the proximity to him messing with my head—and maybe my heart too. Stepping under the scalding water, I try to calm myself further. Jacob's reaction to the Moretti name wasn't comforting at all. Clearly, I missed something. Nothing in my research would lead me to believe they're like a movie mafia family. Maybe to someone who doesn't know him at all, the crinkle wouldn't be obvious. Truthfully, I don't really know anything about him at all. I know his job, that's about it. I don't have any details on his family life, his childhood, his service to our country, or why he founded Blackthorne. Yet I know the ridges and curves of his sculpted body and the feeling of him buried inside me.

On the surface, I know what Jacob's job is—he runs a security firm. I didn't really think about what it means to need his services. *His professional services.* Never thought I would be in a position to need someone to protect me. I also thought Stan was a straight-up guy. How did I miss that? As the heat of the water decreases, I step out of the shower and wrap myself in a towel. After drying off and dressing in the pajamas that Officer Sanchez packed, I move back into the bedroom. The silky pajamas won't faze him. He knows how I sleep, either naked or in something like this. Jacob is talking to someone on the phone and typing furiously on a laptop.

"I don't care what time it is, get it done!" Jacob growls, ending the call. "Better?" he asks me.

"A bit."

"How are you doing?" He pats the mattress next to him.

I don't sit. I pace back and forth along the long edge of the bed. "Honestly?"

He nods as if lying was truly an option.

"I'm scared, pissed, and heartbroken."

"Please explain."

"In the last two days, five men have sought me out looking to silence me. I don't have anything that they want. I follow protocol to the letter. Every time I have a printout, I shred it. Stan took the file from me and removed it from the office server. Despite all of that and my ability to defend myself, I'm terrified. I'm pissed that I didn't see any signs that Stan was shifty. I have worked for him for the last six years. I saw nothing that made me question his integrity. Losing my professional mentor sucks. I worked my tail off to earn partner, and despite my love of certain luxuries, I have the buy in, every single penny. The worst part is, I likely lost my partnership doing exactly what a partner in a well-established accounting firm should do."

"Come here."

There is no room for noncompliance in his words this time. I climb onto the bed and curl into his embrace.

"The only thing I can promise is I will protect you. The rest may or may not end how you want. I'm sorry you might not get your name on the door."

"Thank you, Jacob."

"For what?"

"For coming, for listening."

"I'll always come for you. You're welcome."

There he goes again saying things that make me think there is wiggle room in this no-relationship edict of his. "Can you sit with me until I fall asleep, or are you a pacer too?"

He smiles, a real smile, one that makes that dimple in his right cheek come out in full force. The first one I've seen today. I could fall for this man if I let myself.

"Of course." Jacob sets his laptop on the bedside table and pulls me closer, his arm around me with his fingers grazing the exposed skin of my back.

I settle flush against his side with my head on his chest.

"Sleep, gorgeous."

I nod against his rock-hard chest before closing my eyes.

JACOB

Normally, Norah tucked against me makes sleep come easily. The nightmares and flashbacks stay at bay. Tonight isn't normal. One of the most notorious crime families is after her for doing her job well. It's been a while since my last field assignment. Despite my job requirement to stay focused and awake, I let sleep claim me.

My phone blares near three in the morning. "Yes."

"The Morettis are actively looking for Norah and put a sizable bounty on her head," Blaine informs me.

"Okay. I'll get back to you." I glance down, taking one more look at her before upending her life more.

"Norah, we need to leave." I draw my hand up and down her back. Enchanting, wide, hazel eyes blink open. The moment she recalls why she's with me, she bolts straight up. She throws on a pair of jeans and whips her camisole over her head, leaving her topless. It takes a beat too long before I leave the room to ignore my physical reaction to her ample breasts on display.

After adding the laptop and a few personal items into my bag, I find her ready to go. With a second check of the room, I grab her bag and mine, eliciting another sigh from her lips.

"You will need to explain that later."

She nods and follows me down the stairs. Instead of exiting through to the rear of the hotel, I walk out the side door. Hurrying around the building, I scan our surroundings and find no one of note. Interlacing my fingers with hers, I lead her across the narrow street to the beach parking lot. Questions dance in her eyes, but she says nothing. I'll explain once we leave. She tightens her fingers in mine. I never considered how Norah would react if she were in danger. Perhaps her martial arts training is helping her remain calm. Again I check our surroundings and find our new ride. Last night Captain Ramirez delivered a new rental car for me to use. Once she's settled in the passenger seat, I round the car and jump in.

"Here, please text Connor exactly these words. 'Escape compromised. Need supplies and Tank at Point B.'" I hand her my phone.

After she finishes typing, she asks, "Are you going to explain what's going on?"

"Yes, but we need to move first."

Pulling onto the street toward the row of shops, we pass a restaurant that makes saltwater taffy in the window, a bunch of cute souvenir stores, and even an amusement park. I see why my clients choose to plant roots here. Norah gazes out the window, watching the scenery of her home pass by. Is she from here? I know nothing about her. I know what makes her back arch and what spots on her body elicit moans of pleasure and satiating orgasms. Anything deeper than that, I'm in the dark. My phone vibrates in her hand.

"Can you read that to me please?"

"Roger. Need bp?" Norah recites.

"Please reply 'not yet.'"

Almost instantly, my phone vibrates with a reply.

"Connor replied, 'Roger.'"

I nod and continue driving away from York Beach.

After ten minutes, I pull onto the interstate. Before speaking, I compose the thoughts in my head to share what Blaine told me. When I take her hand in mine, she turns to look at me. The fear of not knowing what I'll say next is in her eyes.

"I will protect you, Norah." I may not want to get married again, but I need to know she's alive and well, even if at the end of this there isn't an occasional us anymore. She deserves the white picket fence. Does she even want that? Either way, I can't give it to her.

"I know. It's hard to grasp how I'm here right now. I don't mean with you. I mean with professional you."

I nod, hoping she'll continue, but she clams up. "That was Blaine on the phone. The Morettis are actively looking for you. They're looking for a ledger that has gone missing. They believe you have it. I had him pause all your credit cards and banking. I also had him deactivate your social media and remove your photo from the Quinn Sterling website."

"I don't have any ledgers."

I nod.

"Escape is me?"

"Yes."

"Why do I get the feeling there is so much more to that nickname than code speak?"

"There is. I don't plan on sharing right now though." It isn't something I ever want to explain to Norah.

We get back on the road, and her gaze returns to the passing greenery, but she doesn't pull her hand away. A few hours later, I pull into a small diner just off the highway. Once we sit, our server, Doris, approaches our table.

"What can I fetch for ya?" Doris is an older woman with short, gray hair and the standard waitress uniform. She's exactly what I picture in my mind for a lifer at a greasy spoon diner. I wait for Norah to order first.

"I'll have a cup of coffee, a water, a triple stack of pancakes, and crisp bacon," she says, looking over the top of her menu.

"I'll have a coffee, a water, and the western omelet."

"What kind of toast?"

"Wheat, please."

Doris walks away.

"Are you going to clue me into your plan?"

"I will, but not here," I reply, gauging her reaction. I've never had a client as compliant and calm as Norah.

"Fair enough. Tell me more about you."

It's fair to say we know pretty much nothing about each other except for bedroom preferences and morning coffee. I also know how her body fills out a custom dress worn to a wedding. Flawless. With her luxury high heels on, we stand eye to eye. She has the perfect amount of curve to her hips and breasts just slightly larger than her frame should possess.

"Why?"

Doris delivers our drinks and saunters away.

"Honestly, I don't really know anything about you other than things I shouldn't mention here. Plus, what else are we going to talk about?"

"You."

"Fine, a question for a question. You can only pass twice."

"Fair enough. You go first," I say, hoping to match the depth of her questions.

"Do you have any siblings?" she asks.

"Not exactly."

"Care to expand on that?"

Doris returns to refill our coffee. As I prepare mine, I consider what harm there could be in sharing true details about myself with Norah.

"I answered your question. You don't get two in a row."

"I was looking for an actual answer, not some crafty way to dodge sharing anything real."

"As far as I know, I don't have any blood siblings. I was left at a fire station when I was a few days old." Only a handful of people know that bit of information about me.

She covers my hand with hers. "I'm sorry."

"Don't be. My parents and siblings are amazing. My father, Benjamin, is a former marine and a cop. Connie, my mom, taught math for thirty years. You will love them." Where the hell did that come from? She isn't going to meet my parents. "I have a younger brother, Cameron, who is a firefighter, and a younger sister, Jillian, who is a teacher. To answer the question in your head, I never sought out my biological parents. I never felt I needed to. My parents are amazing people."

"Are Cameron and Jill adopted as well?"

"Yes. What about your siblings? Obviously, I know Kelly but I don't know Joseph at all."

"Why?"

"Other than the background check I completed when Blackthorne was hired to protect Kelly, we've never met.

"Makes sense. Joseph is my older brother. He works for the regional soccer team. He has a son named James. He's married to his childhood sweetheart, Genevieve, and they have a son named Jackson. You may have seen them at Kelsey and William's wedding but may not have put it together that he's my brother. As you know, Kelly is my younger sister."

"I was focused on you that night. You looked runway ready in that black, silk dress." I was instantly attracted to Norah the moment I met her. That dress pulled the last thread of my resolve. We'd run into each other a few times before anything happened between us. That night I couldn't help myself. I was clear about my intentions—just a purely physical relationship. No dates, no attachments.

"Thank you. You should have been focused on your job."

Doris delivers our food.

"Your sister, brother-in-law, and Mabel were adequately protected." I dig into my plate and shovel the food into my mouth.

"Breathe, Jacob. Your food isn't going to run away."

Smirking, I say, "It's a habit."

"From where?"

"When I enlisted, I learned to eat quickly because we needed to be finished before the person to our right. Unbelievably, I have slowed down a bit."

While I wait for her to finish eating, I scan the room again and consider my next few questions. After paying our bill, I follow her into the ladies' room, locking the door behind us.

NORAH

"I can handle this myself," I say as he follows me inside the restroom.

"I know you can, but I still need to do my job." I sigh and close the stall door.

As we leave the bathroom, two women wink at me. *I wish*. Frankly, I *need* and soon. I understand the distinction he drew last night, but that doesn't change the fact that I want him filling me despite the reason we're together right now. Jacob rounds the back of the car after closing my door. I wonder if he only does that for clients or for women he dates as well.

"What about your parents?" he asks, pulling back onto the interstate. Then he twines his fingers with mine. I'm continually reminding myself that he's simply supporting me. His need to touch me doesn't mean anything. Even so, it's driving me crazy with want.

"My parents were high school sweethearts. They stayed together through college, even though it was long distance for them. Did you go to college or enlist right out of high school?"

"I went to the US Military Academy and got my degree in management with a minor in cyber security. What about you? Where did you get your accounting degree?"

"I went to Boston University for undergrad. I started working at Quinn Sterling as an intern my junior year. While I worked, I got my MBA from Harvard Business School."

"That's impressive."

I smile. "How many tours did you do?" I wonder how deep I need to dig before he uses one of his passes.

"Three. What is your favorite color?" An easy one.

"Violet. You?"

"Green. No-go pizza topping?"

"Anchovies. You?"

"Pineapple. Why did you sigh when I moved your bag?"

"No man I've ever dated acts as gentlemanly as you."

"Meaning?"

"You know I'm capable, but you still want to take care of it for me. You open doors for me, pull out my chair, and carry things. I'm sure it's a testament to your parents."

"Thank you. I'm aware of your capabilities, each one highly attractive, but you shouldn't need to carry, move, or do anything that isn't necessary. My mother would castrate me if I didn't pull out your chair, open doors, and hold them for you. Why did you choose Quinn Sterling?"

I sigh.

"You don't have to answer."

"I know. The firm is one of the best in the northern hemisphere, if not the world. Plus, Stan was willing to take a chance on me."

"You proved him right. Present circumstances notwithstanding, you did the right thing."

"Maybe. No, I did the right thing. I just didn't know it would put my life in danger."

He squeezes my hand tighter.

"Where are we going?"

"Blackthorne has a bunch of safe houses, for lack of a better term, scattered on the eastern seaboard and a few on the west coast. Connor will meet us at Point B with supplies."

"How long before I can let my family know what's going on?"

"Once we meet with Connor and have the supplies, you can contact them. If I need to find another way, I will. It should be today though."

I glance over at him as he drives. He looks relaxed, but he isn't. I've seen him completely relaxed; that isn't it.

"What does supplies include?"

"Basics: food, weapons, and cell phones. Why? Do you need something specific?"

"I may need a coat, depending on where we're going, and some contact solution."

"I gave Connor your sizes. He'll bring everything you need."

"How did you explain that?"

"He knows about you."

"How do you know Connor?"

"Connor and I have been best friends since birth, I guess. We were assigned to the same unit for the entire time we served. He was my first call when I decided to create Blackthorne."

"Did he come up with the nickname?"

"Yes."

"What does it mean?"

"Still not sharing details on that yet."

The longer it takes him to explain, the more intrigued I get.

"What is your plan after that?" It's an *awful* predicament for me to be stuck with Jacob for an indefinite amount of time, especially considering he keeps touching me like we're a couple.

"It's still a work in progress. Right now, I need to get you somewhere I can control and gather more information."

"Thank you. I'm sure my questions are annoying. I feel out of control right now. I'm a planner. Order and predictability are necessary for me to function, especially in my work life. I don't like when my plans go awry. This situation is completely out of my comfort zone."

Lifting my hand to his lips, he kisses it before answering. "I know. This isn't abnormal for me. Well, I haven't taken a field assignment in a few years, but I can handle your situation."

"It's one of the reasons I called."

"Why else?"

"I've watched you work. Hell, I was part of it when the package arrived at Kelly's store. You're thorough; plus Nicholas is hard to impress. If he lets you keep Kelly safe, I will be too." Keeping him at arm's length, considering my attraction to him, is going to be difficult. Our arrangement is perfectly fine. It was anyway. The more time I spend with him, the more time I want from him. *Get a grip, Norah!* He doesn't want a relationship.

"You will. You are," he replies with a quick glance in my direction.

I feel safe with him, although I don't think voicing it is wise. Adding more pressure to this situation isn't a spectacular idea.

"Where are you from?" I ask, changing the subject.

"I was born in upstate New York. I grew up in Pennsylvania. I live near the coast in Maryland. What about you?"

"I was born in Massachusetts, but we spent our summers in York Beach. When my mom fell ill, we moved into the beach house permanently. Joseph purchased it for James from our father soon after her death. Dad went back home."

Jacob cups the side of my face with his right hand, dragging his thumb across my lips. I fail to stifle a deep sigh.

"After college, I had a townhouse in Beacon Hill. Then I started working from home most days, so I moved back to York Beach after finishing my MBA." I caress the delicate necklace my mother gave me as I gaze out the window, watching the snow along the shoulder increase the further we drive. "Thank you for knowing this is important to me. I know I never told you."

"You're welcome." We drive in silence for a while before his phone vibrates in my lap.

JACOB

Baffled by her compliance and calm demeanor, I drive toward our first point. I knew she was smart, but I didn't truly know how brilliant until today. Only in passing did I know about her mother from working with Kelly. Pocketing her necklace was an instinct. I'm glad I did.

"Can you read it to me?"

"It's from Maia. 'K wants to talk to client. I kept her away from the townhouse, but she knows something is up because N hasn't responded.'"

"Please reply, 'Stall as long as you can. I hope to contact K later today.'"

"Maia replied, 'Will do.'" I turn left onto a dirt road near the lake, slowing to meet the speed limit. It's eerily quiet. This area is bustling in the summer months. Fall, not so much.

"Could you text Connor 'Site prepped'?" She sends the text, and as we round the lake, he responds.

"'Yes. About to leave. Need me to stay?'"

Before I can have Norah respond, two black SUVs approach us from behind. My heart rate ticks up. I reach across the seat, pulling her down, pressing the top of her head against my thigh.

"Stay there!" I bellow. "Reply 'Have company. North side of the lake. Need Tank at least.'" I punch the accelerator and move around the lake as quickly as possible. There's a network of tertiary roads winding around to other secluded cabins should we need to move off the main road. How did they find us already? I took the longest route possible, and we switched vehicles. She doesn't have a phone or laptop, nothing to track her with. *Unless*....

As I speed over the dirt road, both vehicles closely behind me, I glide my hand up from her hip, over the dip of her waist, around her taut abdomen.

"Seriously? That isn't helping right now."

I smile inwardly, glad I'm not alone in my sexual frustration. "I'm looking for a tracker. There's no way they found us without one. Did you have any other cuts or spot that felt uncomfortable at the hospital?"

"My temple, the injection site, and the back of my neck." Gripping her soft hair, I shove it to the side.

My phone vibrates again. "Vehicles sandwiched between us. I'll cut them off one by one," she reads aloud.

Pressing along the curve of her neck, across the top of her back, and upward into her hair line, she winces. At the base of her hairline in a small hollow, I find where they inserted the tracker. I reach over to the glove box, pulling out the first aid kit. Without a word, she unzips it for me. Gathering supplies, I set them in the cupholder.

"I need you to climb up here and drive so I can dig the tracker out of the back of your neck."

Moving quickly, Norah climbs into my lap and takes the wheel. Ignoring her against me and the tease of her scent—orchids and vanilla—I refocus on the task at hand. I have never been attracted to a client during an assignment. Now I'm rethinking sending Callen to protect Miss Goldberg.

"Just keep driving around the lake at a steady speed. Try not to slow down too much."

"Okay."

"Can you twist your hair up?" Wrapping my arms around her, I retake the wheel and attempt to focus on our current situation, not her perfect ass nestled against my shaft, which is hardening rapidly. If she notices, she doesn't indicate as much. She takes the hair tie from her wrist and twists her hair into a topknot.

"I'm sorry, this is going to hurt."

She nods curtly, focusing on the road ahead. After cleaning the area, I take the sterilized knife and make a small incision near the implant site. Her hands tighten on the wheel, but she doesn't acknowledge the pain otherwise. Locating the tracker with my fingers, I hold it in place and extract it with a set of tweezers. I set the chip in the cupholder, clean the back of her neck, and add a small bandage. I'll recheck later and determine if it needs a stitch or two.

Twisting to look behind us, I see Connor has successfully eliminated one of the vehicles. I text him before moving Norah back to the passenger seat.

Me: Found a tracker in her neck. Just removed it. Will need to plant it somewhere.

Connor: Roger. Let's get you two out of here.

Curling my arm around her slim waist, I press my lips to her jawline. "Ready?"

"Yes."

I lift her to the right, and she slides across the seat. After fastening her seat belt, she lies back down on the front seat, her fingernails digging into my thigh until the phone vibrates.

After inhaling, she says, "Connor said, 'strip placed, avoid block 58 on next trip.'"

"Please reply, 'Roger.'" Norah sends the text, replacing her hand on my thigh. I set mine on top of hers. She flips hers, allowing me to hold it. As we round the lake, hopefully for the final time, I skirt the strip and come to a stop a few hundred yards ahead. Turning to watch out the rear window, I see the SUV hit the strip and become immobilized. Connor approaches the vehicle, tasing the driver. He restrains the driver with zip ties to the steering wheel.

"You can sit up."

Slowly, she pushes up from the seat as Connor pulls his vehicle behind ours. I exit the truck and move around to the passenger side of the car, opening her door. "You can get out if you want."

Cautiously, Norah steps out of the car.

"Miss Cavallaro, good to see you."

"Connor, nice to meet you in person," Norah says.

"Tank was outside. You're going to have to call him." I whistle and turn in the direction of the cabin. Less than a minute later, Tank comes barreling down the road.

"Good boy. *Freund.*" Tank sits at my feet.

"Norah, this is Tank." She crouches down, pets him, and talks to him as if she has simply been away for a while.

"Thanks for the assist. What are our options now?"

I discuss our options with Connor while Norah and Tank get acquainted. I didn't think to ask if she had a problem with dogs, but I know I don't have the manpower to spare right now. He will protect her and warn me if something is off. Plus, I don't trust anyone else with her life. My team is talented, but I need to handle this myself.

"As long as it's empty, Point M will be fine." I hand him the keys to the truck, and he gives me his. "Drop the tracker somewhere along your route to the office."

"They won't be back for a bit. I'll arrange a grocery delivery for you when I get back to the office." Point M is Connor's parents' home.

"Norah, do you need anything specific?" I ask.

"Food wise, I'm not picky. I need contact solution. Officer Sanchez didn't know to pack it."

"No problem. I'll call you with an update early evening on the other assignments," Connor says.

"Thanks. We should get going." Rounding the car, I open the passenger door for Norah. Tank waits patiently at her heel. He jumps in the back after I open the door.

NORAH

As we pull away, my heart rate starts to decrease ever so slowly. Despite not being able to see everything, something I'm sure Jacob wanted, I pieced together most of the details.

"What's going through your mind, gorgeous?"

"Are you sure you want to know?"

"Yes, I want to know." His response is a bit gruffer than I'm used to from him. I'm sure the situation we're in contributes to that.

"I'm not sure what I was expecting when I called you. I knew you would come for me, but I didn't know what being a job would entail."

"You aren't just a job, Norah."

Meaning what exactly? If I were to spill my guts and tell him that his touch is driving me crazy and I want more, he wouldn't run? Tell him I want more time with him, he wouldn't run? I might run if I said I didn't want a relationship and my booty call asks for one. That's all I am, a booty call. Despite how he's touched me and kissed me in the last twenty-four hours. As incredible as he is, that's all we are. Of course, he'll run as soon as I'm safe on my own again.

"I'll put it this way, I'm having trouble reconciling the sides of you I've seen." My insatiable lover, the protector, and the man with husband potential.

"Ask me whatever you want."

"Don't tempt me." I decide to let the topic drop for now. "When did you get Tank?"

"Is that really what you want to know?"

"No, but I'm not ready to ask the other questions or hear the answers yet."

He nods before answering. "When I was young, we had a few different dogs, sometimes two or three at a time. Once I retired from the military and had a place of my own, I raised him from a puppy."

"How old is he?"

"He's four."

I look out the window as snow starts to fall. "Will we make it wherever we're going before it snows too much?"

"Yes." His mouth is in a tight line. Well, there's another side of Jacob. Sullen.

I watch the snowflakes float to the road as we pull off the rural route onto a narrow lane. As we drive along, a large colonial comes into view. It's picturesque with a wraparound porch and large windows. Jacob pulls in front of the garage door and reaches across to the glove box. He removes a key from a ring and steps out of the truck.

"Whose home is this?"

"Connor's parents."

"It's gorgeous." *Perfect for raising a family*. Where did that come from? I always wanted to have kids, just didn't think it would fit into my life. Now that my life is a mess, I guess all options would be on the table.

"He and I spent a lot of time here." I hop down and open the door for Tank. He takes off running onto the grass along the side of the driveway. I offer to take one of the bags, but Jacob refuses. Instead he hands me the key. I follow him onto the porch and open the door. The exterior of the house is an older design, but the inside is modern. The kitchen has a huge island with stools. The massive fireplace has a stone hearth and a large TV mounted above it. The furnishings are structured but appear comfy.

"Bathroom?" I wait. "Jacob, bathroom?" I ask again while Jacob opens the fridge.

"Sorry, down the hall. First door on the right."

After freshening up a bit, I find Jacob standing on the back deck watching Tank chase a ball. He retrieves it, and Jacob dutifully throws it again. His form is perfect, both his body line and the movement of his arm.

"Quarterback, huh?" Well, just another point in the too-good-to-be-true column for Jacob Blackthorne.

"You like football?"

"Like isn't strong enough. I watch every game I can."

"Do you have a favorite team or just the game overall?"

"I'm a Bears fan despite being from the northeast. You?"

"Same actually."

"So, what now?" I turn to face him. While I still put myself in the barely knowing Jacob category, I would say he's working something out in his head right now.

"I'll have a better answer after I talk with Blaine and Connor again later. For now, let's call Nicholas. You can talk to Kelly for a few minutes but not much longer. Me calling Nicholas isn't out of the ordinary, but it would be if it's too long. While I'm confident that we're safe here and my phones are clean, we still need to be cautious. Give her enough details for her to stop asking questions."

"Okay. Are you going to share what's bothering you?"

"I have a few things going on in my head, but the top two are you and the anniversary of an attack in Afghanistan is tomorrow."

"Want to talk about either one?"

"Later. I'm not a fan of talking about it."

After following Jacob to the kitchen, I watch as he rifles through the bag that Connor delivered. He pulls out a phone and hands it to me.

Taking a deep breath, I dial Nicholas while leaning against the island.

"Hello."

"Hi, Nicholas. It's Norah. Is Kelly there?"

"Sure, are you okay?"

I put the phone on speaker. "Yes, I'm fine. You're on speaker." I won't share any of the details with Kelly about the Moretti's henchmen.

"Hi. Oh my God! Are you okay? Maia wasn't helpful. I tried to visit you."

Jacob settles his arms on either side of me, caging me against the cold granite.

"Breathe, Kel. There was an incident at work and then at my townhouse. I'm fine. I'm with Jacob." *Scared out of my mind but fine.* His nearness is distracting. The heat of him surrounds me, making my pulse increase. All the nerve endings I've been ignoring are screaming for attention.

"Is there anything we can do?"

"No. I'm fine."

"Can you take me off speaker?"

I push the button, lifting the phone to my ear. I try to step out of his arms, but he resists, tightening his arms around me.

"It's just me, Kel."

"Are you going to be okay with Jacob?"

"Yes, it's his job."

"That isn't what I mean."

"I can't answer that." I probably could answer her, but it isn't what she wants to hear. Kelly knows the type of relationship we have, but she also knows what I want for myself. She's just trying to protect me from myself and a broken heart. Normally, that would be my job as the older sister. "I have to go, Kel. I'll call you again when I can. Love you."

"Love you too."

I end the call and set my hands on top of his, linking our fingers. "Thank you."

"You're welcome." His lips press against the nape of my neck, moving to my earlobe. Hell, he knows what that does to me.

"I need you to stop if—"

JACOB

"I don't want to stop, even though I should."

Releasing my hands, she turns to face me, her hands on my chest. Her hazel eyes leaning toward green bore into mine when I pull her curves against me.

"Because I'm a job now."

"While that's arguably true, I couldn't separate the two from the moment I received your text. I care about you, Norah, and I'll lose my mind if something happens to you."

"I trust you, Jacob. Nothing is going to happen to me. We made it through earlier today, right?"

"Yes, but I don't know how that would have gone if Connor wasn't nearby."

"We don't have to worry about that. Connor was there. I'm fine." She curls her fingers and drags them down my chest. She knows the effect that has on me.

"Are you going to share what Kelly asked?"

"She asked me if I would be okay with you."

"Meaning?"

"She knows the nature of our relationship, but she knows me too. Well enough to know…I have only been with you since the Ramirez wedding."

"I haven't been with anyone else either."

Our confessions add weight to this already charged moment. Sliding my hand along her jaw, careful not to press hard against her neck, I pull her lips to mine and claim her mouth as if it's mine to take at will. She opens for me, tangling her tongue with mine. Lifting her shirt overhead, I travel down her jaw and across her collarbone to the point of her shoulder. Walking toward the hall, I break our kiss. Norah whines from the loss but moves to the hem of my shirt. Each exposed inch of skin is rewarded with a lick of her tongue.

"Tank, come." He moves to my side. I taught him commands in English and German. The German commands are for when he is working. The English for when he's simply my dog. "Tank, *halten garde*." Confident he'll alert me if there is a problem, I rip my shirt over my head, and guide her into the guest room.

Norah and I don't dance to bed. Typically our clothes fall to the floor at a furious pace. This time is no different. Moments after stepping into the room, I'm naked, hard as stone, teasing my way up her creamy skin from her perfectly painted toes. Each press of my mouth or skim of my teeth relaxes the tension in the room and in my chest—tightness that I'm choosing to explain based on the bounty on her head, not the confusion in mine. Gripping her thighs, I spread them wide, baring her slick heat to me. With featherlight movement, I graze my fingertips along her inner thighs, ghosting over her core.

"Jacob...." Her voice is dripping with lust and desire.

"Norah." I open her folds with my fingers before dipping my tongue into her center. Her long fingers laced in my hair, her hold tightens as the pressure builds. Tasting her arousal spurs me forward—licking, sucking, and biting. She presses against me. Teasing her tight bundle brings her closer to release, her lips pink, swollen, and aroused from my mouth. She writhes against me. As her orgasm eases, she loosens her hold on me. Moving upward, I stroke myself twice before aligning my shaft with her heat.

There's a look in her eyes I've seen only one other time. I couldn't decipher it then, and I can't now. Palming her breasts, I push forward. Once I'm fully seated, I pull out completely. The loss of her tight walls surrounding me makes me feel bereft. I thrust forward with one long, deep stroke, burying my shaft inside her. Her legs tucked against my sides allows me to hit her spot with each precise movement. I feel her tense as her second release builds in her abdomen. She pulses around me the closer she gets to bliss. Tightness forms for me, but I refuse to come before her.

"Sweet mercy!" Her body convulses around me as she shivers from my tongue circling her nipples one by one. Hooking her ankles behind my back, she draws me even deeper, and I lose the grasp on my control. Sliding my hands around her, I lift her hips off the bed and pound into her harder. My cock throbs in her heat as I forcefully plunge deeper. Her hips meeting mine has me exploding inside her. Breathing heavily, I gaze down at her. Her eyes close tightly as if she's fighting something— holding back emotions that we just stirred up. Emotions about what, I'm not sure, and I don't plan on asking; it would only exacerbate the discord I have in my own head right now. If I'm honest, probably my heart too.

Lowering her to the bedding, I withdraw and gather her against me. Lifting her eyes to mine, I see questions—likely the ones from earlier that she refused to ask. The ones I don't want to answer. I know there are only two options when she's safe again: complete surrender or two crushed hearts. Despite my brain telling me otherwise, I care about her and want her to be happy. There is no scenario where the end doesn't result in two crushed hearts and no more spectacular sex, at least for me.

Tank alerts from the hallway. It's probably the groceries, but I still need to check anyway.

"Stay here. I'll be right back." I kiss the tip of her nose and forehead.

She nods, covering her luscious body with the throw blanket. A small sigh escapes her lips as I pull on my jeans and shirt to check on the alert. Stepping into the hallway, I find Tank exactly where he should be, facing the front entry.

"Tank. *Lindern*. Good boy." Tank and I step into the kitchen and find Connor bringing groceries into the house.

"Connor, what are you doing here?" I say loudly, hoping Norah hears me. I fill a bowl of water for Tank and relieve Connor of the bags he's carrying.

"I tried to get them delivered, but with the storm, no one would deliver today."

"Thanks. What is the expected snowfall?"

"A foot plus for this area, even though it's early in the season. The tractor is in the shed. Keys are still in their usual place."

I nod. "Since you're here, do you have an update?"

"Sure. Callen left for his assignment with Miss Goldberg. I reviewed his plan; it's sound. He intends to stick it out the entire time. How that will play out remains to be seen. Nolan is actively working with Miss Forrester. Her parents are singing his praises. Christoph will be heading out on Saturday for his assignment. Maia will remain in York Beach until Kelly and Nicholas return. Gemma is handling the office well. She's routing all intake calls to me for now and copying me on any necessary information for the team."

"Anything on the Morettis?"

"Nothing new. They're still actively searching for Norah. Eventually, they will realize that the tracker is leading them to a garbage transfer facility. I dropped it in a trash can at a fast-food restaurant. Presumably a worker will empty it and it'll move by morning. The goose chase should continue for a few days before they realize that you removed it. What made you look for it anyway?"

"I was cautious on my way to the cabin. No one was tailing us, no one was suspicious at the diner, and we weren't there long. When Moretti's men arrived at the lake, I knew they must have inserted one after they drugged her. No other explanation made sense. It was embedded in the hollow at the base of her head. You bought us a few days reprieve. She doesn't have the ledger they're looking for. Never did. The bigger question is who does? Why do they think she has it? According to her, she has never seen it."

Tank scurries down the hall as Norah approaches. She clearly heard me. Even though we were a tangled mass of nakedness less than fifteen minutes ago, she doesn't look thoroughly pleasured. Although, I'm confident both of us were in equal measure. Her skin isn't flush, her hair is neatly piled on top of her head, and she's wearing fresh clothes and her dark-rimmed glasses.

NORAH

Deep down, I know a second round would be an extremely poor decision—not that I'm opposed to making it. As I'm waiting for his return, I hear his warning from the kitchen. For whatever reason, Connor is here again. He may know about my relationship with Jacob, but I don't plan on flaunting it or making Connor question Jacob's ability to do his job. Quietly, I pad to the adjoining bathroom and center myself. I can't look satisfied when I finally get to the kitchen.

Approaching the two men, I inhale and slowly release the breath as I get closer.

"Hi, Connor."

"Hi, Norah. How are you feeling?"

"So-so. Still tired from the drugs and not sleeping well."

"Understandable. I should get going." Maybe Connor has a pet or even a woman in his life. Plus, it's snowing harder than before. We must not be far from where Jacob's office is or where Connor lives, maybe both.

"Thank you for the food."

"You're welcome."

I move to the bags and start putting the food away while Jacob follows Connor to the door. Instead of guessing where the items go, I put away the perishables first.

Whatever they are talking about, it's deep. From the looks of it, Connor has the upper hand in this conversation as Jacob scrubs his hands over his face.

I find a knife and start paring the strawberries into a bowl to pull my attention away from their discussion. Jacob will tell me if it pertains to me or if his plan requires me to do something or refrain from doing something.

"Thank you," he says, reentering the kitchen.

"Of course. I didn't know where to put the rest of that stuff," I say, pointing to the items on the island. "Are you hungry? I need to eat soon." I return to cutting the strawberries.

"I could eat."

"I think there are ingredients for fettucine with pancetta, peas, and a cream sauce."

"You cook like that for yourself?" His voice is laced with surprise.

"No, I don't. Maybe once a month I cook a huge meal."

"Do you have family meals?"

Faint recollection of some family dinners zip through my mind, dinners and holidays from long ago. Recent ones have been a bit better, but nothing compares to the meals my mom planned. I see why he asked.

Jacob's strong arms surround me. I set the knife on the counter before gripping his forearms. "I'm sorry. I didn't think."

"It's okay. Eight years is a long time. My siblings and I are working on hosting them. It just isn't the same."

"I imagine they wouldn't be. Nothing would ever compare to the memories you hold in your heart."

Dropping my hands, I twist in his arms and wrap my arms around his neck. I know my heart will break, but I'll take the support and protection he's offering right now just the same. His big hands hold me against his rock-hard chest. It will kill me to walk away when this is over.

Pulling back slightly, I press my lips to his. "Thank you."

He places a kiss to my forehead. I repress a sigh. His actions and his words don't match. We aren't a couple, yet he touches me like we are even outside the bedroom. Inside, nothing has changed. He's just taking care of me for now. "Let's get started on the food."

"Sure, but you'll have to instruct me. My cooking skills are basic."

As I pull out the ingredients for dinner, Jacob puts the strawberries away.

"Could you set some water to boil for the pasta and dice the pancetta?"

He fishes out a pot and fills it with water. After setting it on the stove, he searches for a cutting board and starts cutting. "Diced means small, right?"

I smile. "Yes." It's endearing when he admits he isn't sure about something. He exudes confidence in almost everything he does. I make the cream sauce and wait for the pasta to cook. Once he finishes dicing, I set it in a pan to cook.

After plating dinner, we move to the sunroom. The snow outside is piling up. There is almost six inches so far.

"It's peaceful here."

"It is," he replies softly.

He shovels a forkful of pasta into his mouth. He's careful with his words and who he shares with. I understand; I'm not meant to be a confidant or secret keeper for him. I didn't realize how much that bothered me until I had the opportunity to learn more about Jacob. Damn Kelly for being right.

"What are you thinking, gorgeous?"

Honesty will get you nothing right now, Norah!

"Wondering how I got here. I don't mean literally. I had almost everything I've ever wanted in my life a week ago. Now, I feel... lost. I crave order, and right now, I have chaos." High-paying job—check. Family and friends—check. A man in my life—sort of.

"I don't know how or when this will be over, but you will come out of this. Is there anything I can do?"

"No, thanks. I'm sorry for disrupting your life."

"This is my life, Norah. Well, it was when I was taking assignments. Now I give the assignments out, monitor each job, and travel for certain clients. I'm usually the one who delivers the supplies, or coordinates them at least."

We finish our meal, chatting about nothing important. After cleaning the kitchen, we settle on the couch. Jacob stretches out, and I tuck myself against him to watch something, but the cable is out. Instead, I ask one of the questions pinging around in my brain.

"Will you tell me about tomorrow?" I feel him tense under me. "You don't have to. You still have two passes. Well, one and a half at least. I would appreciate an answer to the nickname question at some point."

JACOB

Admitting what Escape means is heavy, almost as weighty as telling her about Mara. Since Connor isn't here, talking to Norah couldn't hurt. Well, it couldn't hurt me. I don't want to fill her head with awful images though.

"I will tell you, but understand, it isn't pretty."

"You don't have to. Earlier you mentioned that the anniversary of something is tomorrow. I'll just sit here with you if you prefer."

"I don't want you to move either way."

She nods against my chest.

Taking a deep breath, I sort the memories in my head before speaking. "During our third deployment, Connor and I were in a convoy. Our vehicle had three other unit members. Carter was a young kid from Alabama. He was tall, lanky, and enlisted to get away from his controlling father. Jones was a huge, beefy linebacker of a man, who enlisted when he didn't make it in the NFL. Adams was a third generation army legacy with a trust fund. He was assigned to the same unit where both his father and grandfather served. Put together, we were a motley crew of misfits." I have only told this story one other time, and that was to a therapist that the army required me to see before retiring.

As if she senses this is going to get harder for me to say, Norah presses her lips to my forearm.

"We were heading into the city. As we approached the gate, a mortar attack took out the front of our convoy. We were the last vehicle. We moved forward to secure the area but started taking enemy fire. As we fell back, Adams was hit in the leg and chest. Connor dragged him back to the vehicle. Jones and Carter were firing back at the enemy while I radioed for help. After Connor got Adams into the vehicle, I turned to motion Jones and Carter to move. They were shot." I close my eyes to push the images from the front of my mind. Adams bleeding out, calling for his girlfriend. Jones was motionless, and Carter was in agonizing pain.

Norah shifts her knees around my thighs as she wraps her arms around me.

When I open my eyes, she's looking at me with a mixture of concern and pride. Not ready to address that look, I continue. "Connor and I left Adams in the vehicle and pulled Jones and Carter in. Connor took a defensive position while I maneuvered the vehicle out of harm's way." I take a deep breath and slowly exhale before telling the rest.

"We moved forward and pulled four other guys into our vehicle. After a short drive, we started taking more enemy fire. Connor took a round in the shoulder. We switched places, and he drove the rest of the way to safety. He and I were able to be patched up."

"What happened to you?" Her voice cracks, but the look in her eyes hasn't changed.

"I was shot in the arm."

"The jagged scar on your left arm?" I nod, pulling her closer. "Is that why you were eerily calm this morning?"

"I'm glad it looked that way. Generally, I'm calm when things go sideways. This morning I wasn't anywhere near calm."

"Why?"

The more I admit, the harder this is going to be when she leaves. "You."

"Me?"

I slide my hands on either side of her face but resist kissing her—just barely. "I've never been in a position to protect someone I care about. Protecting my brothers in the army is one thing, but protecting you is something else. The stakes are even higher, and failure isn't an acceptable outcome." It's impossible for me to reconcile how I feel about her and my feelings against relationships. Don't she and I have one even though we never said the words? I haven't talked to, dated, slept with, or even fantasized about any woman but her for almost two years.

"I don't know what to say to that."

"You don't have to say anything. I'm going to answer your other question now too." I inhale and compose my thoughts. Hopefully, she won't want to run out of here. "Connor is my best friend, and he knows me better than anyone else. I have flashbacks and sleep issues. I've had them since we redeployed. They increase as the anniversary gets closer or when some other memory triggers them. For the last few years, it has only been the anniversary that has caused problems."

"What does that have to do with me?"

"I'm getting there, sweetheart. Since the day I met you, the dreams and sleep issues have mostly dissipated. It makes no sense clinically, but for whatever reason, having you in my life, even occasionally, keeps my brain settled and calm. Connor started joking that I'm using you to escape from my demons." It hurts to say that aloud. I don't see the flashbacks as demons. I see them as reminders of the price of war. I see them as my penance for surviving. I brace myself for her reaction.

"Do you see me that way?" Her voice sounds strained.

"No, if I did, I would have chucked my 'no relationship' mantra out the window."

"Why don't you want to be in a relationship?"

"I can't answer that right now." I fully expect her to move away from me, but she doesn't. If the situation was reversed, I don't know how long I would be willing to wait for a straight answer.

"Will you answer me at some point?"

A heaviness descends on my chest as I strain to reply, "Yes." Telling her about Mara will likely be the last thing I ever say to her. It's best to wait until she's safe.

Coward.

She's studying my face; for what, I'm not sure. Without a word, she resettles against my chest.

"What do you normally do to remember Jones, Carter, and Adams?" she asks, looking up at me. Her shiny eyes make my heart clench in my chest. I don't know which topic hurt her. It could be all of it. It could have been me.

"Connor and I usually have a beer and share a story or two. Why?"

"Just curious."

Near two in the morning, I carry her to the guest room and set Tank at the end of the hall. Even though I should be fine, I opt for the couch.

NORAH

Waking alone isn't an abnormal occurrence for me, even when Jacob and I see each other. This feels different. He chose to sleep away from me even after sharing about his unit and how I calm his mind. How I have that effect on him is beyond me, but I don't understand his hesitance in telling me. His honest adherence against long-term relationships shows that he isn't using me. Why he feels that way is a different story.

Turning into the hall, I find Tank standing watch. Padding up to him, I pet him on the head, and he dutifully follows me. I check the main floor of the house and outside. Snow is still falling, and there is over a foot already on the ground.

"Tank, where is he?"

Tank pushes his nose against my hand and starts to move. I follow, wondering where he's leading me. I won't leave the house, but Jacob is here somewhere. His faithful companion leads me down a hall on the opposite side of the house. Tank sits at the door. When I turn the knob and open the door, he rushes down a set of stairs and sits at the base.

As I descend, I hear the pounding of gloves on a heavy bag. Jacob is shirtless, dripping in sweat with his back to me. The taut lines and sinew of his back are mesmerizing to watch as he strikes the bag. The taper of his waist and his powerful legs equally draw my attention. I know better than to interrupt someone in the middle of a workout. I sit on the bottom step, and Tank lies over my feet.

The room is a full gym. Weight benches and nautilus machines line one wall with a mat area and a set of bands hanging on the wall as well as the bag. I imagine that Connor and Jacob spent hours down here during high school.

"Morning," he says, turning to face me, removing his gloves. Holy hell! As if seeing his back wasn't enough, post-workout Jacob is like a sculpture. I have painstakingly explored every glorious inch of him, but the ability to stare unabashedly is new.

"Morning. Did you sleep?" I ask as he moves closer to me.

"Some, why?"

"You didn't sleep with me." I stand on the lowest step, looking him in the eye. He drags his hand down his face. The expression left behind is hard to read. Apparently I can only read him when sex is involved. I know if it will be rough, tender, fast, or slow based on his demeanor. This side of him, I'm still learning to understand. The realization that I only know a portion of Jacob nicks me a bit. While he shared more last night, it isn't everything. Whatever the reason he refuses to be in a relationship, scarred him deeply.

"I wasn't sure how to handle your reaction or lack thereof. You're truly not upset about the nickname?"

"Should I be?"

He shrugs.

"For starters, you didn't create it. And isn't it a good thing for the flashbacks to be manageable? Are you using me to chase away the awful memories in your head?"

"No." His gruff response is definite and unwavering. Then there is a flicker of something else. Heartache and pain? The why of those feelings is unknown to me right now, but I have no reason to mistrust Jacob. He was honest from the beginning about what he was looking for with me. It's on me that I want more now.

"I believe you."

His shoulders visibly drop, and the tension in his jaw releases. "You're truly a spectacular woman, Norah. More than I deserve to call my friend, let alone anything beyond friendship."

"I feel the same way about you." I reach out, placing my hand on his cheek.

"You would be wrong." He closes his eyes as he finishes speaking.

"No, I'm not. I may not have all the pieces to the puzzle that make you you, but I'm an excellent judge of character. You, Jacob Blackthorne, are a direct, trustworthy, and honorable gentleman, even if you don't see it yourself."

When he opens his eyes, I see a glimpse of something that gives me hope that I'm not in this alone. The possibility of more when this is over. I lean forward, brushing my lips across his, expecting him to pull away. Instead, he deepens our kiss. I'm likely setting myself up for a devastating heartbreak, but right now, the chance of having a crushed heart over a life with him just tipped slightly to the good. I'm taking it.

When I open for him, he explores my mouth. As he pulls his tongue away, I follow, twisting mine with his. Running my fingertips over his back causes goose bumps on his heated skin. A primal look flashes in his eyes as he lifts my T-shirt overhead, revealing my bare breasts. Drawing his hands down my back, he hooks his thumbs in the waistband of my pants, peeling them down my thighs. After his fingertips graze the front of my legs, he lifts my thigh, hooking it around his hip and pressing his unmistakable arousal against me. Grinding against him, I could make myself come easily. His shaft rubs against my nub in perfect rhythm. He repeats the same commands he gave Tank the last time we were together. Tank moves to the top of the stairs.

"You need to stop if you want to make it to the bed."

"Take me now. Right here," I command. I've never really taken control before. It's a heady feeling when my words elicit a low growl. He pushes his shorts and boxer briefs down, and his erection springs free, grazing my soaked core. Turning, he sets my back against the wall before thrusting deep into me in one hard, breathtaking motion. Reaching between us, I circle my nub as Jacob pounds into me. The coils of a release tighten low in my belly. Jacob reaches down and lifts my other leg to his hip, opening me more. Setting my hands on his shoulders, I bear down, engulfing his shaft as he thrusts upward. I hold on to him tightly as he throbs inside me. As my inner walls constrict, I shudder around him, and he explodes.

Resting my forehead to his, I slowly catch my breath. Sex with Jacob has always been exceptional, but that was somehow more. Slowly, he turns away from the wall, lowering us to the landing of the staircase. As if I weigh nothing, Jacob sets me on the floor between his knees. I tug my shirt on and search for my pants while he does the same.

"Race you to the shower," I challenge, cresting the top of the stairs next to Tank.

"You'll only win if I let you," he shouts from behind me.

"Never." I chuckle, hustling down the hallway.

JACOB

Norah beats me to the shower, but I gladly accept the loss, along with the orgasm she drew from me with her mouth. It's one thing to share your body with someone regularly with no intention of longevity or attachment. It's something else when she is as insatiable as you are. Even more so when it becomes something more intimate.

Over lunch, I share the most recent updates with her. "Blaine and Connor sent updates a little while ago."

She pauses eating her sandwich.

"So far they haven't attempted to use your credit cards or other personal information to access your financial accounts. According to Connor, the Morettis are still looking for you, but they're also looking for Stanley and Delores Sterling."

"Delores is Stan's wife. She doesn't work at the firm," Norah offers.

"She did in the past. She was his secretary before she became his wife. They went into hiding after learning of the break-in at your townhouse."

"Does he know something? Do you think he has the ledger?"

"We don't know where the ledger is. You've never seen it?" I know I inquired before, but she was scared and coming off the injection.

"Not that I'm aware of. When Stan gave me the file seven months ago, it was just a standard internal Quinn Sterling file. Nothing special about it other than the sheer volumes of information. Unless there are some subfolders on the server I didn't have access to, I haven't seen anything that looks like a ledger. Did William say anything?"

"Yes, some of your neighbors have video surveillance and caught some images of the assailants at your townhouse. He's going to send over some photos. They were also able to get a good image of the tattoo. That plus the fact that you injured him, they're hopeful they will find out who he is by cross-checking with hospital admissions."

"I'm still pissed they drugged me. It isn't as if an ordinary woman doesn't know how to twist out of a forearm grab."

"I'm sure they have an entire file about you, including the extent of your training. Nothing about you is ordinary. You're brilliant, ambitious, and stunning."

Her eyes sharpen at the compliments, but she only responds with the blush of her skin and a small nod. I choose not to call her on it.

"Is there anything of significant value at your townhouse that should be removed and secured elsewhere for now?"

"Only things of sentimental value, and that's assuming they didn't destroy them looking for this mysterious ledger."

"I can have Maia pack up whatever is salvageable if you want."

"Very little isn't replaceable. Although, I worked really hard for my—"

"Shoes."

The smile she gifts me is genuine, one I haven't seen in the last few days. "I was going to say my car."

"Liar. Your luxury shoes and lingerie are sexy and seductive. They're part of who you are."

"Maybe I should have Maia get them if *you* love them so much."

"I do, but how much isn't pertinent right now?"

"I don't need her at risk for whatever is recoverable at my townhouse. The only important item, you protected for me." She leans forward and kisses me deeply. So much so that I think we just vaulted over the razor-thin, blurry line we're walking with our words, our mouths, and our bodies.

Just after lunch, the snow slows enough to start clearing it. A few random flurries won't impact the progress of removal. Despite my gentlemanly intention to keep her safe in the house, Norah insists on helping. I relent only after setting a few ground rules. She needs to stay within my line of sight and Tank follows her.

We trudge to the shed and dig out the tractor to plow the driveway. With each pass, I check on Norah who is shoveling the walkway to the front porch. I'm fairly confident we're safe here and the tracker has thrown the Moretti family off. The last place they were searching for her was somewhere in New Jersey—a fact I purposefully neglected to mention when I gave her the update earlier. Nothing will make me relax until the bounty is removed. I have Blaine looking into Mr. Sterling and the other partners at the firm.

As I finish the parking area, I move Connor's truck over and clear around it. Norah and Tank walk in front of me toward the back walkway that leads to the deck. On my last pass with the tractor, I don't see Norah. My heart rate increases. If she were only a client, I would never ever allow her to help. She would be safe in the house doing nothing. We wouldn't be here either. I would have selected another location, something that is less comfortable for her, further away from my real life. Nothing about her or this situation is playing out normally with security protocol. I park and move around the house looking for her. When I reach the corner of the house, she beans me with a snowball. The tension in my chest eases almost immediately, at least as it pertains to her safety.

"Are you sure you want to do that?" I ask when she cocks her arm back to throw another in my direction.

"Why not?" she asks with a devilish glint in her eyes.

"You saw me throw the ball for Tank. I won't miss." Bending down without taking my eyes from hers, I make two snowballs for myself.

"True, but throwing a ball for your dog and hitting a wide receiver at thirty yards is something else. How long since you played?"

"You aren't thirty yards away. Did you just call me old?"

She giggles. It's a wonderful sound that reaches deep into my soul. "No, I'm suggesting you may be rusty hitting a target, and you're making an assumption—"

"Such as?"

"You assume I can't throw because I love La Perla, Agent Provocateur, Louboutin, and Manolo Blahnik."

"Maybe I am. Are you going to prove—" My words are cut off by a snowball hitting me center mass, immediately followed by another in my left shoulder.

"Would you like to select where I hit you next?" Clearly, she has some skills throwing—from where, I have no idea.

"How many more do you have stockpiled back there?"

"Enough." She's armed with another snowball, ready to lob it my way. At this point, I have no doubt she will hit me.

I consider my options, none of them are ideal.

"You have two shots there. Take them."

She's goading me. I lift my arm, ready to throw. The moment it leaves my hand, she jumps down the short staircase and runs into the yard. My throw hits the railing. Instead of giving chase right away, I peek at her stockpile. She was out. Vixen!

I follow her footprints to the base of a large tree. I can't believe the treehouse is still here. Connor, Mara, and I would spend hours just hanging out in this tree. *Mara*. This moment is the first time I've thought about her since we arrived at her childhood home. As I start to climb,

Norah runs out from behind the tree back toward the house. I drop to the ground. She has a few strides lead.

"You're clever, but I'm faster than you." I wrap my arms around her waist, pulling her against me before we fall into the snow.

"Maybe I let you catch me."

I press my lips to hers. "I wouldn't have given up. Where did you learn to throw like that?"

"All-state shortstop for four years in high school."

"Impressive. What other hidden talents do you have?"

"I guess you will have to stick with me and figure them out."

The moment the words leave her mouth, I feel her tense in my arms. *Damn*!

"I'm sorry. I shouldn't have...." She pushes herself up and hurries away from me.

NORAH

I plod back to the walkway and grab the shovel. *What were you thinking?* I wasn't. I was *feeling*. I was being honest. Wordlessly, I walk past Jacob to the shed, replacing the shovel where it belongs.

"Norah," he calls from his spot in the yard. I raise one hand and walk back to the house, Tank hot on my heels.

Get it together, Norah! I chastise myself as I walk directly to the guest room, stripping off the outer coat and boots. I hear the door close, and Tank runs out of the room.

Moments later, Tank returns, but he's not alone.

"Talk to me."

"I can't."

He steps in front of me, his right hand cupping my cheek. "Can't or won't?"

"I promised I could be with you and not.... I can't. I may say something else I can't take back." How on earth am I going to be near him but keep myself in check now?

"I won't push you to talk, but I care about you."

"So you've said, but you aren't looking to be mine, or anyone's for that matter."

"Norah, it's complicated."

"Is it?"

"Yes."

"You said you would explain why. I'll wait until you do, but I need some space to regain my composure."

"Norah, I—"

"Please just give me some space."

Jacob presses his lips to my forehead before leaving the room. The tears fall the moment the door closes. I knew this would happen, but I needed his help. I had no one else to call. I wouldn't be alive if I tried to run on my own with a tracker imbedded in my neck. I can't even talk to anyone right now.

There's a soft knock on the door. As I set my hand on the knob and twist, he starts talking.

"Don't talk too long. You could probably talk to Kelsey longer than Kelly, if that matters." He claims he doesn't want a relationship, but he certainly does the right things—the forehead kisses and knowing I need to talk to someone, even if it isn't him.

I attempt to thank him, but the words catch in my throat. Opening the door, I find the hallway empty and the phone on the floor. A few calming breaths later, I dial.

"Hello."

"Hi, Kelsey." I'm sure William filled her in about my situation.

"What happened, sweets?"

"I...."

"Oh, Nor. Gorgeous, piercing blue eyes Jacob Blackthorne is *the* guy?" Until now Kelsey knew there was a regular exceptional booty call, but not who.

"Yes."

"How long?"

"Since your wedding."

"Wow, you both hid it well."

"I thought I could handle it. Who doesn't want spectacular sex with no strings attached?"

"You... at least not anymore."

She isn't wrong. I was so focused on my partnership. I didn't want anything or anyone in my life to slow me down. Now, my life is in complete chaos. I have no job, my townhouse trashed, and I'm on the run with the one man I want but can't have for the rest of my life.

"All kidding aside, what's changed?" she asks.

"Circumstances and proximity. Before, there were no feelings, at least on his end. His kiss shifted from hot and passionate to reverent, melt into a puddle inside *and* outside the bedroom. I had almost everything I worked for, and now I'm starting over, except for the man in the next room... ugh!"

"You know the answer, sweets."

"I just... he's just so many of the things. Do you know what I mean?"

"Yes, the pieces fit, even the prickly ones. The ones no one wants to talk about: the past, the damage, especially the messy. Do you need me to say it?"

"No." I exhale sharply. "I need to suck it up or tell him that I broke my promise. Then let the dominoes fall, even if it smashes my heart into a million tiny pieces."

"That's my girl."

"Love you, Kels."

"Love you, sweets. Take care. Hopefully, I can see you soon."

I fall back onto the bed and consider what she said. I just needed someone else to say it. Can I be with him without a commitment? Don't I already have one? Not an official one.

The real question is how to handle him now. If I'm headed for heartbreak, I might as well go in with my eyes open and my body humming with pleasure. Resolved to deal with the pain later, I clean up and head out into the kitchen. Apparently, my words didn't only mess with my head and my heart. They messed with Jacob's too.

"Where is he, Tank?"

Tank walks to the top of the basement stairs and sits.

"Thanks, boy. Let's leave him alone." I scour the kitchen for ingredients for dinner.

At least one of Connor's parents knows how to cook well. The spice rack has almost everything I could ever need. I pull out some sausage, rice, and broccoli. After I set the meat to defrost. I search for dessert ingredients. At this point, I'll settle for a box brownie mix since I can't really drink an entire bottle of cabernet. After a successful search, I have the ingredients to make a spice cake with cream cheese frosting. When I turn to throw the broccoli stems away, a car pulls into the driveway. I hustle down the stairs. Jacob is sitting on the weight bench, head in his hands, dripping in sweat. *Holy hell! It isn't going to get easier, Norah!*

His head pops up, his eyes meeting mine. "What's wrong?"

"There's someone here."

He whistles for Tank and asks me to stay put. At first I sit on the landing but move almost instantly. *Time to suck it up, sweets.* I pace the floor, unsure what else to do. I'm sure whoever is here isn't after me.

I hear Jacob talking to someone, likely a man based on the tone of voice. He opens the doors and releases Tank, who runs up the stairs.

JACOB

Six years. I've spent the last six years on my own. No attachments, no relationships until her. I slam the weights onto the bar and repeat on the other side. I was clear from the beginning with Norah. Until her text, I was fine. Two or three times a month, I saw her. A few months, it was more. Sometimes I stayed; other times I didn't. Five reps, then a break. I can't blame her. I don't blame her. I'm confused too.

I need to protect her. Comfort her. I find myself touching her even though I know she's my client. *She was never just a client.* Five reps, then a break.

Hurried footsteps pull me out of my scattered thoughts.

"What's wrong?"

"There's someone here."

"Please stay here." I lean forward to kiss her but pull back. Her sharp inhale makes my chest ache. For the second time today, my heart is in my throat. I grab a towel on my way up the stairs. I'm failing her. I'm off my game, unprepared for this situation. I let my guard down. I'm unarmed. I hear the faint tones of the alarm system. Whoever is here knows the alarm code. My trepidation decreases a bit. No one who knows that code is a threat to Norah.

"Dad, what are you doing here?" I ask, stepping into the living area.

"I could ask you the same thing. Good to see you, son."

"Working. Norah is a friend and now a client. My plan A was compromised, so Connor suggested here. You?"

"Ed and Joyce are travelling. I came to shovel them out. How long have you been here?"

Connor's parents are away on a tropical vacation for their anniversary.

"Two days. Let me get Norah. I'll be right back." I exhale slowly. Everything is fine, at least pertaining to her safety. When I open the basement door, Tank turns his head my way. I release him, and he runs up the stairs. I hustle down the stairs. Norah is sitting with her legs crossed and her feet atop the other leg.

"Everything okay?" she asks without moving.

"Yes, it's my dad. He came to shovel. You can come up."

"Thanks, I'll be up in a minute."

I move away from her and sit on the weight bench.

"You don't have to stay with me," she says without moving or opening her expressive eyes.

"I know." I'm still working out earlier today, and now my dad is here. Norah and I can talk later.

She slowly releases her feet and throws her arms over her legs, gripping her feet. After a few moments, she gracefully stands. I can only watch her.

"What is your dad's name?"

"Ben."

"Same last name?"

"Yes." No one has ever been astute enough to ask that question. Then again, I don't share anything about my life…with anyone. When I set my hand on her forearm, her eyes lift to mine. The storminess has lessened since she asked for space. Whoever she called talked her through her feelings enough that she has regained her grasp on them. Whatever she's feeling, she has locked it up. Where that falls on the spectrum of good and bad, I'm not sure. "Thank you, Norah."

"Of course."

I follow her upstairs. Ignoring the sway of her perfect hips is impossible. My head, my dick, and especially my heart are screaming different things. My head settles on there is a way to work this out. My dick is standing at attention, even though I may never touch her again— never feel her shudder beneath me or the soft press of her lips on mine. My heart is a much more complicated mess right now. When I pull myself out of my thoughts, I notice Norah has kept walking.

"It's a pleasure to meet you, Mr. Blackthorne," I hear Norah say to my father.

"Ben, please call me Ben."

Norah moves into the kitchen and starts cooking. It looks as if she was preparing dinner before she rushed downstairs.

My dad takes a seat at the island. "My son was a tad sketchy on details. He mentioned you are a client."

Norah gazes up at me, looking for permission to share whatever she chooses to. "Yes, he has worked for my sister. I contacted him for help during a break-in at my townhouse."

"Son, why don't you go clean up? I'll keep Norah company."

I look to Norah, and she nods almost imperceptibly. If anyone can provide backup, it's my father. I wouldn't be surprised if he's armed.

"Thanks." I move down the hall to the bedroom. Hurrying through the shower, I clean up quickly. As I towel off, I notice the mountain of white tissue in the trash. *I made her cry.* My heart shreds just a bit more. There is no scenario where I can split my focus again. I was committed to the army and Mara. I failed her. I should have been here to protect her, and I wasn't. I will never repeat that mistake again. I failed Mara, and I refuse to fail Norah. Shoving my thoughts aside, I dress and rejoin them in the kitchen.

NORAH

The availability of cute childhood stories and mischief are almost too much to ignore. But I can't let myself get more attached to Jacob. He doesn't want a relationship. Wrapping my head around that again and separating out my feelings isn't going to be easy.

"You failed to mention that you were also all-state in high school," I say as Jacob approaches from the hall. Despite my efforts otherwise, I note his damp hair, his shirt clinging to his impressive chest, and athletic shorts low on his lean hips. *You can't have him!*

"You didn't ask," he states, moving behind me to the sink. "What are you making?"

"Risotto with sausage and broccoli."

"Can I help?"

"I can do it." *I can't handle you close to me right now, especially with an audience.*

"I insist."

Stifling the sigh and frustrated huff I desperately want to unleash, I turn toward the sink, and Jacob does as well.

"I know the timing isn't ideal. I'm sorry," Jacob whispers, his hand on the small of my back. I increase the space between us and ask him to blanche the broccoli.

"What is your profession, Norah?" Ben asks to ease the tension in the kitchen.

"I'm an accountant."

"You don't look like an accountant."

I consider my attire: yoga pants, a graphic T-shirt, and Jacob's hoodie. He's probably right, at least frozen in this moment.

"What does an accountant look like?" I reply in jest.

"Touché." Ben shakes his head. "What about your family?"

I share details about my family and that I live in Maine as I sauté the sausage and start the risotto. As we chat, Jacob starts cursing behind me.

"Norah, a little help?"

I turn and start laughing. "What are you doing? Do you know how to blanche a vegetable?"

"Nope."

Why didn't he tell me?

"It's easy. You need to boil some water and cook the broccoli for a brief time so it's still crisp but not mushy."

He fills the pan and moves next to me at the stove. I clearly didn't think this through. We're hip to hip, his hand on my back, his shoulders brushing mine. Overall, not sexual in any way except, with him, every touch sets my nerve endings on fire. The heat rolling off him is too much.

Jacob and Ben start chatting while I work on dinner. Thankfully, he moves to the sink to strain the broccoli. I'm losing grip on my rapidly fraying resolve. I'm hurt, heartbroken, and pissed—mostly because the heartbroken part is solely and completely my fault. I broke the promise I made to him and myself. Now I need to deal with this situation and hope it's over soon so I can go home. Alone.

I turn toward the sink and crash into Jacob washing the pan.

"Crap, I'm sorry." There's water all over the floor. My feet are wet, but otherwise fine. Turning back, I grab the pot holder and slip. Thankfully Jacob's reflexes are superhuman. His arm curves around my waist, and he pulls me flush against him. It's impossible to miss his arousal pressing against my ass. Taking two steps back, he sets me on the floor. He dries my feet before drying the floor. While he does that, I move the risotto off the heat.

Thankfully, there are no more mishaps, and we sit down for dinner. Ben shares stories about Jacob as a baby and a few including Connor and the pond behind this property. During dinner, Jacob's phone rings and he excuses himself to answer it.

"Did Jacob give you any idea how long you will be here?" Ben asks.

"Here in this house or with him as my security?"

"Either or both."

I hadn't really thought about it. Until earlier, I was fine being with Jacob indefinitely. Now, not so much. "Actually, I don't know the answer to either. It has only been a few days. We're waiting for the photos from Captain Ramirez."

Jacob returns but says nothing regarding the content of his call. I'm sure he will tell me later.

"Dad, stop grilling her. She isn't a suspect."

"Sorry, old habit."

I nod and move to clear my dish. Both Jacob and Ben stand as I move from my chair. I inhale sharply but don't release the breath until I get to the sink, Jacob following closely behind me.

"Are you okay?" Jacob whispers, even though Ben wouldn't be able to hear him from the dining area.

"Yes." *No, not even close.* How does he do that? How does he know my mind is spinning? I can't stop thinking about what I said. I meant every word, even though I shouldn't have voiced them.

"Norah." He wraps his hand around my arm.

"Jacob, I'm fine." He knows I'm lying. I can see it in his eyes. He slides his hand up my arm and cups my cheek. I lean into his hand even though I shouldn't. "I'll wash these. Go chat with your dad."

Please read between the lines, Jacob, I silently beg. My head and my heart are a muddled mess right now. That isn't even taking into consideration the true reason I'm here.

"Fine, but we need to talk about earlier today and that call from William."

"Okay."

JACOB

The look in her eyes is tortured, pained, heartbreaking, and I put it there. Well, arguably anyway. I grab a water for myself and a beer for my father, and we walk onto the porch.

"I'm sorry that my timing isn't great," my father states as we stand on the porch.

"Not your fault." It's mine. Completely mine.

"I know you said she's a client, but how long have you been a couple?"

"We aren't."

A look of disbelief crosses my father's face. "How long have you been friends with benefits?"

I turn and look my father square in the eyes. I'm not surprised he can see the tension between me and Norah, both sexual and otherwise. I'm a tad taken aback by his use of modern terminology though.

"Almost two years." I set the water bottle down on the railing and stare out into the yard. Images of earlier today rush through my head, from the snowballs to her walking away from me. The fun, joyful moments to the painful one. Two people acting like a normal couple until—

"You've never brought a client this close to home. What's different about her?"

"Nothing...." I grip the railing in front of me with both hands, my knuckles turning white before I manage to mutter, "Everything." I haven't even admitted any of this to Norah.

"You deserve to be happy, Jake."

"Do I? I had Mara. I failed her. I never want to feel that way again." I'm giving up the blissful side of a relationship too, but the anguish and pain—never again. The same pain that reflects back at me in Norah's eyes. The pain I'm causing her right now.

"Do you know how your mother and I met?"

"Of course, you met a few weeks before you deployed to your first active-duty station and you agreed to write and talk while you were gone." That's what I recall anyway.

"That's only partially accurate. We did meet just before I left for my first duty station in Germany for two years. Your mother and I agreed to write and keep in touch. We also agreed we weren't exclusive. About a month after I arrived, I met a woman named Sofie. She worked in a coffee shop near the barracks. After a few weeks of daily coffee runs, both in the morning and afternoon, I worked up the courage to ask Sofie on a date."

I turn to look inside the house. Norah has her back to me, leaning against the sink. Can I handle being alone again when this is over? Do I want to? Will she still want me when I share my past? I refocus on my father's words.

"We became inseparable. Whenever I wasn't on duty, I was with Sofie exploring the country, the culture, and her. Despite all the time I was spending with Sofie, I wrote your mom religiously. After a year, Sofie introduced me to her parents. As you can imagine, it didn't go well. They forbade her from seeing me."

"You didn't listen though."

"No, we didn't. Sofie and I snuck around for the remainder of my tour. Two weeks before I was set to return stateside, I proposed to Sofie and she accepted."

I'm rapt. I have never heard this part of my parents' love story. I glance inside again, but Norah is no longer in the kitchen. A moment later, she walks by, grabs a book from the living room, and walks out of sight again.

"Sofie and I arranged for a temporary visa for her to travel to the United States to join me. I'm sure you can guess what happened next."

"She never showed."

"No, she didn't. I spoke to her just before she was supposed to board, and everything seemed fine. Lovestruck, I drove to the airport and waited for her. Her flight landed, but she didn't deplane. I approached the information desk and asked if she boarded the flight. Even though she shouldn't have, the clerk shared that Sofie checked in but never boarded."

"What happened next? How did you get from Sofie not showing to a solid marriage with Mom thirty-seven years later?" My parents' marriage is stable and still filled with love all these years later. Considering they couldn't have children of their own, it wasn't without difficulties.

"I never heard from Sofie again. Six weeks later, I received a package from Sofie's father containing my engagement ring."

That's awful.

"Did Mom know about Sofie?"

"Yes, she knew."

Incredible. Yet, Mom still chose Dad, even knowing he was set to marry someone else.

"How long?" Quickly doing the math in my head doesn't answer how long between his return and breakup until his wedding with my mom.

"A lot shorter than you have endured. I understand the circumstances with Mara were different. It wasn't her choice, but she was ripped away from you just the same." His words hit me square in the chest.

"How do I forgive myself?"

"Honestly, the guilt you carry is undeserved. You did nothing wrong. Your first love story was cut tragically short. You couldn't have prevented Mara's death, regardless of your penchant for protecting people you love, especially that woman in the house." He believes I love Norah—a notion I have pushed fervently against. A fact I refuse to admit to myself.

"I assume Norah doesn't know about Mara."

"No."

"Have you been with anyone else?"

I shake my head curtly. I'm in a relationship with Norah, just not the kind she deserves.

"Son, you need to forgive yourself. You should be honest with Norah and yourself. Especially yourself. Share Mara with Norah. She taught you how to love for Norah. Tell her you love her, or she will leave when this is over, despite her feelings for you. Then you'll endure two losses instead of one. You have built a multimillion-dollar security business. You deserve to share it with someone who loves you. Mara would want you to be happy."

I nod tightly.

"Thank you for sharing." I follow him to the door.

"You're welcome. Join us for dinner on Sunday. Your mother would love to see you." I don't miss the underlying message—Norah too.

"If it's safe enough, we will, or we can come up with a different plan."

"Please say goodbye to Norah for me."

I nod as he steps out the door. I lean against the door, waiting for the alarm to reengage. After downing a water, I walk down the hall toward her. My chest is tight, and my heart aches. I'm not ready to do this. I should, but I don't know if I can.

NORAH

Space, I just need space to get my head straight. I need to leave and soon. I can't stay with him, considering how loudly my heart is screaming with want. My head is screaming to run. After dinner, I suggest that Jacob talk with his dad. Mostly for me, but a little for him. I'm sure it has been a while since he was able to have a decent chat with his father.

After finishing the dishes, I grab a book and curl up in this chair. It looks as if I'm reading, but I'm not really focused on the words. My mind is pinging back and forth in a host of different directions. Mostly I just produce more questions. Questions about my desires for my life going forward. Losing my partnership after working toward it for six years opens a lot of available options. I can pretty much do whatever I want. Thanks to my diligence, my desire to become a partner early, and Jacob's intuition to freeze my accounts, I could take a break from work for a significant amount of time.

Until recently, being partner was all I wanted. I forwent dates, vacations, and even girls' night out to further my career. I was fine on my own. No drama with boyfriends or the angst of dating. That got even better after Jacob came into the picture offering exceptional, heart-pounding sex, no strings attached, at least twice a month. Perfect. Little did I know it was monogamous on both sides. That just makes this even harder. The bottom line is I broke my promise to him and myself. No feelings, I agreed. As I chastise myself, Tank lifts his head off the floor.

Pushing my thoughts away, I look up at Jacob who is standing in the doorway.

"Thank you."

I don't know what they talked about, but it was heavy. His face is tight and his eyes pained. "You're welcome. What's wrong?"

"Nothing new. That was William on the phone earlier. He sent the photos. We need you to look at them when you're ready. Also, the FBI wants to talk with you. We can do it nearby or we can go to Boston." He's not being completely honest with me.

"Now works. As far as the FBI, whichever option you feel is safer for me is fine." Despite the turmoil in my love life, if you will, I trust Jacob completely regarding my safety.

He pulls out his laptop and reaches for my hand but lets it drop before I can take his. We need to get on the same page, even if it's only for right now.

I follow Jacob to the kitchen with Tank close behind. He boots the laptop and motions for me to sit. Reaching around me, he enters the password. The caress of his breath on my skin and his nearness scrambles my senses.

"Here. William sent these during dinner. Are any of these the correct tattoo?"

Scanning the first set of images, nothing looks familiar. I open the second set and my hands start shaking. I close my eyes to stop the replay in my mind. *I'm running toward the stairs. Just as I reach the top step, a big, meaty hand grasps my left ankle.*

"Norah." Jacob moves to my side, reaching his hand across my lap and turning me to face him on the stool. Against my better judgment, I lean into his embrace. Damn, that feels so right! "Tell me, please."

"The third, fourth, and fifth image are the guy who drugged me."

"Good job, Norah." Once the words leave his mouth, his lips are pressed against mine.

As much as I want his lips on mine, I pull back and look into his expressive eyes. Desire, lust, and confusion are staring back at me. I'm sure mine are saying the same thing, plus a bit of exhilaration from finding the right image.

"I'm sorry," Jacob whispers.

"We need to get on the same page before we do that again."

"Okay. Let me respond to William and get an update to decide where you should talk to the FBI." As if he can't help himself, he softly kisses my forehead. A forehead kiss is so much *less* intimate. He takes the stool next to mine and slides his laptop over.

I push off the stool and move into the kitchen to plate some cake for us and make two cups of coffee. I haven't truly watched Jacob work. I have been in a car chase of sorts, but him doing desk work, his brow furrowed and his focus rapt on the screen or the call, it's another side of

Jacob. It makes him even more attractive. *I'm not getting out of this unscathed.*

After setting a plate and a fresh cup of coffee next to him, I retake my seat while he works. He takes a call from Connor and Blaine and emails William and someone named Callen. Almost two hours later, I wash the dishes, then pad to the bedroom to change my clothes.

Wrapping myself in the blanket from the chair, I return to the living room and gaze out the French doors from the couch. Whoever Jacob is talking to didn't give him the answer he was looking for. After a few choice words, he hangs up and closes the laptop before joining me on the couch.

"There are two options for meeting with the FBI as I explained. Neither option is ideal, in my opinion. Flying to Boston makes more sense, only because it won't give away where we are now. I'll have to find somewhere else to stay and likely for a while."

"I called you because this is what you do. If you feel that flying to Boston is the safest option, then that's what I will do. When are we leaving?" That isn't the only reason, but I don't believe rehashing my feelings blunder is wise.

"I'm waiting on confirmation from Pemberton, but it'll likely be midday tomorrow, and Connor will be joining us. Maia will meet us as well." He's worried if he's using three of his staff to go to Boston, or the Moretti family is exactly as he described. More realistically, both.

"Okay. I don't have clothes to meet the FBI."

"Neither do I. Connor will bring some with him." The look of concern on his face hasn't lessened.

"You're truly worried about this meeting?"

"Yes." The edge on his voice doesn't help calm me at all. It wasn't there before he talked to his father.

"What are the ramifications if I don't go?"

He looks out into the backyard instead of at me. When I set my hand on his, he turns to look at me. The concern in his eyes makes my stomach bottom out.

"Right now, the meeting is voluntary. They just want to talk to you."

"You didn't answer my question. What if I don't go now?"

Jacob inhales sharply, closing his eyes. I tighten my fingers around his. Slowly, he lets out his breath. Releasing his hand, I slide my hands around his face, forcing him to look at me.

JACOB

"Talk to me," she says, her hands cupping my face.

Prohibiting myself from laying her out on this couch becomes increasingly harder each time she touches me. *I'm an idiot!* I have been touching her as if she's mine since the hospital without regard to our agreement.

"I have so much to say. You deserve an answer to your question and to ask as many more as you need, but now isn't the time. Aside from that, my gut is churning. It isn't a normal occurrence when I'm working. It has only happened once before." The only other time I felt this way was the day of the attack in Afghanistan. The problem I'm having now is whether it's an instinct or my feelings for Norah. Maybe it's both.

"Is it me or going to Boston?" she asks softly. Perhaps she thinks I won't answer her.

"Both." Turning my head, I press a kiss to the inside of her palm and slowly rise from the couch.

Her eyes flutter closed, and she slowly releases a breath. As I stare out in the yard, I run through a myriad of options for tomorrow's meeting. Different routes we can take, different groupings of personnel. I can use everyone except Callen. Any way I look at it, I know what I must do. Norah isn't going to like it one bit. It'll keep her safe and keep my head in the game. Turning, I move back to the couch. Norah is using a soft throw blanket as a wrap. I see the thin strap of her red, silky pajamas peeking out at the shoulder. The libidinous side of my brain is screaming to draw it down her arm to expose her luscious.... I reach my hand out to her. She slides her slender fingers along my palm, which makes my chest tighten. Gently, I tug her to standing. "I need to finish the plans for tomorrow. I'll answer your question when we get back. I will tell you everything you want to know."

Norah nods, clasping her arms around my neck. With my arms around her, my fingers graze the exposed skin at her waist due to her outstretched arms. I memorize the feel of her against me. Before I go against what we agreed upon again, I let my fingers slide off her soft skin.

"Try to get some sleep."

She nods before saying, "You too."

I watch her walk away with Tank following closely. I'm jealous of my dog right now—a dog who will at any moment lie beside Norah protectively. Returning to the kitchen, I brew a cup of coffee and start making plans to protect Norah.

"Yeah, Jake," Connor answers on the first ring.

"I need you to get Christoph and Nolan on that plane with you. At a minimum, I need them in Boston tomorrow for this meeting."

"Her or the meeting?" He knows me too well. You would think he would be front and center against my happiness. Never, not once, did Connor blame me for failing Mara.

"Both. Something doesn't feel right about this."

"Let's hash out your plan."

I spend the next hour plus talking through my plan with Connor, the pitfalls, and areas of concern, including leaving her with him.

"She isn't going to be happy about that part of your plan."

"No, she isn't. It needs to be done." I will not be able to manage every aspect of this if my gut turns out to be correct, if this meeting is a setup to abduct Norah.

"Have you told her yet?"

Tell her what exactly? I'm completely in love with her and I hope she won't break my heart into a million pieces when I tell her about my past with Mara. "No, I will after we get back from Boston."

"My sister would want you to be happy, Jake."

"Thanks, C. Take care of her for me." I realize that I'm asking my deceased wife's twin brother to protect the woman I love.

"I will as you would for me if the time ever comes."

"Thank you."

Seemingly satisfied with my answer, Connor hangs up to prepare for this assignment. No more than a heartbeat passes before my phone rings.

"What's going on, Blaine?"

"The Sterlings have been taken from their log cabin in New York."

I pin down more details and dissect the information he provides. "Anything else of note?"

"If the meeting with the FBI tomorrow is supposed to be discreet, it isn't. It was broadcast by a few low-level players in the Moretti Family. Make sure you include some cat and mouse if you plan to bring Norah to Boston."

"I will. Any attempts on her accounts?"

"Just one. There was an internet attempt to get into her personal account where her paycheck is deposited. They were likely fishing in the hopes of getting her personal information. I was alerted, and the attempt was blocked."

"Thank you. Please let me know if anything changes."

"Will do."

After running through the plan twice more, I decide to get some sleep. I recheck the alarm and the doors. Quietly, I call Tank. Sleepily, he saunters down the hall. I give him commands before heading to the guest room.

At the threshold, I'm surprised to find Norah wide awake reading. Wordlessly she closes the book, sets her glasses on top, and pulls back the covers. Ignoring the warring feelings coursing through me, I strip off my clothes before sliding under the covers with her.

Curling my arm around her slim waist, I draw her against me. A shallow sigh escapes her lips. Her arm rests on top of mine, her curves nestled against me.

"Good night, Jacob."

"Good night, Norah." I inhale her vanilla-scented lotion as I drift off to sleep.

NORAH

Every. Single. Day. I want this. He's on his back, and my left leg is across his thigh. I'm resting on his shoulder, and his right hand is flat against my hip. Despite the plan for later today, right now, tangled in Jacob's arms, I feel protected. That isn't to say I'm not terrified to leave here, but with him by my side, I can handle this meeting. Honestly, I'm sure a phone call would be sufficient. I don't have the ledger that the Morettis want. Repeating it over and over will convey my position eventually.

"Did you sleep?" I ask when his breathing pattern changes.

"Yes. You?"

"Enough. When will Connor be here?"

"We're meeting him at the airport. Why?"

"Just wondering how much longer we can stay here like this."

"For a little while longer."

I snuggle deeper into his arms, closing my eyes. I can feel his heart beating against my temple. Even at the prospect of having my question answered, I'm still nervous to hear him out. His conversation with his father changed how Jacob looks at me, or he isn't trying to hide his feelings anymore.

All too soon, an alarm blares on his phone.

Pushing myself up, I sit on the edge of the bed a moment before padding to the bathroom. Jacob turns to watch me.

"You have to tell me something, don't you?"

"The Sterlings were abducted from their cabin in New York late yesterday."

I pause brushing my teeth. "Are they all right?"

"I don't know." Jacob pushes up to sitting.

Holy Hell! Even though I have seen Jacob first thing in the morning, I've never been able to ogle without feeling rushed. His hair is mussed, his eyes are sleepy, but the rest of him looks like it always does—like a work of art carved by one of the world's finest sculptors. The ridges and curves of his chest and abs make my mouth water. If I'm going to have a broken heart, I need to study every ridge and divot for when I'll never be able to touch him again. That notion makes my heart heavy.

In the next moment, Jacob is standing in front of me, snapping me out of my lustful daydream. "Did you hear me?"

"No, not at all. I was… never mind. What?" If he realizes where my head was, he doesn't acknowledge it.

"Would you like coffee?"

"Yes, please."

You would think Jacob walking away wouldn't be worth a second look. You would be wrong. The definition of his back is equally as impressive as his chest, and his ass is simply perfect. I refrain from fanning myself and step into the shower. The steamy water loosens the tension in my neck and shoulders. I can do this. Jacob will help me through this.

When I step out of the shower, there is a hot cup of coffee on the vanity with a sun drawn in the foam. I smile and take the first sip. After surrounding myself with a towel, I pull open the door. Jacob is standing in a towel sipping from a cup of black coffee. His chivalry apparently allows me the master bathroom while he uses the guest suite.

"I forgot socks," he mumbles.

Really?

"Why are you on edge? How you look shirtless isn't a secret. Stark naked isn't a secret either."

His skin turns a bright shade of pink. Him blushing will be the death of me.

"What else do you need to tell me about today?"

"I'm always on edge when moving a client. Sprinkle in the fact that it's you, I'm more edgy than normal. I need to share the plan with you, but not yet. Sometimes things change, so I'll wait."

Stepping into his space, I set my hand on this chest. His eyes close briefly before they settle on mine. "I'll be fine." I trust him to keep me physically safe. My heart is another matter.

"Norah, I—" His phone ringing interrupts our conversation.

"Go."

If he doesn't answer, it will worry whoever is on the other end. I pull out a set of clothes, knowing I'll need to change on the plane. I pack up everything I have here and carry the bag to the kitchen. As I near him, Jacob reaches down and takes the bag from my grasp. I simply shake my head and make us fresh coffee. "Do you want something to eat?"

"Sure, something simple. We need to leave in less than an hour. I'll be right back."

After a quick perusal of the cabinets, I scramble some eggs with veggies and toast sourdough bread. As I finish washing the last pan, Jacob emerges fully dressed and ready to leave with his bag in hand.

"Thanks. That was quick! Do you have any food vices, Norah? You seem to eat very well, no junk. Even though you made the delicious cake, you didn't really eat yours."

Hmm, he noticed that. Interesting. "You're welcome. I do, but I don't indulge often."

"Don't you dare say something about your weight," he commands while levelling his eyes to mine.

Concealing what his words mean to me is difficult. Although, it's impossible to ignore his physical reactions to me. I never questioned his attraction to me or mine to him. The attraction was instant. The first time we were together was straight fire. Every time since then measures up equally. "It is more about genetics. All my older family members are diabetic. I'm careful about how much sugar I eat."

He finishes his eggs. A few bites later, the toast is gone as well. I finish my breakfast and clean the dishes. Jacob refills Tank's water and leads me to Connor's truck. The ride to the airport is mostly quiet. When

I gaze over at Jacob, his face is tight with concern. Reaching over, I take his hand in mine without a word. As we pull into the airport parking lot, Jacob's fingers tighten around mine, but he says nothing. After parking, he ushers me into the lobby.

A very tall, mountain of a man extends his hand to me.

"Norah, this is Christoph. He has been on Kelly's detail, but I don't know if you've met. Christoph, this is Norah, Kelly's sister."

"Nice to meet you."

"You as well." Soon after our arrival, Connor and another young guy join us. After introductions, we board the plane. The young guy named Nolan is one of the newer team members. He's tall, but not as tall as Christoph. Compared to the other team members, Nolan is skinny. I wouldn't be surprised if he's a martial artist as well. We take our seats and wait until we're airborne.

JACOB

When our pilot, Cash Morgan, removes the seat belt sign, the team huddles around a small table. Keenly aware of Norah's presence, we go over the plan step by step. Maia joins our meeting by satellite phone. She's awaiting our arrival at the airstrip in Boston.

"Team A will accompany Norah to the meeting with the Feds. You will leave from the hangar in an SUV. The side entrance has been requested for entry into the building. You will meet with Special Agents Tamara Brown and Stephen Morse. The meeting is expected to take no more than an hour."

Norah is just off to my left. She's close enough that I can smell her perfume but not too close that anyone other than Connor would know about us. I'm not trying to hide my relationship with her; I would just like to know where she and I stand before enduring the commentary from my employees. They may work for me, but I consider each one a member of my family. The balance between the two is delicate.

"Team B will take a longer route to the federal building. Your team will enter the building through the rear entrance. Both teams will meet there before returning here for a flight to the farm. Any questions?"

No one asks any questions. Last night, Connor, who will escort Norah to the meeting, and I discussed contingency plan upon contingency plan in case any part of today goes south. I know my sample set is small, but my stomach is twisted in knots. Something is hinky about this meeting. Now I need to face the even harder part of the plan—informing Norah that I'm not accompanying her.

"Maia, you have the supplies you need?"

"Yes, all set."

Maia will dress like Norah dresses on a workday but with a red wig. If her heels are tall enough, Maia could pass as Norah from a distance to anyone except me.

Connor hands me a bag, presumably containing our clothes. The flight isn't that long, so it's time to break the news to Norah.

"Norah, would you come with me?"

She knows about the clothes, so she doesn't think twice. I don't miss the look exchanged by Christoph and Nolan. Connor will set them straight once Norah is out of earshot.

"Your clothes are in this bag with a red wig. Maia has the same one." Opening the bag, I pull out my clothes and consider leaving. *Man up, Jacob!*

"Norah, I—"

"You aren't coming with me, are you?"

The dejected tone in her voice is impossible to miss. It feels like a stake in my heart. I shouldn't be surprised. She's brilliant. She's everything a man could want in a wife. Smart as hell, ambitious, sassy, fiercely loves her family and friends, and she's a bombshell with perfect curves. Once she knows the truth about Mara, I hope she doesn't shut me out.

"I can't."

She steps closer to me but doesn't touch me. Less than an inch separates us. Her wide eyes stare into mine. All I want is to pull her into my arms and protect her from everything. Lock her onto my property and keep her there. That would never work with a woman like her, someone independent and strong. A sinfully sexy woman who chose to do the right thing, even though it likely cost her everything she has worked for in the last six years.

"Why?" she asks.

How do I explain this without ripping her heart out?

"I let my guard down the moment we were alone. I was not prepared to protect you had our visitor been someone hell-bent on harming you. You make me lose focus. I refuse to be the weak link when it involves your safety."

"I understand."

"You aren't going to argue with me?"

"No. I'm sure your reasons are sound and you don't see another way." Her unflinching faith in me is difficult to fully accept.

"To best protect you, I need you with Connor. Please do what he says. I trust him with my life. For reasons you will better understand later, I trust him with yours."

Before giving her the opportunity to speak, and against our agreement, I seize her mouth. I have no right to kiss her, but I won't walk away without showing her how I feel, even if I haven't said the words yet or if I'm not sure what to say. Threading my fingers into her hair, I coax her closer to me. Her curves pressing against me, a soft moan escapes between us. Breaking my lips from hers, I press them to her forehead before holding her against me. I didn't fathom letting her out of my sight would be heart-wrenching. Pulling back, I look at her once more. When I do, I see my future. Hopefully, it's our future.

Gathering my clothes from the chair, I move toward the door.

"Jacob."

I turn to face her again.

She reaches her hand out for mine. "Bring this back to me." After flipping my hand palm side up, she drops her necklace into it, curving my hand closed around it.

"Norah, I can't—" There's no guarantee I'll be able to return this.

"You will."

Leaning forward, I kiss her softly before walking out the door. I refuse to look back to prevent myself from rethinking this whole plan. I head down the aisle to the front restroom, Norah's necklace still clutched in my hand.

"All set?" Connor asks as I walk past.

"Yes, she's getting dressed."

"You good?"

"Yes." *No, not at all.* After changing, I slip her necklace into my wallet. Ironically, it's safest in the license pocket that also holds a photo of Connor, Mara, and me. When I emerge from the restroom, Norah is dressed and seated with the red wig in her lap. Shortly after I sit beside her, Cash turns on the seat belt sign for descent.

Connor is going over the assignments once again with everyone as Cash lands the plane with the slightest of bounces on the runway. The acid in my stomach just continues to churn. We deplane directly into a private hangar. There's a large SUV and a sedan waiting. Maia is leaning against the sedan with her wig already in place. As Norah walks down the steps, I attempt to focus on something, anything, other than her. The emerald sheath dress and high-heeled shoes are enough to make my heart pound. The red wig makes her hazel eyes stand out. Her eyes draw me in every day. The wig makes them impossible to ignore. This moment right now exemplifies why she must go with Connor.

Connor and Christoph escort Norah to the SUV as I walk toward Maia with Nolan. Norah takes one more look at me as she climbs into the back seat with Christoph. A heaviness settles in my chest as Christoph climbs in and closes the door.

"Jake," I hear in my earpiece. I look over at Connor standing near the driver door.

"Yeah?"

"I'll bring her back to you." Those words from him grab hold of me like a vise. Connor and I have discussed my culpability—or lack thereof, in his opinion—for his sister's death numerous times over the last few years. For him to put his life on the line for the woman I love now, it's an incredible gesture.

I nod sharply as Maia slides into the back seat, followed by Nolan. Centering myself, I focus on Maia who is putting herself at risk right now, based on my gut.

NORAH

I take one more look at Jacob before I slide into the back seat of the black SUV with Christoph. He doesn't trust himself to protect me. My safety is paramount to him, and I make him lose focus. Honestly, I'm not sure how to handle that admission. It's almost as telling as our chosen but previously undiscussed monogamy. The further we pull away from the hangar, the more work I put into locking up my feelings.

"Norah." Connor's voice pulls me out of my thoughts.

"Yes." I lift my head to catch his eyes in the rearview mirror.

"Jake knows what he's doing."

I turn my gaze out the window. My focus needs to be on today, not the history that Connor and Jacob have. Not the questions floating in my mind about how well they know each other and why Jacob trusts him with me. We pass cute row houses decked out in assorted colors to distinguish between one and the next. Bold colors from yellow, red, and blue adorn the façades of the properties. We pass a small hotel and enter through a gated entrance. The building is modern with a mirrored-window exterior. That gate closes and a guard asks Connor who we're here to see. After checking in his booth, he approaches the SUV again.

"You're about fifteen minutes early. Please park in a visitor spot on the side of the building. I have notified Agents Brown and Morse. They will meet you in the lobby," the guard states before waving us through.

Slowly, I release the breath I have been holding since we went through the first gate.

Christoph sets his huge hand on my forearm.

"Again."

I take a deep breath and let it out slowly.

"Once more."

I inhale again and exhale. After Connor parks, he sends a text, then hops out, moving into position near the rear door. Christoph steps out, leaving just enough room for me to set my feet on the ground between him and Connor.

"Stay between us," Connor instructs before we walk into the building. Agent Brown meets us in the lobby and escorts us to a conference room to the right of the entrance.

"Miss Cavallaro, thank you for coming in today. I hope to make this as painless as possible," Agent Brown states. She's a petite woman with flawless skin. Her suit is custom tailored to her figure.

"Thank you."

She motions for us to sit and offers us water. All three of us decline. Connor is standing right behind me, and Christoph is just inside the door.

"I would like to go over the events as we know them. Please correct me if I leave something out or I'm incorrect."

Agent Brown sets forth her version of the events that occurred since I brought the errors to Mr. Sterling's attention. Her timeline of events includes my run-in with Sergio Moretti's henchmen, the break-in, and our race around the lake. She doesn't seem to know where I went after that. Good, that was the plan. She includes additional details from the Morettis' side of the story as well. The Moretti family claims that Mr. Sterling cooked the books on his own and they're looking to clear the family name.

"When was your first review of the Moretti Brand file?"

"About seven months ago."

"When did you notice the errors?"

"Almost immediately."

"Why did it take you six months to alert Mr. Sterling?"

"I have spent many hours over the last six months trying to unravel the discrepancies. Whoever was manipulating the figures hid the pattern well."

As I answer Agent Brown, I feel Connor's grip on the back of my chair tighten. Something went wrong. He must still be able to hear the rest of the team in his ear. Twisting in my chair, I see his poker face is better than I expect.

Agent Brown continues. "How far back do the discrepancies go?"

I return my attention to her. "Approximately eight years."

"When did you start working at Quinn Sterling?"

"A little over six years ago."

A tall, built man enters the room wearing the same type of suit as Agent Brown except he has expensive cuff links and a Breitling watch. The watch alone costs over eight thousand dollars. Pretty steep for a government salary.

"Miss Cavallaro, this is Agent Morse."

I acknowledge his presence.

"Just a few more questions. Regarding the break-in at your townhouse, have local police identified anyone of interest?"

Interesting question. William told Jacob about the FBI request to talk to me. Presumably, they're aware of the status of his investigation.

"Not that I'm aware of."

"Have you been back to your townhouse since the break-in?"

Connor sets his hand on my right shoulder. That's when I see it; Agent Morse has crossed his arms over his chest. The colorful ink of his tattoo is now visible as his sleeves inch up. I can see the tattoo over Agent Brown's shoulder with my peripheral vision. I refuse to tear my gaze away from Agent Brown.

"I don't see how that is relevant."

"The Moretti Family, through their attorneys, claim that a ledger has gone missing. Do you know where it is?"

"I don't have a ledger, nor have I ever seen one." My anger continues to increase the longer I'm in the same room as Agent Morse. "If there is nothing else, I would like to leave."

"I have nothing further. Do you, Agent Morse?" Agent Brown turns to her partner.

"Just one question." His voice echoing in my brain makes my blood boil. I hear his words in my mind from my townhouse. *Immobilize her. She's trained.* Shaking off the memory, I refocus on his question. "Could you identify anyone who assaulted you in the Quinn Sterling garage or at your townhouse?"

"There are cameras at the garage. I'm sure Sid and Carlo, as they identified themselves, are on video. As far as my townhouse, no, I can't identify anyone."

"Thank you for your time. Please contact me if you recall anything further," Agent Brown states, handing me her card.

"You're welcome."

Connor steps back, pulling out my chair. We walk straight through the lobby to the SUV. All the pent-up anger I have is ready to explode. Anger at Agent Morse for having the audacity to question me as if he weren't even there! That man drugged me, held me down, and inserted a tracker into my neck. He's an FBI agent!

As I step off the curb, I trip and catch myself by setting my hand on the small of Connor's back. Christoph grabs my arm, lifting me enough to make sure I don't fall.

"Good?" Christoph asks.

I nod, and we finish the short walk to the vehicle. The moment Christoph closes the door behind me, I announce, "Agent Morse is the guy who drugged me at my townhouse."

"Are you sure?"

"Yes, I recognize his voice, and I will never forget that tattoo. Plus, the cuff links and the luxury watch don't match a government salary. What went wrong?" I ask Connor. He maneuvers the SUV through the two gates but hasn't uttered another word. Even though it's the last thing I want to do, I wait patiently for Connor to answer me.

Once we are on the interstate, Connor utters just four words, "The Morettis took Maia."

Jacob said he didn't feel right about this meeting. He put himself and Maia in harm's way for me.

JACOB

Every decision I make regarding a client puts my team at risk. Today, I'm putting Maia at risk more than ever before. For a client. For Norah. For the woman I love. The fact that Norah is so much more than a client makes this assignment even more difficult.

I pull out of the hangar and turn the opposite way as Team A. We'll take a longer route to the federal building. Once we arrive, Maia will shed the wig and we'll join the others while they question Norah. As we near the exit for the federal building, I note four black vehicles moving together. Instead of turning toward the meeting, I remain on the interstate. Ideally, I'll be able to keep these guys busy until Connor gets Norah to the meeting. Once Norah arrives, I assume these guys will back off.

"Nolan, watch the pattern. Make sure no one deviates."

"On it," he replies.

I speed up to put some distance between us and Moretti's goons. It's late afternoon in downtown Boston. The highway is busy but not gridlock.

Connor: Escorting Escape inside. Will inform when we leave.

Me: Roger. We have company. I'll hold them off as long as possible.

I allow myself a small bit of relief. Norah is safely at her meeting. Of course, that's only the beginning. Connor still needs to get her tucked away afterward.

"Jacob, one of the vehicles left the pattern and exited the interstate," Nolan shouts from behind me. This isn't one of the contingencies that Connor and I planned for. I acknowledge Nolan and consider my options.

"Maia, find a new route back toward the airport, but away from the federal building."

She immediately looks down at her phone. After a search, she sends the suggested map to the GPS.

"Perfect." I slow my speed and follow the route back to the airport. The closer I get to the airport, the less of Moretti's men continue to follow. Once we pull into the parking lot, the last vehicle peels away.

Something is off. Why would they simply stop pursuing? I pull forward, parking near the private hangar. Exiting the vehicle, we follow the same protocol as if Maia is Norah. Stepping inside the waiting area, Maia indicates she needs to use the restroom. After Nolan clears the restroom, Maia enters, and we guard the door.

I survey the room. There is one clerk milling about behind the desk. It's the same clerk who was here when we arrived this morning. She's an older heavy-set woman with graying hair and narrow-set eyes. Sweeping the room again, I note a dirty footprint near the entry door for the front desk area.

Alerting Nolan, I move toward the clerk. She subtly shakes her head as I approach. Then she moves her eyes back and forth toward the restroom door.

Crouching, I move past the entry door. On my signal, Nolan creates a diversion, and I bust through the door. After a short struggle, I subdue a stocky man and zip-tie his hands behind his back. As I emerge with the clerk, Nolan exits the restroom.

"She's gone."

"You cleared the restroom?"

"Yes, the window is still locked from the inside. I checked each stall." I guide the clerk, whose name tag reads Janie, to a chair and examine the restroom myself.

I check the window and each stall again as I consider how someone got in and silently removed Maia from the restroom. Scrubbing my hand over my face, I note one of the ceiling tiles isn't in its place.

"Did you see who was hiding in the restroom?" I ask Janie.

"All I can say is, when the man who is cuffed back there came in, he was with a short, slender woman with purple hair. I didn't see her go into the restroom, but I was more concerned about the gun in my face."

"Are there surveillance cameras in here?" I ask, hoping my gut is wrong, but I highly doubt it. If Janie's description is accurate, the woman who took Maia is known as the Iris, a British assassin for hire.

"Yes, there's an office in the next hangar where the feeds can be seen."

"Nolan, stay here with her and make sure he stays put. I'm going to check out that feed and contact Connor."

Nolan hangs his head.

"All the things that are pinging around in your head—the what-ifs, the blame, all of it—push it away. It won't help Maia right now. Get your head in the room," I remind Nolan.

"Yes, sir."

I run to the next hangar, dialing Connor as I move.

"Yeah, Jake?"

"They took Maia from the restroom at the hangar. I'm going to check the security feeds, but I think Iris took her. They don't know what Escape looks like. Do not bring Escape here. Use option L." Connor is well aware of Iris and what she is capable of.

"Roger. Agent Morse is one of Moretti's men. Escape recognized the tattoo and his voice. He saw Escape at the meeting. I'm having her remove the wig."

"Understood."

"Keep me informed of your location. Option L should be complete in less than two hours. I'll meet you as soon as I can."

"Will do."

"Jake, Maia knew the risks, and she took them willingly. Investigate what you need to. She has a tracker on her. We'll create a plan and bring her back."

He knows me well. I was already blaming myself for this. Norah is safe, and Maia isn't. Maia is a skilled team member. She knows what to do. She knows we'll come for her. My gut was correct. *Damn it!*

"I know. Is N—"

"Shaken but fine."

I let out a breath. Connor would have told me if something went wrong. I know that in my head. His confirmation is welcome, nonetheless.

"See you soon."

Ending the call, I find the security feeds and find a guard bound and gagged in a chair.

"Are you hurt?" I ask as I release him.

"No, sir. How can I help?"

Eddie, the security guard Janie guided me to, plays back the feeds. Unfortunately, it confirms my suspicion. Iris has Maia. My only possible salvation is that Maia isn't Norah. It just might save her life.

NORAH

Connor just talked to Jacob. I would love for someone to fill me in on the contingency plan we're following now. Whatever this option is, I have no idea. I'm sure it means I'll be cooped up somewhere for the next number of weeks. The bigger question is whether Jacob will be with me or not. In the back of my mind, I wonder what is happening with Stan and Delores.

"What is the plan now?" I ask.

"You are getting on a plane and going to the farm with Christoph. I'm coming back here to assist in locating Maia."

"Okay."

I think Connor expected me to argue with him because he asks. "Okay?"

"Yes, whatever you need me to do, I will." It's my fault that Maia was abducted. Not my fault exactly, but because of me. Jacob's instincts are something else. He had a feeling today wasn't going to go as planned. He sent me with Connor for that reason and something else he needs to explain. I won't interrogate Connor right now. He has plenty of other things on his mind.

"I'm going to need you to take off the wig. Agent Morse saw you, so he will inform Moretti's men that you have red hair. Don't change until you get to the farm. Gemma has new clothes for you. You and Christoph are heading there. Mr. Blackthorne will bring Tank to you. You'll stay there until we locate Maia and retrieve her safely. No calls, no contact with anyone other than Christoph, Gemma, and Mr. and Mrs. Blackthorne."

"I understand. Who is Gemma?"

"Jacob's assistant. She's only in the office during business hours. You may not even see her, but I wanted you to be aware that she's allowed on the property."

A short time later, we pull onto a bumpy dirt road. Connor pulls alongside a nondescript building with a domed top. Even though we are in the middle of nowhere, Connor and Christoph flank me as we walk into the building.

Once inside, a stocky man greets Connor with a bro hug and shakes Christoph's hand.

"Norah, this is Wilkerson. He served with Jacob and me on our first and second tours in Afghanistan."

"Pleasure to meet you."

"Likewise."

Christoph and Connor step over to the side and chat for a minute. I can't make out the words, but I'm sure they are talking about me. Regardless of the difference in height, Connor is clearly in charge as he looks up at Christoph, telling him the plan. The only words I can make out are "don't let her out of your sight."

Once we board the plane, Connor tears out of the driveway, heading back toward Jacob. I settle into my seat for the short flight to wherever we're going. Christoph needs to hunch to take his seat. He's an extremely tall guy and built. If Jacob is six feet tall, Christoph has at least another three inches on him. Once we're airborne, Christoph asks, "Do you need anything?"

"Right now? A bottle of Mayacamas 2014. Glass optional."

Christoph smiles. He's quite attractive when he smiles. I can readily admit he's attractive, just not my type. He wouldn't be even if I weren't pining for Jacob.

"Jacob might have that covered for you."

Curious response, but I decide to leave that alone while leaning my seat back. After what feels like five minutes, Christoph is nudging me to wake up.

"Norah, we're here."

I blink to get my bearings. I rise and follow Christoph off the small plane. As I pass, I thank Wilkerson for the ride.

"Anything for my brother."

Even though a wonderful family adopted Jacob, I'm glad he was able to expand his family with the military and his team.

"I'll tell him."

"Thank you, miss."

I step off the plane onto a narrow strip of asphalt. Wilkerson has some serious skills. It shouldn't surprise me. Jacob surrounds himself with the best.

After assuring I'm safely on the ground, Christoph pulls out his phone and sends a text, presumably to Connor or Jacob.

"Where are we?" To my right is a wide, open field leading to what looks like an inlet of some kind. To my left is a sprawling piece of land with a few outbuildings and a gorgeous farmhouse.

"No one told you?"

"No."

"This is Jacob's home."

Oh!

"Follow me. Let's get you settled and find that bottle of wine."

I never considered where Jacob lives. As I stand here looking at this gorgeous piece of land, it makes perfect sense. As I walk toward the house, a car pulls up the gravel drive. I freeze in place. Immediately, Christoph retreats to me.

"Norah, you're absolutely safe here. There's a code at the gate for the private road; there is another at the base of the driveway. Plus the perimeter alarms. There are more security measures than I could list."

I nod slowly and continue toward the house. As we approach, Tank barrels toward me. I bend down to pet him.

"Mr. B."

"Christoph." A look passes between them.

"Ben, nice to see you again," I say in greeting.

"You too, Norah. I would have preferred Sunday dinner instead."

"There's still time."

That reply stung a bit. Why didn't Jacob ask me about dinner? There's nothing he could tell me that would make me run away. Perhaps he doesn't recognize that yet.

The farmhouse is picturesque, like Connor's parents' but more modern. It has a wraparound porch complete with Adirondack chairs. The entryway is flawless with wide plank flooring and a modern light fixture. The living room has a structured sectional bracketing a wood-burning fireplace. There's a young woman in the kitchen.

"You must be Gemma." I extend my hand to her. She's average height and thin with short hair. The ends are pink. It makes me wonder if she had a phase and she's growing it out.

"Pleasure to meet you, Norah. I set some clothes for you in the guest room across from Jacob's. I purchased basic toiletries, including contact solution and a case. I just finished putting some groceries away."

"Thank you."

"I'll be on my way. If you need something before the team returns, my number is near the phone in Jacob's office."

I smile, and Gemma hurries out the door. I wonder what her story is.

Ben speaks next. "I already fed Tank. He should be set until morning. The food is to the left of the sink. If Christoph gives you any grief, feel free to call me."

I laugh. Christoph folds his arms across his chest but says nothing.

"Norah, I know things are unsettled right now. Jacob will be back as soon as he can with Maia." Ben is as good at reading people as his son.

I nod, and Ben leaves out the front door.

"Let's get that wine."

I lift an eyebrow but follow Christoph down the hall and into the basement. The lower level is set up like a cozy family room with a large TV and a few pinball machines along one wall. There are a few doors. One is ajar. Inside, a small powder room. Christoph stops at the middle door and opens it.

Tank doesn't enter the room. He sits by the door patiently. I don't know what I expected, but this wasn't it. The room is a perfect wine cellar right down to the controlled temperature.

"Did this come with the house?"

"No, this property and the house were a mess when Jacob bought it. He refurbished the entire house himself, including building this cellar. What did you say you were looking for?"

"Mayacamas 2014."

Clearly, he has been down here before. I glance to my right and see two bottles of cabernet sauvignon Abreu Madrona Ranch 1997. Jacob clearly knows wine. Just another thing to add to the too-good-to-be-true list. More like a perfect-for-me list. There's no way Jacob knows my favorite wine. Christoph moves over to the wall to our left and scans a few rows before pulling out a bottle.

"Thank you."

Christoph leads me back upstairs and sets a glass and a corkscrew on the granite island.

"Just one?"

"I can't drink while I'm working."

"Sorry."

"It's no problem. After the last few days, you deserve that glass. Hell, you deserve the whole bottle and then some."

I open the bottle and pour myself a glass. I settle onto a chair, looking out into presumably his backyard. The sky is dark now; I can only see shadows.

"Are you allowed to tell me what's going on with Maia?"

"I don't know anything more than you right now. Like you, Maia had a tracker. They will get to her. When I know something, I'll share it with you."

I return my gaze to the blackness beyond the French doors.

JACOB

Norah is safe at home. My home. No woman has ever been in my home. I never wanted a woman there before her. I track Maia to a warehouse in the south end of Boston. Nolan and I are actively working on a plan to make entry. The warehouse has multiple points of ingress and egress. A few more team members would be helpful. Although generally, we're attempting to rescue a client with no skills. Each team member has a unique set of skills. Maia is a combat veteran. After two tours, she shifted to intelligence. She'll be ready.

The clock is ticking. I'm working under the assumption that the Morettis hired Iris to make Norah talk and then kill her. That thought makes chills run down my spine. I was close to losing Norah today, and she doesn't even know how I feel about her. With that in mind, I'm aware the Morettis know that Norah has martial arts training. Neither Norah nor Maia would go easily if attacked. I'm sure they drugged Maia like they did Norah.

Connor: ETA thirty minutes.

Me: Roger. 314

I rehash our plan again with Nolan for the fifth or maybe the sixth time. Then I take a break and send Nolan for some food. Once Connor arrives, we'll go over the plan again and retrieve Maia. I have coordinated vehicles on two egress routes.

Connor arrives soon after Nolan leaves. He gets right down to business.

"What's the plan?" Connor asks, plopping down in the chair beside me.

"Food and then scoop up Maia."

Nolan reenters the room with enough food for a small army. As we dig into the burgers and fries, the guys and I review the plan a few more times. The tracker hasn't moved since she arrived at the warehouse.

Near ten, we load up and trek over to get Maia back.

"Radio check," I say.

"Two," Connor replies.

"Three," Nolan chimes in.

"Let's go get our girl."

Connor and Nolan will enter from the east side of the warehouse. I'm taking the south entrance. As I approach, the guard turns away from me. Subduing him, I move him out of sight before entering the building. I clear a path down the hallway to where the tracker is pinging. Crouching, I glide past the door. As I get closer, Connor and Nolan approach. Testing the knob, I find it unlocked. I feel a tap on my shoulder.

I throw the door open and fan to the right, clearing around the room. Maia is lying in the middle of the room. As I circle her, she doesn't appear to be significantly injured. A few small abrasions on her arms, and she's barefoot. Nolan checks her pulse before handing a folded piece of paper up to me.

Mr. Blackthorne,

Surrender the ledger or Norah Cavallaro dies.

Iris

The note is on thin cream paper with the Moretti Family Brands logo emblazoned across the top.

Fuck! This isn't over yet. "Status?"

"She appears to be drugged. There is an injection site on the side of her neck," Nolan states.

"Let's move out. She needs a doctor. Connor, call—"

"Dialing."

Nolan lifts Maia, cradling her in his arms. An unmistakable expression crosses Nolan's face as he looks down at her. He cares about her more than a teammate. I'll address it later.

With Nolan sandwiched between me and Connor, we move to the south entrance. After another sweep of the grounds, we rush to our vehicle. Nolan sets Maia on the back seat before climbing in after her.

"Smith will meet us at the hotel. He needs an idea of what they gave her."

"They injected Norah with ketamine earlier this week."

I drive as quickly as possible back to our hotel. Connor uses the main entrance while I wait with Nolan at the side of the building.

"Nolan, lock down whatever feelings you have for her until this over. Do you understand?"

"Yes," he grits out.

Once inside the room, Nolan gently lays Maia on the scratchy floral bedspread. Smith joins us and sets to working on Maia. Nolan paces the floor beside the bed. I get where his head is; I was just there with Norah.

"I gave her naloxone. Hopefully, it was ketamine. If you're correct she should wake within the next hour or so. When she does, small amounts of water for an hour. Then she should be fine. You should expect her to be dizzy and unsteady on her feet. She may even have numbness in her hands or feet. It's temporary. She shouldn't be alone for the next eight to ten hours."

"Can she fly?"

"Yes, once she wakes. If she experiences significant changes, give me another call. It's good to see you despite the circumstances."

"You too."

Smith served with Connor and me during our first tour and the third. He dug the bullet out of my arm, stitched me up, and fixed up Connor's shoulder.

"If you ever decide to move on from emergency medicine, give me a call."

"Will do," Smith replies before leaving.

Connor pulls up a chair. Nolan is sitting on the edge of the bed holding Maia's hand.

"We need to check her for a tracker. Nolan, roll her toward you. I'm going to check the same spot they inserted Norah's."

With precision, I guide my hand along Maia's neck, but find nothing. I glide my fingers along the tops of her shoulders, coming up empty.

"My name isn't Norah. It's M...." Maia's eyes flutter open, and she strikes out with her hand, hitting Nolan on the side of his face.

"Maia, you're safe. We've got you."

"Norah, they still want Norah."

"It's okay. She's safe," Nolan offers to calm her down.

"I hit you. I'm sorry."

"I'm fine," Nolan replies. The tension in his voice is unmistakable.

"How are you feeling? Do you recall anything that Iris said?" I ask to move this along. We need to get out of here.

"Dizzy and hungry but otherwise okay. The woman with the purple hair didn't say much. The only thing she said was to someone named Morris on the phone."

Morse. Iris is working with Morse.

"What did she say to Morse?"

"That Norah was at the meeting and I was a decoy."

"Make sure there are no traces of Blackthorne. Think you can handle getting to the car on your own?" I instruct them to make sure the room is clear of all evidence we were here.

"Yes, let's go."

I step into the hallway, Maia directly behind me and Connor and Nolan close behind her. We exit out the side door directly into our car.

"Please call Wilkerson and get us a ride home," I say, handing my phone to Connor. This part is complete, but this assignment isn't over. Not even close. She's still not safe. Where is the ledger? I have no doubt Norah is being truthful. Where else could it be? Who else could have it? As I drive along the interstate, even more questions float through my mind.

Upon landing at the farm, we settle Maia in at the bunkhouse with Nolan promising to stay with her. I'll address his feelings for Maia after this assignment is complete.

"I'll be back at ten tomorrow to plan," Connor says before walking to his truck.

"Let's make it noon. We all need some rest."

"See you then."

I wave backward while opening my front door. I whistle softly for Tank, who runs straight to me. Christoph follows him from the hallway.

"How is Maia?"

"She'll be fine. She's resting in the bunkhouse."

"Good."

"Any issues?" I don't expect any, but still need to ask.

"No, she went to sleep about three hours ago."

"Thank you. We're reconvening tomorrow at noon. Get some sleep."

Christoph nods and walks back down the hall. He moves the chair he was using back into the office and leaves through the front door.

After setting the alarm, I peek in on Norah. She's curled up in my guest room. She's stunning even in sleep. I have seen her dressed for a wedding; even then she doesn't cake makeup on her flawless skin. She doesn't need it. Separating myself from her today was the right call. It was personally painful but professionally necessary. It's seems clear to me that Moretti's men don't know what she looks like. They were tracking me. I set Tank outside her door and shower off the day. Less than an hour later, I slide into the bed behind her.

"Hi," she murmurs softly, pressing her curves closer to me.

"Hi."

"Is Maia okay?"

"She'll be fine."

"Your home is beyond words. Thank you for bringing me here."

"You're welcome. Sleep, gorgeous. We'll talk more tomorrow." I tug her even closer and press my lips to her bare shoulder.

NORAH

Bright rays of sunshine filter into the room. I didn't close the curtains last night. Trying to stay awake was futile, especially after the glass of wine. I'm still wondering how I never learned that Jacob is a wine aficionado. Deep down, I know the answer. We didn't really share about our lives when we were together. Turning slowly in Jacob's arms, I study his face. In sleep, he is completely relaxed. His dimple isn't visible right now, neither is the crinkle around his eyes. The sexy cleft and a day's worth of stubble make for a gorgeous view first thing in the morning. The few times he has slept beside me since sharing about his flashbacks, he hasn't had any.

"Go back to sleep, beautiful. I'm not ready to let you out of my arms just yet."

Seriously, does he need to keep saying things like that? "I just wanted a better look at you. I'm not moving."

"What time is it?" he asks without opening his steely blue eyes—eyes that melt me into a puddle as easily as his touch. I have forced myself to avoid speculating on why he refuses to be in a relationship.

I crane my neck to read the clock. "It's near eight."

"Good, the team isn't returning until noon."

He slides his arms around my waist, pulling me against him. My head tucks under his chin. Fresh, clean bodywash teases my nose. His impressive arousal rests against my hip. I attempt to stifle a sigh but fail. Pushing away his effect on me is impossible while in his arms. However, I need to hear him out first. Even this is skirting the line I drew in my mind. Then again, so was that kiss on the plane. It's times like right now, I wish my mother were still here. I need to talk to someone who had a strong, lasting relationship. While my mother died young, they were married for a long time beforehand.

Settling my thoughts, I decide to enjoy being with Jacob and fall asleep again.

Tank barking wakes me out of a deep sleep. Jacob is on his feet and already tugging a shirt over his head before I even register what's happening. A quick glance at the clock indicates it's almost ten. Either someone is early or has arrived unannounced.

"Please stay here. No one shows up unannounced." Jacob leaves the room.

Sitting up, I lean against the headboard. I hear talking but can't make out the words. Then I hear the alarm reengage.

"That was Gemma. She wanted to check on you," Jacob says, taking a seat on the edge of the bed.

"That was nice of her. She's super cute and thoughtful."

"She's a great kid. Her father was my commanding officer. He said her teen years were tough. I hired her when I opened Blackthorne. The structure works for her."

"How are you?" I ask, sliding my hand along his jaw. I resist drawing my thumb across his lips. He looks tired, but I know he hasn't slept enough in the last week.

"I'll be fine when you're safe. How are you?"

"I'm handling it. The chaos is a bit much for me, but I'm doing my best to keep my need for order in check."

"Honestly, you're handling this better than most clients."

"Thanks. What do I need to know?" I'm afraid to ask, but I need to know what I'm up against. I assume they took Maia thinking she was me. If so, this isn't over yet.

"They took Maia because they thought she was you. Thanks to Blaine, they didn't have a photo of you. Moretti's men were tracking me to get to you. Either they believe I don't trust my team, or they think we're together."

"Your instinct was right?"

"Yes."

"Have they been watching me that long?" That thought makes me angry. I didn't notice anything. Although, I suppose if he or she were doing their job, I wouldn't see them.

"It's likely. There's no other way for them to know about us."

A look or something must have crossed my face because Jacob stands, scoops me into his arms, and resettles us on the bed with his arms holding me snug against his chest.

"That's terrifying. I didn't have any idea someone was watching me."

"Yes, it is."

"What else?"

"How do you know there's more?"

"You paused too long."

He inhales before speaking again. "The Morettis, through Iris, the woman who took Maia, left a note. They threatened your life if they don't get the ledger."

A chill runs through me. Turning my head slowly, I look into his eyes. He's concerned.

"I don't have it! I've never seen it!" Bringing the errors to Mr. Sterling's attention was the right thing, even if it caused this.

"Breathe, Norah. I believe you. Either way, we must find it. Later, when the team arrives, we'll figure out a starting point. I'll have Blaine start looking as well."

"Can I call my family at some point today?"

"Yes, you can call later. Why did you choose this room?"

"I didn't. Gemma did."

Seemingly satisfied with that answer, he continues. "Your bag is in my room. If you need anything let me know. We can send Gemma, or you can order it and have it shipped."

"I don't have access to my money. Plus, I owe you a bottle of Mayacamas 2014."

"I'll give you mine. Christoph shared my secret room, huh?"

"Is it a secret if Christoph knows about it?"

"I suppose not. Why that bottle? There are plenty of excellent choices."

"When we were on the plane, Christoph asked what I wanted and that was my reply. Had I known you have stellar taste in wine, including my favorite, I would have chosen that one. I was just joking around. Then he led me downstairs."

"What is your favorite?"

"My favorite cab is—"

"Let me guess. I have it downstairs, right?"

"Yes."

"Abreu Madrona Ranch 1997."

"How on earth? I never told you that's my favorite."

"No, you didn't. There are two bottles in your wine rack at your townhouse."

I smile, leveling my gaze to his.

"We should get moving. After I meet with the team, I'll give you a proper tour of the property if you don't mind walking in the snow."

"Okay."

He moves to leave but stops when I call him.

"Jacob."

"Yeah."

"Thank you. For so many things, most of which I can't list right now."

"You're welcome."

JACOB

The meeting with my team went well. Even Maia was up to joining us. Blaine is searching for the first mention of the ledger. Connor will work to find who has been tracking Norah and when they started. Christoph is headed out to LA for an assignment escorting Miss Forrester to an event. At the end of the meeting, Norah brought Maia over into the living room. I couldn't hear their conversation, but by the end they were hugging, so I gather it went well. Before we set out for our walk, Norah calls her sister Kelly. She was quick in sharing that she's fine and would call again when she could.

Near one, we walk side by side along the driveway. Tank runs circles around us, every now and then our fingers graze one another. As much as I want to take her hand and share my home with her, I need to lay everything out. As we pass each building, I explain what's inside.

"How long did it take you to refurbish the house? Did you do all the work yourself? It's perfect. The bathroom is spa worthy."

I smile. Out of all the rooms, the master bath is the one I'm most proud of.

"About two years. I did all the work myself. It helped me to have something to do after my last tour while I was building Blackthorne during the day." I have never admitted that to anyone other than Connor.

"It's gorgeous. You should be proud."

"Thanks. Let's sit." I pull a blanket out of the bag and lay it on the ground on the edge of the shoreline. There's barely any snow cover on the sand. I sit facing Norah, her legs bent over mine. Our fingers intertwined between us.

"You don't have to tell me. I just need to know if you don't want me, a relationship, or a marriage. Even though I promised you and myself I wouldn't fall for you, I did. I want to be with you, even if it's just for now. When it's safe for me to be on my own again, I'll leave. When I do, we will be over."

She's everything I don't deserve. "I want to tell you. I need to tell you. After talking with my father, I realized that we're already in a relationship, just not the kind either of us deserve, especially you."

Her eyes soften a bit. I watch her throat move as she swallows hard.

"Connor's mother, Joyce, is a social worker, my social worker. She facilitated my adoption and my siblings'. Connor was my first true friend. Mara, Connor's twin sister was always around. There was no mistaking they were twins. Both have light features and light blue eyes. Both tall too. The three of us spent hours at the pond, running roughshod all over the Michelsons' property and hours upon hours in their tree house."

Her eyes widen at the mention of the tree house, but I press on.

"Mara and I began dating when we were juniors in high school. I even asked Connor for his blessing. The three of us were inseparable." My grip on her hand tightens slightly as I continue.

"During Christmas break of my junior year of college, I proposed to Mara. We got married a week after we graduated. Even though my parents have a stable marriage, I didn't think I would ever find someone to love me like that. Mara never cared about where I came from, my biological parents, or my adoption. She loved me for me." I wish I could read Norah's mind. Her poker face is phenomenal. I would expect a myriad of emotions and questions running through her mind right now. I cast my gaze out to the water before I continue speaking. "During my second tour…."

Norah reaches over and turns my eyes to hers.

"I couldn't protect her. I failed her, and she died."

"How did she die?"

I have never said any of these words out loud to anyone ever before. My hands are shaking in Norah's, causing her to tighten her grip. "During a seizure, she hit her head on the corner of her desk in her classroom. She didn't make it to the hospital."

"Breathe, Jacob."

Closing my eyes, I take a few deep breaths.

"Why do you blame yourself?"

"I wasn't here. I couldn't protect her." A tear falls down my cheek.

Inexplicably, Norah leans forward, kissing it away. "If you were here, would you have been in her classroom?"

She's the only person who ever asked me that. The first person to point out the disconnect in my logic. I suppose it isn't logic. Either way, my heart was ripped out of my chest. My wife was gone, and I couldn't stop it.

"No."

"Does Connor blame you? Do Mr. and Mrs. Michelson?"

"No, they don't."

"You sent me with Connor yesterday because I make you lose focus."

"Partially." I take a deep breath. "I sent you with Connor because he knows firsthand what it would do to me to fail you. You are the only woman who has ever made me question if I deserve a second chance to be blissfully happy in love. You have awakened parts of my heart and soul that I buried six years ago. I gave my whole heart to Mara, and I promised to love her until death do us part. I wasn't prepared for it to be so short. I didn't think I could love another woman as completely as I did Mara. You deserve my whole heart. I don't know if I possess it in its entirety anymore to give it to you."

"Oh, Jacob. You should honor her memory, not run from it. She was loved during her life. You gave that to her."

Her words cut through me. Not one shred of angst, jealously, or hurt lace her words. She's truly a gift—a gift I'm not sure I deserve.

"What are you afraid of?"

"Feeling pain of that magnitude again," I answer honestly.

"Is it worth forgoing all the bliss that comes with sharing your life with someone? The joy of little everyday things. Inside jokes and watching your children reach milestones."

I never considered having a family. It was a topic Mara and I never discussed. "No one gets once-in-a-lifetime love twice."

She leans forward, brushing her lips across mine.

As I open my eyes, Norah whispers, "Maybe you were her once-in-a-lifetime love. What if I'm yours?"

For a solid minute, I let her words settle in my head and in my heart. I fulfilled my promise to Mara. Could I give the same thing to Norah?

"Norah, I—"

She sets her index finger on my lips. "Figure out what you want. What you deserve. Forgive yourself for something you had no control over. Think of all the people you have protected since then—including me." Norah rises from the blanket and walks back toward the house. Her words sit on my chest like an elephant, making it hard to breathe.

NORAH

As I walk away from Jacob, my heart breaks for him and for me. I can't make him forgive himself. I'm unsure what he thought about losing his wife I would find reprehensible. I guess my extraordinary sex partner now has an expiration date. I expedited that all on my own. *Great job, Norah!*

I'm steps away from locking myself in his guest room to pull myself together. Just three steps from his idyllic front porch.

"Norah, wait," Jacob calls from behind me.

I stop but don't turn to face him. His arm rests on my waist as he makes me look at him.

"What changed?" he asks.

"Me. You. Us. I had everything I thought I wanted until a few weeks ago. The dream job, a roof over my head, a few luxuries, and you. Since my text, everything has changed. The dream job I have worked my ass off for over six years is gone, my home trashed, and you...how you touch me, how you kiss me, has changed. Maybe I'm imagining it. That's fine—"

Jacob claims my mouth with his. His possessive, toe-curling kisses take hold of my entire body. Heat rushes to my core as I wrestle with the thoughts in my head. *Just feel, Norah. You don't know how much longer you have with him.*

Wrapping his arm around my waist, Jacob twists the knob, pushing his front door open. After Tank scurries inside, Jacob sets my back against the wall and arms the alarm system. Without breaking our kiss, he unzips the parka and hangs it on the hook near the door. As I draw the zipper on his jacket down, he toes off his boots. His lips sucking southward on my neck as I hang his jacket up next to mine.

Jacob grips my hips with his large hands, lifting me. I wrap my legs around his waist, hooking my ankles. He takes a few large strides and sets me on the edge of the island. As I work the buttons of his shirt, he stares at me hungrily. When I reach the last button, Jacob grabs my wrists in one hand, lengthening them to the ceiling. With his free hand, he tears my shirt up and off.

"So sexy," he murmurs against my skin at my lingerie.

This set is a sheer red with crisscrossing straps, each with a button. If unfastened, each button will expose my nipples. Generally, he just strips me naked as quickly as possible. Today's slow exploration is different. Feels more intimate. I push that thought away as Jacob nips my nipple through my bra. The material against my taut pebble combined with his teeth is decadent. Holy hell that feels good!

Releasing my wrists, he unfastens the clasp of my bra, pulling it away between us. I dip my hands beneath the collar of his shirt, pushing it down his corded arms. Palming both breasts, Jacob lowers his mouth to my collarbone, then down the valley between them, dragging his tongue along the underside of my breast while pinching my nipple between his finger and thumb. He follows my rib cage and down to the dip of my waist. I struggle to keep still as he nears one of the spots on my body that makes me squirm. A spot only he knows exists. One that will turn me into pliable clay in his capable hands.

Fumbling with the snap of my jeans, he pops it open, drawing the fly down. Grasping the waistband, he attempts to expose more skin to his mouth. Frustrated he can't do it here, he pulls me off the island and sets me on the floor. I grab his wrist and undo the button there, repeating with the other arm. He lets the tailored shirt fall behind him. I set my hands on his sculpted chest, digging the tips of my fingernails into his skin and drawing downward.

"Norah," he growls, falling to his knees before me. Over the last two years, I have learned things that make him squirm too. Without finesse, Jacob tugs my jeans over my hips. Lifting each foot, he pulls the leg off, casting my jeans aside. I look down at him at the same time he gazes up. The hunger in his eyes is more palpable than I've ever seen before. Tearing his gaze away, he drags the side of my thong down my hip and presses his mouth just inside the point of my hip, followed by a stroke of his tongue. Chills rise beneath my skin.

"Jacob, again."

I feel his mouth curve upward into a grin before he draws his tongue along my hip once more. Except this time, he continues down the front of my thigh, pulling my thong off ever so slowly. When it reaches my toes, I step to the side. Rocking back on his heels, Jacob stands before me.

"Tank, *halten garde*."

Taking my hand, he leads me down the hall. Most of our clothes are scattered near the kitchen island on the floor. He pauses at the threshold into his room. While I wait for him to continue forward, reaching around him, I unsnap his jeans, unzip his fly, and push his jeans and boxer briefs to the hardwood. Sliding my hands along the front of his powerful legs, I draw the tip of one fingernail along each side of his shaft before settling my hands flat against his chest. All my curves press against his back.

Turning to face me, Jacob leads me to the chair near the fireplace in his room. After sitting, he slides his hands beneath my knees, pulling me forward on the seat. His blue eyes stare straight into mine. Starting at my toes, Jacob kisses a path up my leg with excruciatingly slow precision to the inside of my left thigh. Inch by inch, his mouth moves closer to my core. Pushing outward, he lifts my left thigh, setting it atop his right shoulder. My nerves are wound so tightly that the first touch of the tip of his tongue sends spikes of pleasure straight through me. He drags the flat of his tongue from my pucker to my clit, followed immediately by his finger. Him repeating this in reverse order a few times has me on the verge of splintering. The moment he spreads my folds and spears me with his tongue, I convulse against him. He presses his splayed hand on my lower abdomen to prevent me from squirming away.

"Let go, gorgeous."

My orgasm rips through me, the intensity harder this time. There is no reason other than I shared my feelings with him. Before I have the chance to recover, Jacob turns me away from him, placing my feet on the floor. Immediately, his fingers enter my core and tease my nub. I'm dripping with arousal as Jacob withdraws his fingers, filling me fully with his shaft from behind. Threading my fingers over his, we rub my nub in a tantalizing rhythm. He glides his hand from beneath mine, sliding it over my hip and the curve of my ass, resting his fingers against my anus. I continue circling the sensitive bud with my thumb.

"Norah?"

"Yes, fill me completely."

With my words, Jacob pushes forward with his index finger. The feeling of him buried deep inside me to the hilt and filling my ass is intense. The fullness is beyond anything I've ever felt before. He has penetrated my ass before, just not at the same time as his hard length is deep inside me. I feel the rush of a hard orgasm building at the base of my spine.

Jacob thrusts into me harder than ever before. My inner walls tighten around him as my orgasm spirals. His fingers dig into the flesh on my hip as his release mounts. His finger and shaft move in unison as we explode together. After a few shallow thrusts, he gently withdraws, gathering me against his chest before carrying me to his bed.

I refuse to let the possibility that we're going to be over soon cloud what we just shared. The list of men with whom I have shared myself completely is miniscule. It contains only one name—Jacob Blackthorne. I wasn't a virgin when we got together, but no one has ever given me pleasure like him. I promised to give him time for whatever he needs to sort out. However, as soon as I no longer need his professional services, I could very well be alone with a crushed heart and walking away from the most spectacular lover I have ever had.

JACOB

Honesty is the best policy, right? Right. If I'm being honest with myself, sex with anyone else, though it's a brief list, never felt like it does with Norah. Not even Mara. I'm sure there is something twisted comparing my sexual partners, but it matters. It matters that my connection with Norah, both sexual and otherwise, is different than Mara.

Sliding her soft, long tresses over her shoulder, I press my mouth to her bare skin. A satiated sigh falls from her pouty lips. I continue pressing kisses down her spine while massaging her breast, plucking her nipple, as she rocks against my hardening length.

Twisting, Norah cranes her neck to kiss me. I climb over her, settling between her creamy thighs. As my gaze settles on hers, I see the emotion written all over her face. Lowering my mouth to her toned belly, I kiss upward to her lips. Sliding my hand around her neck, I ravage her mouth, tasting her with a desperation that I have only felt for her. She slides her hands down my chest, gripping my shaft tightly.

"I need you."

After aligning us, she drags her hands up to cup my face. After kissing the inside of her hand, I secure her wrists above her head and bury myself into her hot center with one deep thrust. Our eyes remain locked on one another as her walls squeeze and convulse around me.

The pressure builds as I pump into her harder and faster. A pleasured moan fills the air around us as we explode together. After a few long bursts, I release her wrists and slowly lower myself on top of her. Moments later, I curl my arm around her waist and roll us to our sides.

There are likely plenty of appropriate words for me to say in this moment, but they escape me. The shift from taking her on the stairs to now is unmistakable. Her surrender is complete and unequivocal. If I'm honest, mine too.

I hear my phone ringing faintly from the kitchen.

"How long until you have to answer that?" she asks, her lips against my heated skin.

"Not long enough." I pull back slightly to look at her.

"Go, you know whoever it is will just call back in ten minutes."

"Please stay here."

She nods, pulling the soft sheet up as I rise from the edge of the bed. After pulling on some shorts, I pad to the kitchen and release Tank.

As I lift my phone to check the voice mail, it rings in my hand.

"Yeah, Blaine." I listen to Blaine list what he learned and his next steps. Ending the call, I dial Connor.

"What's up, Jake?"

I fill him in on the details from Blaine, and he offers a few more of his own. "Also, are you coming to dinner tomorrow? Our parents are having a joint meal, and we're all invited, including Cam and Jill."

"I want to but don't think it's safe to move her unnecessarily."

"Have it at your place."

It's a good suggestion.

"Have you talked to her?" he asks after a brief pause.

"I told her about Mara. The rest, we need to talk more. Let me ask Norah, and I will let you know."

"Listen to you, so domesticated."

"Really, C?"

"Jake, I'm happy for you. I hope it works out. You have spent enough time blaming yourself for something you had no control over. You're my brother. If Norah makes you happy, you need to hold on to her."

"I'll text you after I talk to her." I hang up, grab waters, and move back to my bedroom. As I step in, my eyes are treated to a gorgeous sight. Norah is kneeling on my bed—her silky hair falling like a sheet down the small of her smooth back, her perfect ass bare to me, and her front draped in my sheets. Although it's almost dark, she's staring out the bay window.

"Is everything okay?" she asks, looking over her shoulder toward me.

"There have been some developments, but there's nothing you need to do yet."

She returns her gaze out the window. The trust she places in me is incalculable.

"What do you say to hosting a family dinner tomorrow?"

"I thought you were going to your parents'?"

"How did you know that?"

"When your father brought Tank, he said he would have preferred seeing me again at family dinner."

"How did you respond?" There's an edge to my question that I didn't intend.

"That there was still time for you and your team to get back."

"Thank you. You didn't have to cover for me."

She nods without looking at me. I set the bottles on the night table. Placing my hands on her hips, I turn her to face me. The sheet puddles at her knees as she sets her hands on my chest.

"I don't think we should move you unnecessarily. I'm absolutely confident that you're safe here, but I won't risk you, my family, or Connor's."

"Okay. I'll stay here. You go to dinner with your family."

"No." I drag my hands down my face, my response a bit harsher than I plan. "I'm not very good at expressing my feelings."

"I disagree," she murmurs, lifting her eyes shyly to mine. "I think you express your feelings with your body perfectly. Your words, not so much."

A small grin appears on my face. "Norah, will you host a family dinner with me tomorrow?" I just hope my family is on their best behavior and doesn't make Norah feel uncomfortable.

"Yes. How many people are we talking about? Do you have everything you need?"

Leaning forward, I pull her against me, kissing her thoroughly. "Let's shower quickly and then make sure we have everything we need to pull this off."

The shower takes longer than planned. One would think we would be sated for a little while. That would be wrong. We finally check my pantry for staples. According to Norah, I have all the ingredients for dinner except for fresh bread.

Me: Norah is willing to cook. Please bring fresh bread and tell everyone.

Connor: Roger.

I can only imagine the thoughts running through Connor's mind right now considering how long it took me to respond. I set two glasses on the island and divide the remainder of the bottle of Mayacamas Norah opened a few days ago.

"Are you going to tell me what Blaine's update was?"

"It's not overly substantial. The Sterlings are still missing. Blaine found the first mention of a ledger two years ago."

"Now what? We just wait?"

"Pretty much." I take a healthy sip of my wine as Norah swirls hers.

"Can I use your computer? I need to order some clothes."

"Sure, come on." I slide my fingers in hers, leading Norah to my office, so she can start shopping. "Just don't use your account. Shop as a guest just for an extra layer of security. "I'll be right back." I walk to my bedroom and grab my wallet.

Less than fifteen minutes later, Norah is ready to checkout with some clothes. The cart has jeans, a few tops, and socks. I stand behind the chair as she adds silky pajamas on another website. She opens a third window and adds lingerie to the cart.

"Are you sure about this?" she asks. "Do you have any idea how much my lingerie costs? I'll pay you back."

"Yes, I'm sure. As long as you don't buy lingerie *and* shoes today, it'll be fine. Use the office address. Gemma will deliver your packages when they arrive."

After placing her orders, Norah and I sit side by side in front of my fireplace enjoying our wine. As much as I'm fighting it, having her here feels real and perfect, despite the threat on her life.

NORAH

Carefully, I slip out of Jacob's bed, pull on his hoodie, and pad to the kitchen. Tank follows me once I step foot in the hallway. I scoop out his food and brew some coffee. Coffee in hand, I pad to the French doors overlooking the back yard and let Tank out. I feel Jacob before he touches me.

"Morning," he says, sliding his arms around me, his lips against the nape of my neck.

"Morning. I tried not to wake you."

"It's fine. I heard the alarm. Who gave you the code?"

"I watched you. Why?"

"Just wondering. Remind me later, I'll give you the others as well. I should go to the gym anyway. Want to come with me?"

"Sure." I return to his room, stripping off my clothes as I go.

"Norah," he grits out. I'm bending over, searching in my bag for something to wear in nothing but a pink lace thong.

"What? I need to change. My clothes are in here."

He moves behind me, drawing his hands up the back of my thighs, sending ribbons of need through me. His hands come to rest on the flare of my hips.

"You need to stop touching me like that if you want to work out before we need to cook dinner."

"Touching you like what?"

"Like you want to do sinfully delicious things to my body."

"I do."

"You can't have both."

"Why not?"

"You're very thorough."

"Is that a complaint?"

"No, hell no."

He slides his hands from my hips down the front of my thighs before drawing upward, pausing at the apex, his low growl indicating he noticed the wetness of my panties.

"What were you thinking about?" he whispers near the shell of my ear, raising goose bumps across my skin.

"You."

"Don't move." He rushes out of the room. I hear him talk to Tank before returning. "I said don't move."

I've stepped out of my thong and turned toward the door.

"I heard you, but isn't this better?"

He latches on to my right nipple while lifting me into his arms. We fall onto his bed and feast on each other until there's very little time to shower and prepare dinner before our guests arrive.

Near two, I slide the veggie lasagna into the oven while Jacob finishes chopping the greens for a salad. Connor saunters in first. I'm not sure what he thought he would find, but he seems surprised that Jacob is helping in the kitchen.

"Hey. Here is the bread you requested," Connor says, handing me two loaves.

"Thanks. Jacob, can you slice it and put it in that basket?"

"Sure."

The look of amusement in Connor's eyes is hard to miss. It makes me wonder how Jacob was with Mara. They were so young, and his deployments made for limited time together when they were married. I didn't expect him to have no dating history. Considering his service and his profession, widower wasn't something I thought would be listed anywhere near Jacob's name. Ben and a petite, dark-haired woman, who I deduce is Jacob's mom, enter the house. Jacob washes his hands quickly and moves to greet them. He pulls his mom into his arms and gives his dad a bro hug. Jacob moves behind me to introduce me, but Ben beats him to it.

"Norah, lovely to see you again. This is my wife, Connie."

"You as well, Ben. Pleasure to meet you, Connie." I extend my hand to her. After the introductions, I busy myself with the appetizer plates, and Connie rounds the island, stopping near me. She stands there appraising me before speaking again.

"You failed to mention she's gorgeous, Ben."

"Not as gorgeous as you, darling."

"Thank you, Connie. I see where Jacob gets his smooth lines from," I say, and Connie's face lights up as she walks away.

"I never used any lines on you," Jacob mutters from behind me where he is gathering dishes to set the table. I don't think anyone heard him but me. He leans near my ear. "You aren't the type of woman to fall for a line."

I turn my head and whisper, "What type of woman am I?" My eyes rise to meet his.

"Everything about you is beyond what any man would expect to find in one stunning being."

Speechless, utterly speechless. My desire to kiss him right now is exceedingly high. However, we didn't have time to discuss PDA, or much of anything, before our guests started arriving.

"Come closer."

I want to make sure only he can hear me. He lowers his head level with my lips, effectively blocking anyone who happens to look this way from reading mine.

"I want to kiss you senseless right now." I press my mouth high on his cheek. He smiles and lifts his head, looking straight at me as if there aren't other people nearby.

The remainder of our guests arrive at the same time. Edward and Joyce, Connor's parents, are making the rounds. Edward is tall with graying blond hair. Joyce is tall for a woman with salt-and-pepper hair and a bright, kind smile. Cameron and Jillian, Jacob's siblings, are hovering near me in the kitchen. Cameron is average height, stocky build, and brown eyes. Jillian is slender and petite with gorgeous blonde hair down to her waist.

"How long have you been dating our brother? Do you want to get married?" Cameron asks.

"Do you want a family? What do you do for work?" Jillian adds.

"Why are you a client?" Cameron follows up.

I was wondering when and where the inquisition would come from. I inhale deeply and start to respond. "Well, I met Jacob—"

"Guys, leave her alone."

I'm thankful for the reprieve, but I would like to know how he would answer some of those questions.

I pull dinner out of the oven and set it on the counter before turning to grab a spatula to serve it. Jacob is immediately beside me.

"I don't know how to answer some of their questions. I don't know what you want to share or not share," I whisper, facing the corner of his kitchen.

"I know. We should have discussed it earlier."

"We were otherwise tangled up."

His face and neck turn a dark shade of red. Damn, that blush is sexy!

"Yes, we were. We need to focus on getting through this meal without divulging too much or something we aren't ready to share."

"What do you suggest?"

Unfortunately, our guests are clamoring for food, and we don't get to finish this discussion. Luckily, the rest of our meal passes with jovial conversation and no major questions asked of Jacob or me. The parents, if you will, chat amongst themselves. Jillian and Cameron argue about the Bears' defense and what could be done to improve it. When I offer a different option, they're shocked by my allegiance, considering where I live, but happily include me in the conversation. I excuse myself to the bathroom once we finish eating. I simply need a few moments to gather my thoughts.

Family gatherings like this is what I miss most since losing my mother so young. Joseph wasn't equipped to host so soon after Mom's death. Kelly was in school. Now that all of us have the ability, we haven't been able to pull it off successfully, at least not with the same atmosphere. The last great family gathering I recall is the Christmas before she died. She decked the beach house out as if we were home in Massachusetts, complete with a real tree. The three of us snuck downstairs and tore into our gifts instead of waiting in our rooms. At first, I thought our mother was going to shout, but she didn't. Our parents sat at the landing of the stairs watching us. I think she knew then that her time with us was limited.

Leaning against the sink, I splash water on my face. Like earlier, I feel him as he enters the room.

"Who said something inappropriate?"

I crack a small smile. "No one."

"Thinking of your mom?"

I nod as he pulls me into his arms. The steady beat of his heart calms me. I want him every day. How well he knows me has grown exponentially since I became a client. Odd, but true. If he decides he can't give himself permission, I'm going to be nursing an obliterated heart.

"I miss this part of my childhood so much, these gatherings with no holiday attached. Do you have them often?"

"Usually every other month, especially if Connor is on assignment."

"Your family is wonderful, Jacob."

"They are." He lightly presses his lips to mine before leaving as quickly as he appeared.

JACOB

Norah has made an impression on my family, especially on Joyce. After I return from checking on Norah, Joyce corners me, forcing me to talk with her, how every mother figure can. My father also pulled me aside earlier in the evening to see if I shared Mara with Norah yet. When I admitted that I had, he told me not to screw it up. Apparently, that was the totality of his advice. Joyce has much more to say on the subject.

"How are you, Jake?"

"I'm well, Joyce. How was your trip?"

"It was wonderful. You know that isn't what I'm asking you, young man."

"Do you have any idea how difficult it is to talk to you about my personal life?"

"I have known you since you were three days old. You're family, but I understand why you feel it's odd to talk to me about Norah."

She's asking me to divulge my feelings about a woman who isn't my wife, her daughter.

"I failed her."

"Did you?"

"Of course, I wasn't here. I couldn't protect her."

"Jake, if you were standing right next to her, do you believe in the depths of your soul that she would have made it to the hospital?"

"I don't know."

"She would have died in your arms."

I can't fathom that image at all. It was hard enough hearing the words "I'm sorry to inform you your wife has died," getting an emergency flight home to bury her, and sleeping in our bed alone. Mara was willing to sleep alone in our bed if I didn't come home from my deployment—a sacrifice that all military wives understand they could potentially endure. I never thought it would be me. Her hospital records, the autopsy, and every shred of documentation I could get my hands on say the same thing—instantaneous death upon impact. I can wrap my head around that. Both Joyce and Norah astutely pointed out that I couldn't save her even if I were here.

"Jake, I love you like a son. Were you unfaithful to my daughter?"

"No, absolutely not."

"Did you give her a false sense that your service was without risk?"

"No."

"Did you love Mara?"

"You know I do." Do or did? Will it ever be did? No, I will always love Mara.

"You honored your vows?"

"Yes."

"Mara is gone. You gave her your whole heart for her lifetime. It was short, but her lifetime, nonetheless. I know from experience, you'll never get it back completely, but you can and must give your heart to someone new."

"You lost someone too?"

"Yes. My first husband, Martin, died in a military training accident just six months after we married."

"Joyce, how did you move on?"

"A wise old woman—"

"Nona?"

Nona was a spunky woman who wielded so much power, both literal and figurative, in her tiny, barely five-foot-tall frame. She was Mara's favorite person. Mine too if I'm being honest.

"Yes, Nona. She pushed me to see that I fulfilled everything I promised to Martin. I believe you loved Mara sincerely, and she loved you. There is a vast difference between the first love you shared with Mara and forever love. Your first love didn't have the opportunity to blossom into forever love. Jake, you deserve forever love. You never looked at Mara the way you look at Norah."

"How?"

Joyce sees I love Norah too. I need to admit it to myself and her.

"It's how you talk to her, how you interact with her. It's you making sure she was okay when she walked away from the table earlier. I hope we didn't push her."

"No, her mother died of cancer about eight years ago, and family gatherings are hard for her."

"Yet she agreed to host one with you for your family."

She didn't even hesitate. In fact, she was willing to risk her safety for me to attend without her. She's....

"She loves you Jake."

Joyce is right. Norah told me herself.

"The only person you need permission from to let her in completely is yourself. You deserve forever love and happiness, Jake."

"Thank you, Joyce." I hug her tightly.

"You're welcome." Joyce rejoins everyone in the dining room.

Turning to gaze inside, I see Norah chatting with my sister near the fireplace, her hands animatedly explaining something and Jill laughing at her response. I watch a bit longer before heading back inside.

The remainder of dinner, dessert and drinks, passes with ease. Afterward, while I wash the dishes, Connor approaches me.

"You good?"

"Your mom is a wise woman."

"She is, but you already knew everything she said to you."

"I did."

He's right. Permission, I just need to give myself permission to love again. That isn't true. I love Norah. I need to tell her. I need to give myself permission to tell her out loud and for the world to see and hear. Honestly, I don't know enough about her to gauge what type of reaction

I might get, even if she did say she loves me, just not in those words exactly.

"I'm heading out. Are you working from here tomorrow or are you bringing Norah to the office?"

"She's safest here. The less movement, the better. We don't know how long the search for the ledger is going to take."

"Good point."

"I'll contact everyone later, let them know we're meeting here. Nine work for you?"

"Sure, see you then." He pauses before saying, "Jake, let me know if you need me."

"Thanks, C. I will."

As long as we're here, I don't think I need backup to protect Norah. Not human backup anyway. The list of people who have access to my property is short and tightly controlled.

Soon after Connor leaves, my family departs in a steady stream. Norah and Jill are whispering as they make their way to the front door.

"You'll be my first call," Norah says, glancing over at me. Great, my... girlfriend, lover, client... Norah and my sister are joining forces against me. I'm sure that isn't good for me.

"Care to share what that was about?" I ask as the door closes behind our last guest.

"It's not a big deal, Jacob."

"You and my sister conspiring against me isn't a big deal?"

"She just offered backup if I need it. I assured her I can hold my own with you."

I shrug, moving closer to her. She looks up at me. "Okay, I give. Are you up for a walk?"

"Sure."

Less than fifteen minutes later, we're walking hand in hand along the driveway.

NORAH

With our fingers intertwined, we casually stroll along the driveway toward the inlet. Tank ambles along just ahead of us. This time, Jacob turns right instead of left.

"Where are we going?"

"To my favorite spot," he replies, offering nothing further. As it gets darker, he hands me a flashlight.

"What happens now with the Morettis?"

"We keep searching for the ledger. It's the only thing that will remove the threat. How does your job work?"

"I crunch numbers."

He laughs softly, hanging his head. "When you're retained by a new client, what typically happens?"

"If it's my client, I open a file, gather as much back data as I can, and interview the client regarding the areas they need assistance. Then I review everything and create a plan based on their needs, such as a restructuring or trimming expense."

"Do you have anyone else review your work?"

I'm trying my best to focus on his questions and not the tension in my body. The push and pull of my brain and my heart. I only hear peacefulness here. It's silent other than Jacob's questions and the sounds of nature. The water nearby, the crunch of the snow beneath my feet, and my heart pounding in my ears.

"If it's my client, someone I brought in myself, then no. If it's a file assigned to me as an associate, then yes."

"You said the Moretti file was assigned to you seven months ago. Have you worked on it before that?"

"Yes, but nothing substantial."

"What did you do?"

"I recall reviewing a few filings for the SEC regarding some stock transfers and the split of one company into two new entities. When a member of the family attains the age of thirty, the parents create a company for him or her based on their skill set or splits one that already exists."

"When was the first time you ever saw the Moretti file?"

"Three years ago, give or take."

After I answer him, Jacob comes to a stop. We had walked up a small hill and are standing on an overlook.

"This is spectacular."

"It is. It's equally as gorgeous during the day, but the stars now are unmatched. Stay there." Jacob steps away from me, taking about ten long strides. Not long after, he returns with a thick blanket, which he spreads out on the wooden platform to my left. "Join me."

He takes a seat on the platform, patting the spot beside him. I sidle up against him; then we lie down, staring upward, taking in the midnight sky dotted with what seems like a million stars. He sets his hand over mine, and Tank rests his head on my ankles.

"I haven't seen this many stars maybe ever."

"Thank you, Norah."

"I didn't do anything. I should be thanking you."

"You did." He turns on his side to face me. "I shouldn't have asked you to host dinner with me. It was selfish."

"I could have said no when you asked. I don't want you to change your life because I'm here. I gather from your family that I'm your only client who has ever been here." He nods slowly. "Why?"

"I've never had a client who was more than a passing acquaintance until you. You're in a category of your own." He leans over, lifting his hand to my face. "My family is taken with you. You made quite an impression today."

"They're wonderful. All of them. Were your parents and Connor's parents friends before your adoption?"

"Yes. I think my mom's relationship with Joyce was one of the deciding factors in pursuing adoption."

"Would you consider marriage again? You don't have to answer me if you don't want to or aren't ready."

He inhales sharply. I knew what I was getting myself into when we started seeing each other, but everything is different now, at least for me.

"Before I talked to my father last week and Joyce today, I would have said absolutely not. You know better than anyone that I wasn't looking to share my life ever again. They offered sound insight into us, even after meeting you briefly."

"Like?"

"It boils down to me giving myself permission to be happy again. Only I can do that. Only I blame myself for being in Afghanistan when Mara died."

"Tell me about her."

A look of surprise crosses his face. "She was tall like Connor with the same light features, which makes sense because they were twins. Mara was a tomboy. She played in the dirt with trucks. She sat through our games, both football and baseball, regardless of the weather. Connor was my offensive lineman. She would run routes as we prepped for football season. A teacher was the only thing she wanted to be. You would think we talked about having a family, but we never did."

Based on this little bit of information, Mara sounds like a cool chick. "Do you?"

"Giving myself permission also means deciding what I genuinely want. Do you?"

"Since I started at Quinn Sterling, I had the single focus of becoming the youngest partner ever. I knew it would mean forgoing many things. I opted out of dating, vacations, parties, and so many other things to focus solely on work. Now that is gone, and I have nothing to show for the first chapter of my career other than a small fortune with nothing to spend it on. I don't even know what I'm going to do for work when I'm free to make that decision. I suppose the answer is, at one time, I would have said no because it would prevent me from attaining partner. Now, I would say yes."

"A small fortune?"

"I assumed you reviewed the data that Blaine provided when he paused my banking."

"For any other client, I would have. I have no reason to mistrust you or invade your privacy, so I decided not to open the file. I trust that Blaine froze everything."

"I appreciate that, but it wasn't necessary. The buy-in for partner at Quinn Sterling is two and a quarter million dollars."

"Damn, good for you!"

"Thanks."

"Do you want to go back to Quinn Sterling?"

"No. I'm certain I don't want to be a partner there anymore. I also don't think I can work there after the way Stan mistreated me. He was using me, and I didn't see it. Plus, I'll always be looking over my shoulder there, wondering which file will cause problems next."

A gust of wind sends chilly air up my back. I shiver. Instantly, he pulls me closer. I struggle to suppress the sigh that is ready to fall from my lips.

"Do you want to go back?"

"No, but we probably should. Thank you for bringing me here." I mean here right now and his home, but I'm not sure I conveyed that adequately.

"You're welcome."

As we walk back, he informs me that he'll be working from home and the team will arrive daily by nine. Although Maia, Christoph, and Nolan live in the bunkhouse, they don't show up without calling first or for a scheduled meeting.

When we enter the house, he sets the alarm before we turn in for the night.

JACOB

The last two weeks have felt normal, except for the fact that Norah is still being sought by the Moretti family. Over that time, we have talked and learned a bit more about one another. Each day, Norah and I hit the gym and make breakfast. I handle my morning meeting at the house, then work in my home office. Norah typically curls up on the couch in my office with a book. I'm sure she's bored out of her mind.

It has been lightly snowing all morning. The longer she is here, the more likely she will miss Thanksgiving with her family. We need to talk about how to handle that and her townhouse. Whether she wants to keep it, move, or upgrade her security system.

On one hand, I have a sense of dread, waiting for the next issue. Yet on the other, I have hope we're going to locate the ledger.

Late afternoon, I receive an urgent call from Blaine. The moment Norah hears my tone of voice, she sits up straight against the arm of the couch.

"Give me an hour to review this and discuss it with Norah. In the meantime, work your magic. Find out everything you can about this video and where it was sent from."

The pit in my stomach is back. After I watch this, if I need to get Connor here, I will. The question is, do I watch it alone first?

"That was Blaine. Your personal email address received an email from someone with a video. Do you want me to watch it first?"

Norah lowers her head slowly. The fear that just crossed her face has me on my feet immediately. In two steps, I have her curled into me, her hands flat on my chest.

"I won't let anything happen to you." I won't survive if I fail her. "If I need to have Connor here because I don't trust myself, I will."

Norah nods against my chest, and I loosen my hold on her. The cold fear in her eyes has lessened some, but not enough for my liking. I kiss her forehead and then her lips. After sitting back behind my desk, I pull out a set of earbuds, inserting them just in case this is something awful she doesn't need to see or hear. I inhale sharply and press play.

The video is grainy, but Stan and Delores are front and center. Both look despondent and disheveled but largely unharmed. The background is a nondescript room with a crack in the wall. It looks like a newer warehouse, but that's something Blaine will figure out.

"My name is Stanley Sterling. Delores and I are being held until Norah Cavallaro releases the ledger to the Moretti family. Norah, they don't want you; they want the ledger. Please, wherever you stashed it, retrieve it, then deliver it to the FBI building in Boston by Friday at 5:00 p.m. If you fail to comply, they will kill Delores. I can only imagine how you feel about me, but please save my wife."

Absorbing his words, I lift my eyes to Norah. She's moved over near the window that faces the backyard.

Throughout the entire video, Delores sat beside Stan, her right hand covering his, her left hand gripping the armrest. She sat debutante straight in her chair, head held high with a grim look on her face. Even though it appears he's reading from the paper in his hand, Stan is composed and steady. The paper isn't shaking and.... He's lying! Stanley Sterling knows where the ledger is but won't give it up. He's trying to draw Norah out! I want to murder him.

Get it together! Right now, she's your client. Not the woman…

Before I think it through, I dial Connor.

"Yeah, Jake."

"There has been a development."

"I'm on my way."

Rising from my chair, I walk over to Norah.

"Is it that bad?" she asks warily.

"Depends on your definition of bad."

"It must be pretty bad if you called Connor before telling me."

"After watching and taking a few minutes to digest the footage, I feel rage building against the person speaking in the video. I need Connor to make sure I'm not reacting because of my feelings for you. He'll see the footage for what it is, without regard for feelings."

"Should I watch?" Her voice is strong, unwavering. She may not know what she will see, but she isn't afraid.

"Probably, but let's wait for Connor's opinion."

She nods before pulling my lips to hers.

"What was that for?"

"I wanted to. Plus you just shared feelings with words."

A grin spreads on my face. Leaning closer, I kiss her again, but more deeply. I lose control easily when her lips are on mine. Thankfully, Tank lifts his head and runs into the hall when Connor arrives. I would prefer to avoid any awkward moments until after Norah is safe. Kissing her softly once more, I step away from her.

Connor steps into the office as Norah retakes her spot on the couch.

"That was fast," I say.

"Hi, Norah."

"Hi, Connor."

"I was already on my way here to use the range. What's up?"

"Blaine sent me this about thirty minutes ago." I hand him earbuds as he sits at my desk. After he watches it in its entirety, he backs up about thirty seconds to review the end again.

"Did she watch?"

"Not yet. What's your take?"

"She should watch before I say anything. I don't want to steer her."

Norah sits at the desk. As she watches, her emotions play out on her face. I see them, maybe Connor does, but the betrayal, the anger is all bubbling beneath her calm surface.

"That son of a bitch! I don't have the ledger. He's lying! Why?" she shouts.

I move behind my chair and set my hands on her shoulders. She leans into my forearm slightly, then pulls back to straight. Maybe because Connor is here.

"I agree. He is too composed; the paper isn't shaking," Connor states.

"It isn't me?"

"No, you have every right to want to murder Stan after watching that." Connor assures me.

I start to formulate some type of plan. Although I'm not sure there's anything else we can do. I believe she doesn't have it, or maybe she doesn't know she has it. Either way, I don't know where else to look.

"What do we do now?" Norah asks, looking back and forth between Connor and me. Connor doesn't speak up right away.

"I believe you. You don't have it, but Stan is indicating that you at least have access to it," I admit.

"Neither Stan nor Delores has ever been to my townhouse. The only things from work that were at home are my laptop and access reader. Everything else I use—the printer, shredder, and pens—are mine. William has my laptop, and the access reader is smaller than a deck of cards. I don't see where they could hide anything in there, and it still works properly."

"Blaine should continue his search as well as picking apart that video," Connor adds. "We need to know as many details as possible. The closer we get to the end of the week, we may need to consider responding in some way to stall or suggest that we have the ledger but they need to let Delores go."

Norah pushes up out of her chair, circles around me, and starts walking back and forth behind me. After the first two passes, I step back so she is in front of me.

"As heartless as this may sound, I don't care what happens to them. He lied to me, used me, set me up to look complicit in a money laundering scheme with a notorious, albeit alleged, crime family. All I care about is clearing my name, restoring my reputation, and forgetting everything about Quinn Sterling and everyone who works there."

"Well, then that is what we have to do," Connor says, watching Norah who has stopped pacing to look at him, "but first we need to find the ledger. I realize we keep returning to it, but Sterling thinks you can get to it. So, let's locate it."

"Okay, what do I need to do?"

"The only thing I can think of is going through your interactions with Stan over the last two years or so to recall a time when he gave you something or you feel something was off about him." Before I can say more, my phone rings. Seeing it's Blaine, I answer.

"Yeah, Blaine."

"I'm working on isolating the sounds in the background and checking if there's anything unique about the video. Whoever sent it to Norah's personal email address has serious skills. I haven't been able to find the origin yet."

"Thanks."

I update Norah and Connor.

"There's nothing else we can do right now other than let Blaine do his thing," I inform them.

Connor nods. "I'm headed to the range. I can stop by again before I leave."

"That works," I reply.

"See you later, Norah."

"Bye, Connor."

I hear the front door close, and Tank returns to his spot at Norah's feet. "Will you take a walk with me?" she asks.

"Yes, whatever you need."

"What I need is to strangle Stan, but I'm pretty sure that would land me in jail for a very long time."

I laugh. "It would, but I would love to see you tell him off at some point."

"I would like that myself."

NORAH

After donning coats and boots, we walk out the back door. Tank opts to remain in the house. We cross the yard in silence. As we near the edge, we exit through a wrought iron gate. After stepping through, Jacob grabs my hand.

"Are you up to talking about Stan and the ledger, or do you want to talk about other things we need to discuss?" Jacob asks.

"Such as?"

"I realize that all of these are indirectly connected, but are you planning to go back to your townhouse? I had the front door and French doors replaced with added security locks. I can have someone clean it up and remove the damaged furniture and other items."

"Thank you. I don't know. I feel like I could choose anything. Honestly, it's pretty scary and exhilarating at once." As we talk, Jacob guides me to the right on a leaf covered path into the woods.

"Did you always want to be an accountant?"

"No, does anyone?" I smile, and Jacob laughs heartily. It's deep, honest, and unguarded. Considering the reason we're walking, unguarded is surprising. The sound of his laugh warms my soul. I don't know that I have ever seen Jacob relaxed during a regular day and not after a hookup.

"What is your dream job?"

"I'm sure if you dig for writings from my childhood, you will find I wanted to be everything from an astronaut to a lawyer. Truthfully, I always wanted to own a bookstore. A bookstore where you don't necessarily have to buy a book to enjoy the space, a library of sorts. I would have books for sale but also a lending library as well."

"That sounds amazing."

"What about you?" I ask, wondering if he always wanted to be in the military.

"From an early age, I wanted to serve like my father. When I returned from my last tour and retired, I considered becoming a cop, but I didn't want to put myself at risk every day for my job. Connor and I were lucky, our injuries were recoverable. Carter, Jones, Adams, and the others were not. The look on my mother's face was too much to bear when I finally returned home. I can't take a risk like that every single day."

"Aren't you taking risks like that right now—" I swallow hard. "—for me?" I stop walking and turn to face him.

"Yes."

"Why?" *Because you asked him.*

He scrubs his hand down his face before sliding it along my jaw, his fingers trailing to the back of my neck. His eyes soften as he looks into mine, the blue of them serene and calm. A place I could get lost if I allow myself. I would be lying if I said I wasn't already.

"Up until your text, I was fine being here alone with no one to share my nights. I was fine with my life if you were happy. Fine if you were safe. If I could see you when it worked for both of us, it was working for me. I was stuck feeling guilt for something completely out of my control. Guilt I unnecessarily placed on myself. Now, I can't go back. I don't see how I can let you go when this is over. I don't want to."

"Jacob—"

"Could you be happy here?"

"What do you mean here? Here as in living here or here as in with you?"

"Both, I think." A hint of doubt creeps into his voice. That wasn't the intent of my question. I know he can't leave here. He built his business here. I would never ask him to leave for me.

"Jacob, I want you. I—"

He pulls my mouth to his, pouring every ounce of his heart into his kiss. The warmth and heat of his tongue tangling with mine makes my knees weak. He has kissed me more times than I can count, but this kiss…. He's staking his claim, admitting that we have something worth fighting for. We could have a future together. A soft moan seeps past my lips as he gently pulls back.

"Norah, I—" His words are cut short by his phone ringing. "I'm sorry."

I attempt to take a step away, but he pulls me back against his body. Sweet mercy! His large hand is flat against the small of my back, digging in just enough to make sure I know moving isn't an option.

"Okay, I'll talk to her and see what she remembers from that time frame and get back to you," I overhear Jacob say to whoever called. It's probably Blaine. I wonder what he found.

"What did Blaine find?"

Dropping his hand, he silently takes mine, leading me a bit further along the path. At a small clearing, there is a group of tables and chairs. He takes a seat in a chair, guiding me into his lap. He ignores my question and continues what he was saying before the call.

"I want to take you on a proper date, but there are two issues with that. First, I haven't been on a date in way too long. Second, you can't leave here yet."

"I understand." I smile and press my lips to his briefly. "Any idea how much longer I will not be able to leave?"

"Do you need something?" There is an edge to his question, letting me know if he can fix whatever it is, he will.

"Jacob, our circumstances are unique. I appreciate that you'll do whatever you can to make this more palatable for me, and you have. Your home is idyllic and comfortable. I want you. I want to be with you, but I also want the freedom to see my family and friends. You can't control that, and I understand completely, but I need to let Kelly know about Thanksgiving soon."

"Okay. Hopefully, we'll have a better idea in a few days how we'll handle the ledger, or lack thereof, by Friday and if they follow through on their threat regarding Delores. Blaine indicated there's a mention of the ledger in an email from Sergio Moretti to Stan dated about two and a half years ago. It mentions something about a prize and stashing the ledger with the prize. Does that mean anything to you?"

"Not off the top of my head. Is there a way for me to get into my personal email safely?"

"Maybe. What are you looking for?"

One hand is digging into my hip while the other is threaded with mine.

"My calendar is linked to my email. I might be able to recall something if I could review it."

"Are you okay with Blaine downloading it and sending it to me?"

"Yes, that's fine. Anything else?"

"Not right now." I bring my legs over the arm of the chair and snuggle deeper into Jacob's embrace. Aside from learning more about this caring protector with insane blue eyes, I need to figure out what I want to do with my life, at least professionally.

JACOB

Sharing some of my feelings with Norah was easier than I thought. Now, I just need to make her world safe so she can go back to it, at least to visit. It takes Blaine less than an hour to send me a copy of her calendar back three years.

We're walking back when I receive the copy. Tank meets us at the gate, his tail wagging. We aren't alone.

"Who's here, Tank?"

He barks before taking off back toward the house.

"How do you know someone is here?" Norah asks.

We need to work on her observation skills.

"Tank was inside when we left."

We step onto the porch and remove our boots. I glance inside before we enter, but don't see anyone.

"Oh, there you are." My mother comes into the main living area from down the hall and hugs us both. I watch Norah in my mom's embrace. Her expression is hard to decipher. I'm not sure if she's sad or happy. Sad because her mom isn't here, but happy that mine is willing to welcome her.

"Hi, Mrs. Blackthorne. How are you?"

"Please call me Connie. I'm well, and you?"

"Same."

"Is everything okay, Mom? You don't normally just stop by."

"Joyce fell on some ice at the courthouse this afternoon. I just left her at the hospital."

"Is she going to be okay? Is she home? How badly is she injured?" I ask a slew of questions rapidly.

"Connie, could you excuse us for a minute?" Norah asks to slow down my questions.

"Of course."

Norah takes my hand and leads me into the bedroom. "Is one of your staff here?"

I run through the assignments in my head. Callen is with Miss Goldberg. Christoph has returned from his event with Miss Forrester. Nolan is unassigned right now, and Maia isn't due back to Maine for another week.

"Probably, why?"

"Call them. You need to see Joyce with your own eyes. It's the only way to make that look dissipate."

"What look?"

"The uncertainty you have in your eyes. It's the same look you had on the plane when you told me I was going with Connor before you kissed me. The look was different after you kissed me. Have one of them or all of them come stay with me."

"Are you sure?"

"Yes. As much as I would like to go with you, I can't. But you need to go."

She would be willing to come with me. This woman is beyond what I deserve.

"Do you have a preference who stays with you?"

"No."

Reluctantly, I dial the phone at the bunkhouse. "Hello, Jacob. What's up?" Christoph answers.

"I need at least one of you to come keep Norah company. I need to visit Joyce."

"Give us ten minutes," he replies before hanging up.

I turn back to the woman beside me. "Thank you, Norah. I'm sure this is awkward for you."

"Not at all. Joyce holds a special place in your life, not only as your social worker but your best friend's mother and your mother-in-law."

"I have no words right now to explain what's going on in my head." My heart too if I'm being completely honest with myself. I slide both hands along her jaw and kiss her thoroughly, her lips plump from mine as I pull away.

"Hey, boss man. We're here," I hear Nolan call from the foyer. I also hear my mom greeting them. I press my lips to Norah's again briefly.

"Go. I'll be fine."

I don't want to leave her, but I'm grateful she understands my need to see Joyce with my own eyes.

"I'll be back as soon as I can." I hurry out of the room with my wallet and keys in hand.

"Will Mrs. Michelson be okay?" I overhear Nolan asking my mom.

"Eventually, yes," my mother replies as I step into the kitchen.

"Thanks for coming, Nolan. She'll be right out."

"No problem. The others will be here momentarily."

"Ready, Mom?"

"You're coming?" she asks, grabbing her purse.

"Yes."

We pass Maia and Christoph on our way out the door.

"Where is she?" I ask my mother as we walk to our cars.

"She was being discharged when I left to come here. She's just getting home now. Is everything okay with Norah?"

"What do you mean?"

"The threat is still out there?"

"Yes, it's why she is staying here."

"She suggested it?"

"Yes." I let that just hang there. I know what my mother is getting at. *Norah cares about you; don't screw it up.* "Okay, I'll follow you there."

I settle into the driver's seat and exhale. It's imperative that I find that ledger or some other way to get the Morettis out of Norah's life. Every day I spend with her, I learn something else that I love about her. Her insistence that I visit Joyce is admirable and selfless. My past doesn't bother Norah at all. She deserves everything she wants out of this life.

One of the things she wants is me. I'm willing to try again with her as soon as she is safe.

A little over thirty minutes later, I pull into the Michelsons' driveway. Closely after my mom, I enter their home. Joyce is sitting on the couch with her cast right arm and her left leg wrapped in a brace propped up on a pillow.

"Oh, Jacob! You didn't have to come."

"Yes, I did."

"Where is Norah?"

"She stayed with my team. It still isn't safe to move her more than necessary."

"Yet she insisted you come?"

A look of surprise must have crossed my face.

"Don't look so surprised. She's special, Jake."

She is. "Enough about me. What happened?"

Joyce retells the story of her injury for probably the fiftieth time today. Edward is making some snacks in the kitchen with my mom and Connor.

NORAH

That look when Connie told Jacob about Joyce was too much. Pushing him to leave me with his team was necessary. His concerns about my feelings are difficult to understand. Everyone has a past. I wouldn't expect Mara's family to never see him again after her sudden death. The fact that her family and Jacob's parents have a relationship reaching before their children were born, it's natural they would still be part of his life.

"Thank you for coming guys. Does anyone know where Jacob has cards, games, etc.?"

"I do," Maia says. "Come on."

I rise and follow her down the hall. She steps into the room on the left past the guest bedroom.

"How are you, Maia?"

"I'm fine."

"What's going on with you and Nolan?"

Shock appears on her face. "What? Nothing. Why?"

"It's just something I see when he looks at you. Is that against the rules?"

"Not that I'm aware of, but there's nothing going on. What do you mean how he looks at me?"

"He looks like he wants to devour you."

She looks away from me. "You mean exactly how Jacob looks at you." I'm sure my face is bright red. "There is no denying it, don't bother trying."

"It's complicated."

"No, it isn't. You clearly care about him if you sent him to visit Joyce."

"I do. It isn't complicated on my end."

We chat more while browsing the games in the guest closet. We opt for Yahtzee and return to the living room. The guys have turned SportsCenter on and gathered some snacks. Maia and I sit on the floor near the ottoman and set up to play.

"Norah, what do you want to drink?" Christoph asks from the kitchen.

"Water would be great, thanks."

Christoph brings a round of waters into the living room. The anchor is talking about tomorrow's game between the Bears and the Vikings.

"There's no way the Bears can win that game. This sportscaster is crazy," Nolan blurts as if the anchor could respond.

"You're wrong," I say, much to everyone's surprise. All eyes cast in my direction.

"You're a Bears fan. You poor thing. You and Jacob are made for—"

Maia elbows Nolan, who abruptly stops talking. Apparently, everyone believes there is a personal relationship between Jacob and me.

"The defense will have no problem keeping the running game in check," I inform him, quickly changing the subject. "The Vikings running back will be lucky to hit fifty yards. The Vikings quarterback needs a balanced game to win. His wide receiving core is weak at this point in the season, so many injuries. Do you even have a first stringer left?"

Christoph rolls a Yahtzee on his first roll of his second turn.. He jumps up and does a little dance around the couch. It's nice seeing the less serious side of Jacob's team. Maia rolls next and gets a full house.

"Care to make a wager?" Nolan suggests.

"Whatever it is, it can't be money. I don't have access to mine right now," I remind him.

"Loser prepares dinner for the entire team. It must be an actual meal, not takeout or delivery."

"Deal. Just so we're clear. I'm betting the Bears win, and you're taking the Vikings to win."

"Yes," Nolan replies.

I shake Nolan's hand and then roll a Yahtzee. A good omen, perhaps. We continue the game.

Christoph wins the first round by a huge margin, and Maia cleans house in the second game. Near nine, Tank's ears perk up and he runs to the front door. Moments later, Jacob strolls in.

I consider the appropriate response to my… my what… boyfriend coming home while I'm hanging out with his employees. *Bodyguards,*

Norah. Don't fool yourself, they're here to protect you. I decide to wait until later to ask Jacob about it. I want to throw my arms around him and ask how Joyce is, but Nolan beats me to it.

"How is Mrs. Michelson?"

"She'll be fine eventually. Her arm is broken, and her knee is badly sprained."

"Glad to hear it's nothing too serious. Did you know that Norah is a Bears fan?"

"Yes."

"She bet me that the Bears are going to win tomorrow over the Vikings," Nolan states as if it's an impossible feat.

"She's correct. What is the wager?" Jacob asks.

"The loser prepares a home-cooked meal for the entire team."

"I hope you can cook, Nolan." Jacob winks at me as I pass him with the empty water bottles. "Thank you for coming."

"It's no problem. We were hanging out in the bunkhouse. Plus Norah's so much easier going than most of our clients," Maia states as they get ready to leave.

I recycle the water bottles and wash the few dishes, setting them to dry. I wonder if all their clients are difficult. Perhaps it's because only Jacob is really dealing with me regarding the mess in my professional life.

After he closes the front door and engages the alarm, he moves to me faster than I've ever experienced before. His lips cover mine like he hasn't kissed me in months not hours. Regardless of how often he kisses me, it feels like it's just the two of us. Everything else falls away. Nothing else matters. Not the fact that I have a bounty on my head or the fact I have Delores's life in my hands, without the ability to save her. My professional life is in shambles, yet everything else feels like it's finally falling into place.

"Hi," I whisper when he eases his mouth from mine.

"Hi." He sets me on the counter, resting his hands on my hips.

"How is Joyce, truly?"

"She'll be fine. She will hate the physical therapy and likely her therapist, but her spirits are surprisingly good."

"Did you know that Nolan has feelings for Maia?"

A slight moment passes before he speaks. "I saw a brief glimpse when he realized she was taken and then another after she was drugged. He looked exactly like I did while I was waiting with you. Why?"

"I asked Maia if there was anything going on. She replied no but pressed why I thought that."

"What did you say?"

"I told her Nolan looks at her like he wants to devour her."

"What was her response?"

"She said, 'You mean the way Jacob looks at you.'"

"She isn't wrong. I was fooling myself thinking my feelings for you were well hidden. Hell, my father saw it when he showed up at the Michelsons."

"Do you have a rule against them dating?"

"No, but I won't compromise a client's safety because of their relationship."

"Makes sense. Are you and I a secret?"

"Clearly not if Maia is asking questions."

"True, but we aren't acting like a couple in front of anyone."

"Meaning?"

"If we aren't a secret, I would have kissed you when you got home regardless of who was in the house."

"Norah, at the risk of sounding cheesy, will you be my girlfriend, which would allow me to kiss you and touch you as I wish regardless of our audience?"

"Yes."

JACOB

Stepping even closer, I scoot her forward so my hard length presses against her core. Lowering my mouth to hers, I worship her mouth. Wetting her lips with my tongue elicits a low whimper. Noted. I lift her cotton tee over her head and feast my eyes on her breasts.

"Damn! I'll never get tired of finding new lingerie beneath your clothes."

"Don't say things you don't mean!"

"It's worth every penny. Your sexy-as-sin shoes too!"

This bra must be the one she ordered a few weeks ago. I've never seen it before. Red silk with black lace holds her perfect breasts up high and ready for tasting. Heat creeps into her cheeks as I dip my head, sucking the curve of her mounds. Hooking my finger under the strap, I pull it down her arm, following it with my tongue. I travel inward along the side of her breast to her nipple. Pulling it between my teeth, I bite down a tad harder than I planned.

Instead of wincing in pain, Norah's fingernails mark the back of my neck. As I swirl my tongue around her taut pink bud, she unclasps her bra, dropping it to the tiled floor. I drag my thumb over her other nipple, watching it tighten with arousal. Her fingers grip the hem of my shirt and drag it up to my shoulders. I release her just long enough for my shirt to fall over her bra on the floor.

Curving my arm around her ass, I draw her forward, lifting her high in my arms so her breasts are level with my mouth. The tips of her long, dark hair tickle my forearm. With precision, I move upward with open-mouthed kisses to the curve of her neck, teasing her earlobe. Slowly, I lower her to the floor before gliding my hands over the dip in her waist. Sliding my fingers to the front of her jeans, I pop open the snap. I pause when her hands skim down the front of my body to cup my shaft.

Covering her hand with mine, I say, "Norah, wait. We're going slow tonight."

It may kill me, but I'm going to explore every inch of her tonight. Curving her fingertips, she draws her hand up. As each tip scrapes my shaft, I grow harder, which I didn't think was possible.

Sliding my hands into her jeans, I cup her cheeks before pushing her jeans to the floor. She steps out of her jeans before kicking them to the side near our other clothes. I let my gaze roam from her bright red toes, up her long, toned legs, to the matching red, silk thong soaked through with need. I continue moving my eyes upward to the smooth curve of her toned abdomen, over her luscious breasts, the small group of freckles along her collarbone, to her hazel eyes. I cup her face in my hands and kiss her softly before leading her to my bed.

After stepping into the bedroom, Norah opens the snap of my jeans.

"Norah . . .."

"It's unfair that I'll be totally naked in the next minute and you have half of your clothes on. At least the jeans need to go."

I look into her eyes and realize there is no room for noncompliance with her request. I throw my hands up in surrender. She peels my jeans down my legs; her hands flat against my skin makes my length jump.

"Better?"

"For now."

To avoid giving up any more ground, I tug her flush against me and walk until her legs hit the foot of my bed. Wrapping one arm around her rib cage, I set her on the mattress and climb up, straddling her thighs. Lifting her once more, I set her down in the center of my bed clad in only her sexy red thong. I brush my lips across hers before moving down her luscious body. Knowing it will drive her crazy, I kiss from her shoulder down to her fingertips. Rising, I lick down the center of her chest to her belly button. Dipping my tongue inside makes goose bumps rise on her skin. That's new. With each trail her hands grip my comforter. Moving over to the point near her hip, I draw my tongue south but stop short of the lace edge of her panties. I repeat on her other hip. Deep sighs fall from her lips.

"Are you trying to drive me to insanity?" she murmurs, lifting her head to look down at me.

Looking up, I reply, "No, I'm taking my time."

This is the first time I don't feel rushed. I want to savor it. I want to savor every inch of her flawless skin. Seemingly content with my answer, Norah lowers her head to the mattress. I tuck my fingers beneath the sides of her thong and lower it toward her feet, kissing and nipping down her leg.

As I caress the inside of her thighs, I part them slowly, making room for my shoulders. First, I drag my index finger just outside her core on the left and then the right. That slight touch has Norah squirming. Running my finger from the top of her slit down to her tight pucker causes a low whimper of approval. I lean forward, blowing onto her sensitive bud, knowing she will attempt to move way. I hold her thigh against the mattress before drawing my tongue from the bottom of her core to the top, nipping and sucking her clit between my teeth.

"Jacob…."

I tease her more than normal before dipping my tongue into her folds. It doesn't take long before her thighs are trembling and her fingers are pulling at my hair. Even before she completely recovers, I push two fingers deep into her core while sucking her nub with my mouth. Moving forward and back, she pushes against my hand until she convulses in pleasure.

"Jacob…."

"Hmmm," I reply against her swollen folds, the vibration of my response clearly adding to her euphoric state.

"Holy hell."

I hum again, causing her to writhe against my mouth. After she relaxes a bit, I climb up her body, leaving a trail of kisses along the way.

I shimmy out of my boxer briefs as she says, "I need—"

I know what she needs. I need it too. I interrupt her by sliding deep into her heated center. She lifts her leg onto my shoulder, pulling me deeper while curving her other leg around my waist. Thrusting in and out, I feel her tighten around me. Moving her leg from my shoulder to my waist, I lift her hips higher, allowing me to bury myself deeper. Every muscle in my lower body contracts as I get close. I feel her tense beneath me as her release grows in her body. As I push forward, Norah bears down. At once we fall over the edge into complete bliss.

I have no idea how many times I've been with Norah, but the last few times, it's more. So much more. I couldn't possibly fathom that it's still getting better. I suppose what they say about sex without love is true. At least when both people admit their feelings, it's more fulfilling.

I lower myself, pressing my lips to hers. The emotion in her eyes is screaming at me. I can only imagine what mine are saying to her. She unwraps her legs and sets her feet on the bed. Languidly, I roll us so she is lying on top of me.

Hours later, I wake with Tank pushing his nose against my hand. Sliding to the right, I slowly move Norah onto the bed and cover her. I pull on my boxer briefs to let Tank out. After downing a bottle of water, I gather our clothes from the floor and set the alarm before climbing back in bed with Norah.

NORAH

Dim sunlight brightens Jacob's bedroom. I burrow deeper into his warm, hard body, refusing to acknowledge that it's morning and I'm getting closer to seeing if the Morettis will go through with their threat. If Delores is lucky, I'll find something in my calendar to produce a plausible place for the ledger.

I set my hand on Jacob's thigh, drawing my fingernails in circles. He presses his mouth to my shoulder while sliding his hand down my belly. It's impossible to ignore his impressive morning wood flush against my ass. His fingers graze my nub. He moves his thumb in circles as I rock against him. Pulling myself up to straddle him, I grind against him until my orgasm claims me. Gripping one hip, Jacob continues flicking my nub, keeping me on the razor edge of another orgasm. Lifting, I grab his length and stroke it before sinking down until he's buried inside me. Leaning forward, I angle my hips back, taking him even deeper.

"Holy fuck, that feels good!"

I smile down at him, setting my hands on his pecs, and slide along his shaft. I feel him swell inside me, the tip hitting a spot that only he has touched before.

"Norah, don't stop." His face tightens, and his fingers brand my hips.

Moving faster, I convulse around him as he empties into me in long bursts. I glide my hands up to his shoulders as I lower my chest to his.

"Good morning to you too," he says against my neck.

I giggle softly. "I could have just gotten up."

"No, that was the perfect way to start a day. Hell, every day."

"Is it now?"

"Absolutely."

I lift my head, pressing my lips to his.

"We should get moving. It's already after seven."

I frown and start to move, but he pulls me in for a toe-curling kiss. If we weren't already naked, we would be after that kiss. I may not know when this issue with the Morettis will be over, but I want to be wherever he is.

"Why don't you shower while I feed Tank and make coffee?"

"That's not as much fun," I say with a pout.

"I agree, but we won't be ready when the team arrives if we step in there together. While I don't plan on hiding our relationship, we need to be respectful too."

"Fine." I wink as I move into the bathroom. I step into the steamy enclosure and enjoy the heat of the scalding water easing some of my delicious soreness. I'm working to keep my expectations in check. That gorgeous, blue-eyed, flawed man making coffee is my boyfriend. I haven't had one in years. If that isn't a reason to call Kelsey, I don't know what is. I would have already if I had a phone. Ugh! Still need to be off the grid. As I shut off the water and step out of the shower, I find Jacob leaning on the counter with a steaming cup of coffee in his hand and a second cup just beside him. "How long have you been standing there gawking at me?"

"Not that long. Is it gawking if I have permission?"

I dry off as we talk. "When did I give you permission?"

"The moment you agreed to date me exclusively."

"Still not a fan of 'girlfriend,' huh?"

"Not at all. It isn't enough."

I'm speechless. What does that mean? We can't just jump to anything more significant than that, can we? Arguably we have been together for more than two and a half years. It was undefined, but still.

I decide to shift off my title, if you will, for now. Wrapping myself as best I can with his small towels, I step over to the side, allowing him access to the shower. "You should get in. I need my gawking time too." I smile before kissing him softly.

I enjoy my coffee and the view a bit too long. Plus, getting ready at the same time isn't conducive to keeping my hands to myself.

I'm still cooking when Maia arrives before nine.

"Morning," she says, stepping inside and patting Tank on the head.

"Hi, Maia."

As I plate the food, Jacob comes into the kitchen and refills both our cups. He kisses me tenderly as he sets a fresh cup down for me. When I turn with the plates, I get a look from Maia—the look from a female friend that says, "We need to discuss that in detail."

No offense to Maia, but I would prefer to talk to Kelsey. Maybe I can call her later.

Soon, the rest of the team ambles through the front door. Everyone except Maia opts for a cup of coffee. Not surprisingly, Jacob finishes eating, washes his dish, and is ready to begin the meeting precisely at nine.

JACOB

During the meeting, I update everyone and give Nolan a single event assignment for Mrs. Lynn Smith. She worked with Nicholas on his last movie and needs security for an event in New York tomorrow night. Her previous security company folded, and she recalled Blackthorne's presence for Kelly Barnett. Fortunately, I'm able to accommodate her last-minute request.

After holding the morning meeting, I briefly chat with Connor before he leaves.

"Are you aware of Nolan's feelings for Maia?" I ask.

"I noticed them acting more friendly than colleagues but nothing overly concerning. Why?"

"Norah mentioned something after they stayed with her last night."

"About that, thanks for coming to visit. You didn't need to leave her with the team. Mom will be all right."

"You're welcome. Norah insisted."

"I assume you finished talking with her."

"Yes."

"I'm happy for you, man. We need to get the bounty off her head."

"Thanks. We do. She needs to be able to make decisions for her life." Ideally, those decisions including her work will be here, not in Maine.

"Let me know if you find anything in her calendar. As far as the deadline tomorrow, what's your plan?"

"I won't put Norah in harm's way again. I won't bluff that we have it to save Delores. Besides, I fully believe that Stan knows where the ledger is or at a minimum knows that Sergio Moretti hid it somewhere."

"Agreed. Let me know if you need anything."

"Such as?"

"A bodyguard so you can take her on a proper date."

"Thanks. I'll consider it. I could also plan one here." That's on my agenda for later today—plan a date for Norah here at home.

After everyone leaves, Norah and I move into my office to review her calendar. She starts at the earliest entry, which is about three years ago. Scanning each day, she moves through at a decent pace. I know it shouldn't bother me, but I notice the dates she's gone out with other men listed in her calendar. Admittedly, there aren't many, perhaps one a month, but for some reason, it ticks me off a bit. I reel in that train of thought rapidly. I didn't even know her then. I have no right to be judgmental.

Mara does not threaten her, yet you're upset about some random dates? There are a few GNO listed on Fridays each month. I push my thoughts away as she gets close to the Ramirez wedding. That is about the time that Blaine indicated a prize of some sort in connection with the ledger. I note on her calendar that her weekends are devoid of dates except for a J listed sporadically throughout the months. She hasn't dated anyone since the wedding either.

"You haven't been on an actual date since before Kelsey and William's wedding?"

"No." She doesn't even look up.

I set my hand on her finger hovering over the arrow keys. "Why?"

"I wanted the partnership. Plus I'm not a one-night stand kind of woman. Never have been."

I'm not sure how to respond, so I lift my hand, and she continues scrolling. Weeks pass as she scrolls.

"Wait, what's that?" I ask, pointing to a four-hour block of time on a Friday evening.

"That's the yearly awards ceremony for Quinn Sterling. I got an award for the highest billings and revenue."

"What came with it?"

"A plaque and a sizable bonus. Why?"

"I wonder if the prize was the bonus. But that doesn't make sense. Presumably you deposited the money, where is the plaque?"

"All of the awards I have ever received from Quinn Sterling are in the bottom two drawers of the left filing cabinet in my office. The bonus money helped fund a scholarship I created for girls in my hometown."

"That's amazing, Norah. What is the purpose of the scholarship?" Another reason she's incredible.

"It's for girls who choose predominantly male fields of study like engineering or science-based professions."

"You never brought the awards home?"

"No. Awards are meant for a hero like you, not an accountant who billed the most hours."

"I'm not a hero, Norah."

"Yes, you are. You saved Connor in Afghanistan. You tried to save Adams, Carter, and Jones. You brought all those men home to their families. I'm willing to bet you earned military honors for your actions during your third tour."

Like her, I put my Purple Heart and Silver Star in a drawer. I never looked at them again.

"You and I are similar there. You're correct. I did receive medals for my service, but...." My eyes drift off to the right of the screen toward where the medals are stored.

She reaches out and turns my gaze to hers. "I get it. Not everyone made it back, but you did. You deserve to be recognized for your service, even if you think you failed them."

"How?" No one other than Connor understands how I feel about that day. We did what we expected others to do in the same situation. An award doesn't change the outcome.

"What?" she asks, drawing her thumb across my lips.

"How is it you can put my feelings into words so much better than I can?" I lean forward, kissing her softly. "Thank you."

"You're welcome."

We finish scrolling through her calendar until the beginning of this year before taking a break. Norah makes lunch while I make plans for our date on Saturday night. My only concern is, after the outcome of tomorrow, whether she will be willing to go on a date.

NORAH

Clearing the rest of my calendar is easy. The only event of note is the awards dinner. To me, nothing seemed out of the ordinary with the plaque. It was the same as the others I've received in the past.

"Are you going to join me to watch the game?" Jacob asks.

"Absolutely! I need to see who is making dinner on Sunday. Plus, I get to watch with you."

After preparing a feast fit for football, I turn on the game and take a seat. I hear Jacob's phone vibrate. After pulling it out of his pocket and glancing at the message, he hands it to me.

Nolan: I hope your cooking skills are on point, Norah.

Me: My cooking skills aren't relevant, although I'm rather good.

Jacob reads the text I sent and smiles. He settles into the corner of the couch, pulling me close. I curl into his chest and enjoy the game. Is this what a normal relationship is like?

"Can I ask you more questions about Mara?" I tilt my head back to look at his face.

"You can ask whatever you want." He leans forward, kissing my head.

"Was she your only relationship?"

"Before you, yes. Why?"

This man. Seriously, he just acknowledged that he and I are in a relationship. It's a huge statement from him. I consider whether I should ask my next question or not. Suppressing my concerns, I ask anyway.

"I was trying to determine what normal is. Aside from my need for your professional services now, what does a normal dating relationship look like?"

"Why do you ask?"

"My last relationship was during college. Ethan was also an accounting major, and he lived across the hall in my apartment building. We started off as friends, hanging out in groups. Eventually, he asked me out. We dated off and on for almost two years. We went to college parties, campus sporting events, and occasional movies. That ended when he asked me if I wanted a family. At the time, my sole focus was my name etched in glass."

Jacob nods, likely because we already talked about how my opinion on a family has changed since then. The crowd noise grows on the TV. We both look toward the television and see the Vikings quarterback complete a fifty-yard pass. We watch the next series where the Bears' defense stops them in three downs.

Content the game is back in hand, he says, "Keep going."

"During my first year at Quinn Sterling, I met Timothy. He was eight years older than me and hopeful he would curry favor with Mr. Sterling by taking me under his wing. Over six months, we went out once a month, sometimes twice. Mr. Sterling paired us together on a joint file.

Tim arrived the morning of our presentation hungover. Not only did he take credit for the work, but he told Mr. Sterling that I wasn't up to the task of handling a file of that size on my own. Thankfully, the firm requires all work to be initialed before it's saved on the company server. Soon after the presentation was complete, Mr. Sterling called me to his office and asked specifically if Tim did any work. When I indicated he did not, he was fired. Based on my limited experience, normal is something I have no basis for."

"Mara and I were young. We spent a lot of time just hanging out at the Michelsons' or my parents. Pizza and movie dates happened often. During college, we were apart, spending tons of time on the phone. The amount of time we actually lived together was remarkably short."

"I'm sorry. I didn't mean to dredge up memories."

"Don't be. Mara and I were together a long time ago. I've never shared her with anyone. We truly only spent time with a few people during high school. I never met any of her college friends or roommates. She never met mine. Overall, we were together for almost eight years, married just shy of two. When I first told you about Mara, your reaction floored me. Not only about my feelings of guilt, but you weren't angry, jealous, or concerned about her. Just me."

"You told me when you were ready. Until a few minutes ago, I never mentioned Ethan or Tim."

"I never asked because I didn't really care until you agreed to date me. You and I have been together for over two years. It wasn't what most people would call traditional dating, but it worked for us, especially me because it didn't require me to face my guilt about Mara. As far as whether this is normal," he says, gesturing back and forth between us, "it feels normal to me."

If how Jacob and I interact is normal, I'm fully on board.

The game has been a defensive struggle since the opening kickoff. Nolan has been largely silent. He hasn't sent another text yet. The Bears are winning three to zero at halftime. I scoot forward to clear our dishes.

"Where are you going?"

"To take these to the kitchen?"

"Halftime is not for dishes."

"It isn't?"

"Nope, come closer."

I lean in, and he tugs me against his chest, our lips a mere inch apart.

"Halftime is for kissing, except for the Superbowl. Then it's for watching if the performer is halfway decent."

"Noted." I eliminate the space between us. It would be a lie to say we were prepared to watch when the second half started. There is just something about his kiss that drives me to distraction. His touch sends sparks straight southward. Plus, whatever spicy cologne he uses smells divine. Our clothes pile up on the floor until we're both clad in only our underwear. "Are you sure no one will show up unannounced?"

"Fairly confident, why?"

"I want to stay like this." We're lying on the couch, which faces the French doors to the backyard.

A wide grin spreads across his face. "Works for me."

Apparently, any amount of exposed skin is an invitation for Jacob to touch me. I'm not complaining, but we don't finish the game. It also keeps me distracted from the fact that I can't help Delores. Even though I expressed my anger, I truly don't want anything to happen to her because of her husband. I certainly don't want to help Stan, but in the handful of times I've spoken to her, Delores has been nothing but genuine to me.

When I reach up for Jacob's phone to set an alarm, I find a text from Nolan.

Nolan: Well done, Norah. Dinner Sunday will be catered by me.

Smiling, I set an alarm for seven thirty tomorrow morning. Pulling the blanket over us, I lie across Jacob's chest, his heart beating against my temple and his breath calm and even. Even though I want to avoid tomorrow evening, I close my eyes and fall into dreamland—dreams filled with the life I just might be able to capture with him by my side.

JACOB

Nothing about falling for Norah is what anyone would term normal. I can't even say when I fell. That isn't true. The moment she asked for my help, I knew I would protect her until my last breath. I need to tell her. First, we need to get through this day. I hope the Morettis' threat is empty. I don't believe that she won't blame herself if they follow through.

Norah has no idea where the ledger is. Aside from Blaine's information regarding the prize, we have nothing to indicate where the ledger is. Her calendar gave us nothing other than when she received the award. However, it gave me more insight into the phenomenal woman plastered against me.

Waking with her is worth savoring. Her head against my chest as her long locks fall down my flank. One hand resting on my shoulder, the other against my rib cage. The scent of her shampoo wafts up to my nose. It isn't her normal shampoo, which smells like coconut and something beachy. This one is vanilla.

She's brilliant, which I already knew, but the scholarship, her understanding about Mara, and her concern for us regarding her inexperience in relationships. Laughable if you ask me. Neither one of us has any good recent experience except with one another. Yet even that isn't a good basis. When I stayed over, I didn't stay much past a cup of coffee. Tomorrow night will be a good start.

Ranking clients, Norah is the best. She hasn't complained about not having access to a computer, phone, or her own things. I'm sure it was easier for me to accurately request what she needs because I know her intimately, but Gemma or Connor handled the basics at least initially. Later today, I'll be able to determine how much longer she needs security. Well, I plan to be around indefinitely, but she'll be able to go wherever she wants without worry.

My phone vibrates above my head. When I move to grab it, Norah stirs. Lifting her head slightly, she looks up at me through her long lashes. Without a word, she starts trailing my chest with hungry kisses.

"Norah."

"Don't let me stop you. You go ahead and check that. I'll just keep finding spots to put my lips." Immediately, she draws my nipple between her teeth. I check the time and set an alarm, so we're appropriately dressed before the team arrives at nine. Her mouth moves across my chest, down my flank, to the point of my hip. I stifle a groan, knowing there isn't enough time to worship her properly.

"Norah, we don't have time right now."

Her sultry gaze shifts to mine without removing her mouth from my hip. That look tells me she doesn't care, but I do. Despite my desire to allow her to continue her downward path, I reach down and haul her mouth up to mine. I drop my lips to hers to quiet her protest. If I have learned anything in the past few weeks, it's that I can make her weak with my mouth. Dipping my tongue between her lips, I explore her mouth. A soft moan escapes her lips. Pulling back, I catch her lower lip between my teeth. She moans deeply. That is apparently on par with drawing my tongue over her lips. Learning her is fast becoming my favorite pastime. How did I miss these spots over the last few years? She pulls back, reclaiming her lower lip long enough to scold me.

"You can't kiss me like that and expect me to relent."

"Like what?"

"You know damn well what I mean."

I do but watching her flustered, especially naked, is fun. An alarm blares on my phone. "Is it really already that late?"

"Unfortunately, yes. We need to move."

"Why can't you just cancel the meeting so I can move back down where I was before you made me melt into a puddle with your skilled mouth?"

"As much as I would love to do that, we have work to do." She frowns, but I'm undeterred. "Plus, I'm not sharing any of your spectacular curves. . . ever. I'll race you to the shower."

"How are you going to beat me if I'm on top of you?"

"Not as difficult as you think."

Before she can reply, I wrap my arms around her and stand. Once she's on her feet, I release her and run down the hall.

"Jacob!" she shouts as I reach the threshold of my bathroom. I start the water. When she walks into the bathroom, she has a wide smile on her face. "Is this payback for me beating you at the Michelsons'?"

"Maybe." I step in the shower, and she follows immediately after. Unfortunately, there isn't enough time for me to make her orgasm with my tongue like she did at the Michelsons'. I just hope by the end of the night, we have more answers.

After the morning meeting and a few hours in my office while Norah paces like a mom waiting for her daughter to get home from prom, I decide we need to leave the house.

"Go change into something you're willing to get sweaty in." She raises an eyebrow. "No, that isn't what I mean. Your clothes will stay on."

"You're no fun."

"Liar!"

She smiles and walks out of my office. Once she changes, I lead her to the gym.

We warm up and spar for a bit before Maia and Nolan enter the gym. When they finish warming up, we take turns practicing releases and holds. Norah and Maia go toe to toe for a half hour before Maia opts to take a break. Honestly, that match up could have gone either way. It takes years of training to achieve the level of skill Norah possesses. Then she easily tripped up Nolan in less than five minutes.

"Your turn, Jacob," Nolan says after rising from the mat and high-fiving Norah.

"Not happening, we need to get back and clean up before the deadline."

"Afraid your woman can take you?" Nolan states.

My woman. I don't plan to address him calling Norah that. Honestly, I'm fine with it, at least in the sense that she's mine.

"I'm sure she can, but this session was to stop her from wearing a hole into the carpet in my office, not to see if she can defend herself. I know she can." She probably would, considering I'll never hurt her. "We'll see you on Sunday. Let me know what time you will be over to use the kitchen."

"Congrats again, Norah. I have never met anyone who analyzes a football game like you did before it was even played," Nolan says, honorably accepting defeat.

"Thanks. It's mostly that I love the game and a wee bit the stats."

I hand her my sweatshirt as we leave the gym.

"I wouldn't go easy on you," she says with a smirk on her face.

"I know, but I'll never put you in a position to defend yourself against me."

"I know."

NORAH

My nerves have been on edge since the calendar didn't provide any insight into the location of the ledger. As the close of business approaches, my anxiety increases exponentially. I'm grateful Jacob noticed and made me leave his office. Sparring with Maia and Nolan was fun and did take my mind off the ticking clock about to expire.

After cleaning up, I grab water from the kitchen and return to his office. He's standing with his back to the door, arms crossed over his chest. His shirt stretches across his back. In this moment, how hot he is shouldn't even register in my brain, yet it does.

"Thank you. I needed to get out of here. What if they kill Delores? I did everything I could."

He surrounds me with his arms, and a muted sigh leaves my lips. I could stay here. I want to stay here. The bigger question is will he be able to move on? Am I willing to stay without a commitment of some kind?

"It isn't on you. It's on Stan. Honestly, I think he knows where the ledger is or at least how to guide you to it."

"Why wouldn't he give me all the information I need to solve the puzzle?"

"I don't know. The threat of losing his wife should be enough."

Tank runs out of the office.

"Jake?" Connor calls from the hallway.

"In the office," he answers, refusing to let go. He leans back to look into my eyes.

"I'm good for now."

As if he doesn't believe me, he slides his hand up, cupping my face.

"Truly, I'm as good as I'm going to get."

Pressing his lips to my forehead, he releases me.

"Hi, Norah," Connor says as he joins us in the office.

"Hi, Connor."

"Still waiting?" he asks.

"Yes," Jacob replies just as his phone rings. "What have you got, Blaine?" He listens for a moment, nodding his head. "Okay, I'll call you back." I watch his chest inflate, and he slowly releases the air filling his lungs. Looking at me, he says, "There is another video. Same as before?"

I nod curtly, lowering into the client chair and pulling my legs against my chest, hugging them close.

Connor rounds the desk, standing beside Jacob as he presses play. I consider turning away so I can't read their faces, but I don't. It doesn't matter anyway; their expressions are devoid of emotion. A few minutes later, Connor and Jacob look at one another, shaking their heads.

"Well?" I ask.

Connor raises his hands as if to say, *you're the boss.*

"I don't think you should watch this. You should listen to the first part because Stan is talking to you, but not the entire video," Jacob states.

I nod slowly, and Jacob restarts the video.

"Norah, I would like to apologize for my treatment of you. I thought withholding the ledger would save Delores, at least I hope it will. You will find the code in Red Star and the prize. Decipher it and deliver the ledger, Norah. Our lives depend on it. You have one week. Despite all the drama of the last few days, please help save my wife." There are some mumbled words by someone else; then the playback stops.

"Was there more?"

Jacob looks over at Connor who tilts his head to the side. Clearly, they have their own language. One I need to learn.

"Delores and Stan are both dead," Jacob murmurs.

Speechless, I stare him down, trying to grasp the roiling in my stomach. Unfolding my legs, I push off the chair, leave the office, and walk straight out the back door after shoving my feet into Jacob's slides. I run halfway to the gate before screaming at the top of my lungs. It doesn't make me feel any better. I do it again. Still not feeling better. That bastard just increased the bounty on my head!

"I'm sorry, I—" I begin when I sense him approaching me, but he doesn't let me finish.

"You do what you need to. Scream some more, throw punches at me if you need to, but let it out."

I turn to face Jacob, not only to find him two feet behind me, but Connor standing on the porch.

"That bastard! Why didn't he give me that information three days ago? I'm not saying I would have been successful, but I would have tried like hell despite my disdain for him."

"I know. Can I...?" He opens his arms.

I step into them as he closes them around me.

"What can I do?" he asks.

"I need to stay here for a few minutes."

He nods, tightening his arms around me. The safe cocoon of him is exactly what I need.

"Norah, I l...." Jacob looks up at the darkening sky, letting out a jagged breath.

"I know."

He brings his eyes level with mine before closing them.

"You tell me when you kiss me, when you touch me, by not allowing me to watch the end of that video, by chasing me out here, by asking me what I need."

"How do you see that?"

"You're afraid to voice it because it'll make the possibility of experiencing that pain again real, very real." I may have read his mind.

He casts his eyes down to the ground.

"Will you ever be ready?" I ask, not sure I want the answer.

"I don't know. Probably... when you're safe."

"Then let's make that happen. But first." I snake my hands up his chest, sliding them to cup his face. I pause a breath away from his lips and look into his blue eyes. I'm expecting the storminess I see in them. The cause of his uneasiness is hard to determine. I brush my lips across his, giving him the opportunity to walk away. When he doesn't, I kiss him deeply, pouring every ounce of love and confidence I have into him, into us. "Let's go. We have work to do."

When I'm halfway back to the house, I notice Jacob isn't following me. Connor is still standing watch on the porch. I retreat to Jacob, take his hand in mine, and wait him out.

"You. Are. Everything. Even though I slammed the door to ever being happy again, I let you in. I gave you the ability to crush me. Instead, you make me stronger. I don't know when you will be free to leave here, but I want you to stay even after you are."

"Jacob, I—"

His phone cuts my words short. I may not get the same words in response, but I want to say them.

"Yeah, Blaine." When he finishes his call, he threads his fingers in mine and takes off back to the house.

Connor follows us inside. As we walk, my brain is spinning. What is Red Star?

"Can Blaine access the Quinn Sterling server or safely get me access? Maybe my log-in still works."

"What else do you need?" Jacob asks, walking straight into the bedroom. He drops my hand long enough to grab me a hoodie, retake it, and lead me into his office. Connor is sitting on the couch waiting for us to return. Jacob may not be able to say the words, but he certainly knows what I need.

"If I can't access the server personally, I need a lot of information. My billings for at least the last three years."

"Why three?"

"The award and the prize were from two years ago. Hopefully, it's near the time. I also need access to Stan's files for the last three years, specifically the Moretti Family Brand and Red Star, if there is such a file. I need to see the award; maybe William has some friends in Boston who can retrieve it from my office. I need to see at least the front of the bonus check. If Blaine needs access to the scholarship fund, let me know."

"C, can you call Blaine and ask for all of that data she needs?"

"On it," Connor replies.

"I'm going to call William," he states.

I zip Jacob's hoodie up and pad to the bathroom. I throw some water on my face and let out a harsh breath. When I return, he's finishing his call with William.

When I step back into his office, Jacob appraises me carefully. He asks without words if I'm okay. I nod tightly.

"Anything else?" Jacob asks with a serious look on his face.

"Pizza and wine. Do you have decent pizza around here, wherever here is?"

He smiles at me, a genuine smile. Rare and breathtaking. "That depends on your definition of decent. I absolutely can pull off the wine. Go grab some wine, and I'll order dinner."

JACOB

Terrifying. I have never felt fear this deeply rooted for another person, not even my brothers-in-arms. Not even Mara. Clearly, my feelings are written on my face, at least to Connor. That isn't accurate. Norah sees them too. She saw right through me outside. I love her completely, but I can't bring myself to say it in words. Her astute observation and acceptance make me love her more.

"Jake, you good?" Connor asks.

"No." My response is a bit harsher than I intend. "Sterling just put her deeper in jeopardy. He should have shared that information days ago, but he didn't. I don't see his angle for waiting. Do you?"

"The only angle I see is within the Moretti family. Whichever Moretti is—was—holding the Sterlings clearly wants the ledger for some purpose other than protecting the family. He or she wants to either keep the profits for themselves or expose the entire family. Hopefully, your woman loves puzzles and can find the ledger while we figure out how to take down the Morettis at the same time."

"You too?" My woman. It sounds so simple when someone else says it.

"You haven't told her yet."

"Not in those exact words."

"Of all the people in your life, have I ever lied to you or not told you something straight?"

"No, never. Neither have I."

"Jesus, Jake! You have been lucky enough to have two incredible women love you."

"What if something happens to her too?"

"That's what you're afraid of?"

"Yes. More than anything."

"Giving your heart to Mara didn't cause her death, Jake. Opening your heart to Norah won't change what happens in your life or hers. No one knows how long we have with someone. You shouldn't deny yourself the happiness of loving her because you're a coward."

"I am not a coward."

"Regarding her, you are."

There's no adequate response. Connor's right. Absolutely right. A short time later, my phone indicates there is a delivery at the gate.

"Did she come back up yet?" I ask.

"No, I don't think so. I'll get her. You get the food."

I hesitate.

"Go, Jake. She's fine. Your collection is extensive. She's a woman, probably couldn't make up her mind."

He's right. She's fine. She wouldn't leave. I grab my keys and drive to the road to pick up dinner.

When I return, Norah and Connor are chatting in the kitchen, dishes out, glasses poured.

"What took you so long?" I ask.

"First, you have an expansive cellar downstairs; plus, I didn't know what you ordered. So I found a red and a white." A small smile crosses her face.

"Fair enough. Dig in."

We slide pizza on our plates and sit at the dining table. Like me, Connor inhales his food. We've polish off three slices each while Norah is barely starting her second. My phone is pinging with emails from Blaine. Then it rings with a call from Captain Ramirez.

"Hey, Captain. Thanks for returning my call." I put the call on speaker.

"What do you need in Boston? I have some connections with Chief Walker," William says.

"I need Norah's office at Quinn Sterling emptied, but mainly I need the awards that are in her office, left filing cabinet, photographed and then sent to me. I need chain of custody preserved and each award fingerprinted, please."

"I'll get that done as soon as possible. Anything else?"

"No, not right now."

"Is Norah available? Kelsey wants to talk to her."

"Sure."

Norah takes my phone and moves away from us. I wouldn't expect her to stay, especially with Connor here. I'm not even sure she would talk to Kelsey with me nearby considering I will likely be the topic of conversation.

NORAH

"Hey, girl! How are you?" Kelsey asks.

I curl up in the chair in the bedroom. It's the room farthest away from Jacob and Connor. "I like order, Kels. My life is a mess both personally and professionally."

"You told him, didn't you?"

"I did. His reason for avoiding relationships is significant and understandable. He asked for time." It isn't my place to share Mara with Kelsey. If Jacob wants to share with everyone, that's fine.

"Your current situation with the Morettis isn't helping matters either."

"No, it isn't."

I don't plan on sharing anything more in depth with Kelsey. She likely knows more than anyone else. I'm sure William has shared with her. I don't want to alarm Kelly or Joseph any more than they already are.

"Do you need anything?"

That's a loaded question. I need to solve this puzzle so I'm free from the Morettis. Then I can work on everything else.

"Nothing you can do for me, but thanks."

"Of course, sweets. Will you be back for the holiday?"

"Probably not. I was hoping to have an answer today, but instead I have more questions and another puzzle to solve."

"You've got this!"

"Thanks, Kels."

"You're welcome. Figuring out what you want isn't going to be easy, Nor. I promise, it's worth it."

"I know what I want. I just may not get all of it. Love you, Kels."

"Love you too, sweets."

I end the call and glance out the window. It's dark now—the same hue hanging over this day like a storm cloud. Stan and Delores are dead. My life depends on unraveling Stan's message and finding the ledger. Honestly, I'm sure there is more to the Moretti issue. I won't be safe simply by finding the ledger. That is a terrifying thought. Taking a deep breath, I return to the kitchen.

Everything from dinner is cleared and washed. I don't see Connor anywhere. Jacob is standing in front of the French doors staring into the darkness. His crossed arms stretch his shirt across his sculpted back. Setting his phone on the ottoman, I slide my arms around his waist, gliding my hands flat on his chest before setting my temple against his back.

"All set?"

"Yes, thanks."

"How are you?" he asks, turning in my arms.

"Angry. The thing is, even if I knew I would be in this position, I would do it all over again. I would share the discrepancies I found with Stan. I don't know how to feel about that."

"You have every right to be angry at Stan. You should be proud that you would do it again. You have integrity and a strong belief in doing the right thing, Norah. Both are downright attractive as hell."

I nod against his chest before lifting my eyes to his.

"Do you want to get started tonight or wait until the morning?" he asks.

"I should at least sort everything tonight."

"Okay, most of it should be finished printing." Kissing me softly, he takes my hand as we walk into his office.

Connor is setting stacks of paper on the floor and the couch as they come off the printer.

"Thanks, Connor."

"You're welcome. I set each file in its own pile. Otherwise, I have no idea what any of it means."

I chuckle softly. "No problem. It makes sense to me. Hopefully, I can figure out the clues sooner rather than later."

I walk past the stacks of paper on the couch. First, I grab the printouts of my billings, stacking them from newest to oldest. Chances are the clues are not from this year. Next, I set up the Moretti file from oldest to most recent for each of the six companies. Oddly, but luckily, Stan scanned my work about the discrepancies and added it to the company server. At least I don't have to redo it. I take a seat, waiting for the printer to catch up.

Jacob sits next to me on the couch. When I lean against his shoulder, he puts his arm around me, pulling me closer. When the printer runs out of paper, he kisses my temple and moves to refill it. He just kissed me with Connor in the room. The kiss wasn't anything obscene, but Connor is Mara's brother, Jacob's brother-in-law and best friend. Connor must have said something. I'll accept assistance from any willing party.

When the next file finishes, Jacob's phone rings. He listens and then ends the call.

"That was Blaine. Any idea what Red Star could be?" he asks me.

"You mean if it isn't obvious like a file named Red Star?"

Jacob nods.

"No, never heard it before today. I gather there isn't a file named Red Star on the server."

"No, Stan didn't make it that easy."

I sigh. "I'll add it to my list of puzzles to solve. The bigger question is where to start. Probably there since I don't have the other pieces of info anyway."

"Makes sense if Red Star is the only part you have everything you need to start working on it," Jacob replies.

"If that's all, I'll head out for now. If you need me to come back in the morning, let me know," Connor says after adding to the final file on the floor.

"Bye, Connor," I say, turning back to a piece of paper with Red Star written across the top. Jacob follows Connor out. As I hear the alarm engage, I refocus on the paper, rearranging the letters of Red Star to form different words. I get "treads" but have an extra r. "Dears" or "dares" with an extra t and r. I keep scrambling and unscrambling the letters.

"Do you always pull your lower lip between your teeth when you're working?"

I look up and find Jacob watching me with a glass of wine in each hand. I didn't even realize I was doing it.

"Not purposely. Why?"

"It's hot."

I feel my face turning red.

"So is that."

"Stop." I have an odd feeling. The longer I'm here, the more we act like a normal couple, not where one of us needs personal security.

"Not a chance. I believe this is the first time I've made you blush outside of a bedroom. I'm savoring this moment." A genuine smile graces his lips as he approaches the couch.

I can't help but smile too. "You may be correct. Thanks," I say, taking a glass. I swirl my wine before taking a healthy sip.

"Any progress?"

"I guess. It isn't as if I have a desired outcome, at least not for this part. I have only found one other way to rearrange the letters to "starred." If that is the answer, what is starred? I have no clue. There aren't any stars on the Moretti file or my billings. But… wait . . ."

I hop up from the couch after setting the glass on the coffee table.

"Norah?"

"Hold on, I need to check something." I flip through the Moretti file, specifically through Sergio's company file. There is an RS typed after the Quinn Sterling employee who input data into the file. I keep flipping through the pages. Almost every time there is an RS, its preceded by SS for Stanley Sterling. I keep flipping and find another entry with RS, but it has RQ before it. Robert Quinn. He's dirty too? "Can I have that paper?"

Jacob hands it to me.

"Norah?"

I ignore him as I scribble down the names of the Moretti family members. Gustavo and Maria are the parents. Their children are Sergio, Mario, Rosalie, Vincenzo, Giovanni, and Rosita.

"There's an RS after entries on some of the Moretti family files. If the RS corresponds to family members, I have narrowed it down to Sergio and one of his sisters. The other interesting part is a few entries were signed by Mr. Quinn."

"You're amazing!" He leans forward, kissing me hard.

I could really get used to him kissing me whenever he feels the urge. Honestly, though, I don't know where he and I stand. True, he asked me to stay, but what happens in six months or a year and he still isn't ready?

It would be a lie to say I don't want a commitment, especially if he decides he wants a family.

"Mr. Quinn too?"

"Is it possible he did the work without knowing it was to launder money?" Jacob asks, likely to assuage my concerns that both named partners at my firm were dirty... are dirty.

"I suppose. I found his initials only a few times."

"Come on, let's go finish this glass away from work. You're pretty much stuck at this point, right?"

"Yes, I'm as far as I can go right now." I rock up to my feet and follow Jacob into the living room.

He's likely concerned that I'm not okay.

I set my glass on the ottoman and curl into him on the couch.

"Do you need anything?" he asks.

"Nothing other than the information William is working on."

"Want to try again?"

I lower my head into his lap, looking up at him while balancing my head between his muscular thighs. "How?"

"I'm exceptionally good at reading people. You... are a whole different book, one I'm getting more skilled at reading each day."

"I'm angry. Now it's more like a simmering pot that won't relax until removed from heat. In my case, until I figure out where the ledger is. Even when I find it, then what? I still won't be free. The Morettis aren't going to forget I know their deepest, darkest accounting secrets."

"I've never met anyone like you who sees where the pieces fit so far in advance, especially a client. You're correct. That won't be the end. Connor and I are working on that aspect of this. From what we can gather, there are two factions in the family. One working to maintain the status quo and one attempting to go legit."

"How do we figure out which is which, and how do I trust that whoever doesn't go down will truly leave me be?"

He leans down, brushing his lips across mine. My hand slides up to cup his jaw. He deepens the kiss before hauling me up onto his lap, staring into my flecked hazel eyes.

"You'll be safe when this is over, I promise," he murmurs. I nod before pulling his lower lip between my teeth. A low groan escapes his throat.

I release his lip and say, "Now you know."

"Yes, I do. Do it again."

I comply. He rises from the couch, carrying me to the bedroom. I continue to kiss and tease him until he's hovering over me on the bed.

"Your turn."

He pulls my lower lip between his teeth before thoroughly searching my body for other spots to make me scream.

JACOB

Near six in the morning, I turn to find Norah missing from the bed. Setting my feet on the floor, I start to look for her, ignoring the panic that's building in my body. She won't leave the compound. She probably won't leave the house. She's fine. I walk to the kitchen. I don't see her, but the coffee maker is warm and Tank's food bowl is wet. The living room and porch are empty. I hurry downstairs and come up empty. My concern level increases exponentially the longer it takes to find her. I take a deep breath outside my office door.

"Jacob?" she calls from inside. No wonder I didn't see her. She's sitting on the floor near the corner of my desk. Just the top of her head is barely visible. Tank's head is resting on her thigh.

"How long have you been up?"

"About an hour. Come check this out."

I settle behind her, pulling her against me so I can read over her shoulder.

"I went through Sergio's company paperwork and found these ten companies mentioned. Rosalie's paperwork only mentions two companies in common with Sergio. Rosita's company mentioned twelve companies overall, but ten in common with Sergio."

"Sergio is likely teamed up with his youngest sister, Rosita. We just don't know which side of the equation they're on."

"Right, the only thing we know for certain is Sid and Carlo were sent by Sergio. We don't know who abducted Stan and Delores."

"Blaine will figure it out. How about some breakfast before we work more?"

"Sounds good to me."

She follows me into the kitchen and makes two fresh cups of coffee while I tackle some pancakes. After breakfast we clean up and spend much of the day in my office, Norah searching through her billings for the last few years for any indication that she missed something. I suspect she'll come up empty. She's diligent and conscientious. She didn't miss anything. I check in with Jill about my plans for tonight.

Jill: Everything is set for 6 pm. The gorgeous flowers are on the porch.

Me: Thank you so much for your help.

Jill: She's wonderful, Jake. I'm glad you finally let someone in.

Me: Thanks. Me too.

I just need to tell her. Connor's words truly shook me. Not about two women loving me, although that was a shot. *Coward.* He called me a coward. He's absolutely right.

"How much more time do you need to finish that file?"

"I'm pretty much done, why?"

"Perfect, we're going on a date."

She turns her head to look at me. "We are?"

"We are."

"Let's get ready."

As difficult as it is, I keep my hands to myself while we get ready. When I finish, I start to leave the bedroom.

As I approach the door, she asks, "Jacob, can I have my necklace?"

I reach into my pocket, pulling out my wallet. I cross the chain in front of her as she pushes her hair to the side. After clasping it together, I press a kiss to the back of her neck. A soft sigh signals it's time for me to step away or we'll never leave the house.

"Thank you." She turns to face me.

I press a kiss to her forehead and walk out of the bedroom.

Just before six, I step out the front door and pick up the flowers I ordered for Norah as she comes out into the kitchen. I have no idea what type of flowers Norah's likes, only that her favorite color is violet. I opted for Picasso calla lilies, blue moon roses, and white roses. I hurry back outside and ring the doorbell. Laughing, Norah lets me inside, accepting the flowers.

"Thank you. These are beautiful." She kisses me high on my cheek near my ear. "Do you have a vase?"

I smirk because there's one on the front porch. I've got to hand it to Jill, she knew I didn't have one. I open the door, grab the vase, and give it to her. Shaking her head, she moves to the sink, adding warm water before setting the vase on the island.

"Ready?" I offer her my arm.

"Yes."

I grab our coats and head out the front door, leading Norah to the barn. I couldn't check out the setup before now, but I'm impressed. String lights hang around the huge door as well as along the interior of the barn. There's a table set up with a small heater warming around it. A large screen hides the second part of our date. I glance up to the loft which appears to be prepared exactly as I asked too. Jill is a rock star.

"How did you pull this off?"

"I enlisted a little help from Jill for the execution, but the idea and planning I handled myself." Some of it cost more than normal due to my time frame, but I don't care. I have been saving most of my earnings for the last decade. A little extra cost to make this date happen exactly as I want is worth it.

"Thank you." She leans over to kiss me softly.

I nod and pull out her chair. After sitting, I open a bottle of her favorite wine and pour two glasses.

"Isn't that your last bottle?" she asks.

"On hand, yes. I ordered more. It will arrive in a few days."

"You don't have to go to all this trouble for me."

Setting my glass down, I place my hand over hers before bringing it to my lips. "I want to."

I watch her chest rise and fall slowly as if she's afraid to believe I want her. She's afraid I will crush her heart. I completely understand. I haven't been clear. My words and actions don't match, I own that. I will fix it tonight.

Rising from my seat, I move over to the side of the barn where Jill informed me our food was set up.

"Where are you going?"

I lean back from behind the door and grin at her. She laughs as I bring out our food. I set hers down and then mine. She waits to pick up her fork until I'm seated. I watch as she savors the first bite of her dinner. Her plate has pasta with chicken, bacon, peas, and a carbonara sauce. Mine has a steak with mashed potatoes and asparagus. "This is delicious. Is the restaurant local?"

"I'll tell Jill you thought her food is restaurant worthy."

"Jill cooked? I thought you said she was a teacher."

"She did and she is. Cooking is her way to deal with chaos. The steps, the order, the beginning and end of a recipe are calming to her, at least they were when we were younger. Now it's her passion hobby."

We finish our meal in companionable silence. Not awkward, just quiet. This isn't a typical first date. We have learned a lot about one another since her text. That doesn't factor in any of the time before that. True, we didn't really talk about anything important, but we spent time together. Plus, I'm sure talking about work isn't high on her list of ideal topics right now, considering the reason she's here in the first place revolves around her professional life imploding.

"How do you feel about winter sports?" I ask her.

"Like skiing and sledding? Not a fan of skiing but tubing down a ski hill is fun. Why?"

"We're just getting started." I stand, offering her my hand. I peek around the screen to orient myself. There's a bench on the other side of the screen with skates and a speaker connected to my phone. "Close your eyes."

Reluctantly, she closes her eyes. I guide her around the curtain, telling her to step over the edge of the ice. Gripping her hips, I step in front of her and lower my lips to hers. I intend a short kiss, but instead I savor her lips, mouth, and tongue until we're breathless.

"There's a bench behind you, please sit." Slowly she lowers herself to the bench, I reluctantly remove my hands from the perfect curve of her hips as she sits. "You can open your eyes."

"Jacob, wow! How did you know?"

"Know what?"

"I love ice skating."

"You do?" I had no idea. Sheer stroke of dumb luck.

"Yes!" She stands, throws her arms around me, peppering kisses all over my face and neck.

I lift her into my arms, accepting the feel of her lips on mine and her soft hands cupping my face. During a brief break in her kissing, I set her down.

"There is a pair of skates under the bench for you." I join her on the bench, tugging off my shoes and shoving my feet into my old hockey skates. "When is the last time you skated?"

"Last winter. A park in the next town floods the tennis courts every year."

Once she finishes tying her skates, she pushes off the bench and is across the barn before I even stand. Apparently, she has skating skills too. She glides back to me as I stand. I pull out my phone and select the playlist I created. If I can't say the words, at least one of these singers can convey my deepest thoughts for me, share how I feel about Norah. I included "Must be doin' Something Right" by Billy Currington, "Sinning with You" by Sam Hunt, even "In Case You Didn't Know" by Brett Young. The music fills in the empty space around us.

"Are you rusty?" she asks me.

"Don't think so, but I'm not nearly as graceful as you."

I slide my hand into hers, and we move around the ice in a circle, laughing and having fun. At one point, she is a few lengths ahead of me. As hard as I try, I can't catch her until I cut across the middle and cut her off. Surprisingly, I'm still able to skate backwards. I haven't worn these skates in years. Connor and I played recreational hockey in the winter between football and baseball season to keep busy. I slow down enough to bracket her waist with my hands. Inch by inch, I draw her closer to me. She sets her hands on my chest as we spin around the ice, the twinkling string lights overhead casting our shadows on the wall.

Once she is safe, we could live carefree every day. I could take her on an actual date with other people around. Although, if I'm being completely honest, just us is incredible. I feel a buzz against my thigh; Norah does too.

"Do you need to get that?" There isn't a thread of anger in her voice, but I would never answer during a date.

"No, that's Jill's reminder that dessert is ready."

"Your sister is amazing."

"Funny, she said the same thing about you."

A slight blush reddens her skin. "What did she make?"

"I don't know. Want to find out?"

"Not yet, let's skate a little longer. I like skating with you."

I lower my mouth to hers, pushing off slowly. We glide along the ice, our lips locked. As we near the edge, she slows us down and pushes off, sending us back across the ice. Following that pattern, we cross the ice repeatedly, lost in one another. A while later, we sit on the bench removing our skates.

"Jacob."

"Yeah?" I turn to face her.

"This was fantastic! Thank you."

"You're welcome, but we're not done yet."

A small smile graces her gorgeous face. After we remove our skates, I grab the wine and our glasses from dinner and lead Norah around the ice.

"Up you go. Trust me, it will be worth it." I watch her climb. I'm always turned on when she is near me, but this view is tempting.

I owe my sister a huge debt for helping me pull this off. As I crest the top of the ladder, I find the loft ready for dessert. The hay was already up here. Jill brought blankets, pillows, and a small fruit crate to act as a table and opened the loft door to the backyard, allowing the moonlight to shine in.

"This is a very close second to star gazing in your favorite spot."

"Up here or the whole evening?" I ask.

"This is by far the best date I've ever been on. As far as spots go, the loft is second to your favorite spot."

"Fair enough. Let's see what Jill made." I open the basket near the crate and find two dishes of something chocolate with raspberry garnish, two spoons, and fresh napkins. "I can see your mouth watering. You don't have to wait for me."

She dips the spoon into the ramekin and offers the first taste to me. I want her in my life. I reach up, holding the spoon with her. A look of concern crosses her face.

NORAH

Holding the spoon near his lips, he draws it into his mouth. He reaches his hand up taking mine.

"Jacob, what's wrong?"

"Nothing."

"Want to try again? You're shaking." I have only seen Jacob vulnerable twice—when he shared about his third tour in Afghanistan and when he told me about Mara for the first time.

"Nothing's wrong. Everything is right. I don't want to wait anymore, Norah. I have so many benchmarks. I always have. A list that must be complete. I need to accomplish this before that. This needs to happen before…. I'm not making any sense, am I?"

"Not really, but you'll get where you need to go. You always do." My heart hurts with all the possible scenarios of where he is going with this.

He kisses me tenderly before adding a bit of space, so he's looking into my eyes, his hand around my jaw. Inhaling deeply, he pauses before saying, "I've fought hard to get where I am today, both professionally and personally. You make me believe that I'm worthy of a second chance. My head is telling me to wait until you're safe to choose me, but you already have. My heart is telling me to wait until I know you're safe, but none of that matters anymore. I'm giving myself permission, Norah. I need you. I want a life with you. I love you."

A single tear falls down my right cheek. He kisses it away, waiting for me to respond with words.

"When we're together, we can conquer anything. Your touch makes me feel protected and cherished. Your lips on mine make everything else fall away. When we're tangled in each other, I know we're meant to be together. I love you, Jacob."

After a moment to compose himself, he threads his fingers into my hair, luring my lips closer to his. The moment his lips touch mine, everything quiets. I only hear his heart and mine. I surrender completely, knowing here is where I belong. He is where I belong.

Dessert forgotten, I open his shirt button by button followed by open-mouth kisses from his chest to his abdomen. With excruciating precision, he lifts my shirt overhead, pressing his mouth to my exposed skin. Immediately, his hands find the front clasp of my bra, baring my breasts to his needy tongue. While he laves my globes with his mouth and teeth, I work to remove his jeans. Once I successfully strip him naked, I stand and push my pants to the bed of hay below me.

"You're stunning," Jacob murmurs, beckoning me closer.

One step forward and his mouth is teasing me up the front of my thigh. As I lower myself with one leg on each side of his hips, his tongue grazes my swollen nub, the tip of his length teasing my core. Looking directly into his eyes, I impale myself. His eyes widen as I take him deep into my center. He drags his calloused hands down my chest and over my belly before gripping the flesh of my hips. He rocks against me. As he lifts, I push down. A spiral of need tightens at the base of my spine. The closer I get to release, the harder he thrusts into me.

"Let go with me, baby."

"Don't stop."

I feel my walls constrict around his hard shaft plunging in and out of my heat. I grip his forearms and tremble as he explodes inside me. Sliding my hands up his arms, I press my chest to his, my lips against his neck. After catching our breath, Jacob surrounds my waist with his arm and lowers us to the blanket. We spend the rest of our evening intertwined in each other under the moonlit sky.

A shiver wakes me. It takes me a moment to regain my bearings. I turn over, resting my chin in my hands. I gently nudge Jacob. His eyes fly open to meet mine.

"Morning, gorgeous."

Leaning down, I lower my lips to his. "Morning. Roll over. Watch with me." He flips over just as the sun peeks above the horizon. The sky brightens, casting rays of purple and pink on the snow-covered grass. A new day is bathed in beautiful sunlight. Jacob presses his lips to the cap of my shoulder.

"We should go inside," Norah murmurs.

"We will... in a bit. I'm in no rush for our date to be over. Plus, it's Sunday. No one will be around to bother us."

"I agree that would be amazing, but you're forgetting one thing. Nolan is cooking today."

A momentary frown appears on his face.

"We can sleep out here again next weekend," I suggest.

"We didn't sleep very much," he replies, dragging his finger down my arm, teasing the side of my breast.

"No, we didn't."

"Fine, we can go inside."

I slither backwards to get my clothes. I find my panties, shirt, and his jeans.

"Are you on my jeans?"

He shrugs, pulling me on top of him. Kissing me breathless, he rolls over, caging me beneath his hard body.

Looking over, he nods. "Yes, I was on your jeans."

I laugh before pressing up to kiss him again. After a long, shared shower, we dress and watch pregame while Nolan starts dinner. Shortly after he arrives, Maia joins him in the kitchen. I cast a look to Jacob who simply shrugs.

"What do you think about today's games, Nolan?" I ask him.

"I'm never wagering with you about football ever again!" he replies, busying himself with food preparation.

I laugh and snuggle deeper into Jacob's arms.

After the rest of the team arrives, Nolan serves dinner—buffalo wings, ribs, mashed sweet potatoes, and coleslaw. I don't know a lot about Nolan's background, but I would guess he's southern born based on his choice of meal. We dig in and chat.

"Great job, Nolan. These ribs are fantastic!" Jacob exclaims.

Nolan nods, returning his gaze to his plate. I feel Jacob's phone buzz in his pocket.

"I'll be right back." He kisses my temple before leaving the table. Maia casts an "I told you so" look across the table. A small smile grows on my face as I move to clear my plate. After washing my dish, I see Jacob has returned to the kitchen.

"Everything okay?" I ask.

He tilts his head to the side. "William sent the photos of the awards. We can look at them later."

"Keep going."

He simply shakes his head before continuing. "Someone went through your office at Quinn Sterling."

"There's nothing of importance in my office. I was wholly honest with you when I indicated I only needed my necklace."

"I know, but the fact they're still looking concerns me. Now they think the ledger is or was in your office. It also means there's another player involved. Someone we don't know yet. Someone who gave a member of the Moretti family access to your office without regard for you."

I hadn't really thought about it that way. Maybe Robert Quinn is just as dirty as Stan. Shoving my emotions aside, I focus on our guests. The outcome of this mess will remind me of the people of character in my life. I'm certain Stan wasn't one of them. Hopefully, I'm wrong and Robert is on the good side of this, but that's still to be determined.

Grabbing a drink, I move back into the living room to watch more of the afternoon game. As the game wraps up, the team leaves one by one. Joining Nolan, I assist in cleaning the kitchen.

"You don't have to help. You won the bet."

"I know, but I don't mind. I need to keep my hands busy. The pace here without my work is considerably slower. I'm not complaining, just getting used to having more time."

"Workaholic?"

"Sort of. I wanted the partnership, so I worked extremely hard to get it. Now I don't want it anymore."

He sets the last dish on the drying rack. "Being able to adjust your path isn't a terrible place to be."

Interesting and astute observation for a young guy. "Thanks, Nolan. Have a good night."

He leans down to hug me before walking out the door. When I turn from the door and set the alarm, Jacob is scowling at me.

"What was that?" he asks.

"What? A hug. Seriously?"

He raises an eyebrow.

"It isn't as if he and everyone else doesn't see we're together, Jacob."

"Don't like his hands on you."

"How cute, you're jealous."

"Not at all. I just didn't like him hugging you."

"I want you. Nolan was just being friendly."

"Still didn't like it."

"I love your 'protect my woman at all costs' attitude, but Nolan isn't going to hurt me. Would you freak out if William hugged me?"

"No, I trust him."

"You don't trust Nolan or is it because William is happily married?"

Realization crosses his face. "I give." He hauls me into his arms before kissing me possessively. "Ready to take a look at the photos?"

"Sure." I follow him to the office where a large stack of photos is piled on his desk.

JACOB

Never once have I ever felt jealous. Not only did I feel jealousy but possessiveness and a tiny bit of rage. It isn't that I don't trust Norah and Nolan, but whatever they were talking about led Nolan to believe she needed comfort. That is solely my domain. Reeling in my thoughts, I follow her to the office.

"You weren't truthful when I asked about awards."

"Yes, I was. I said they were in the bottom two drawers in my office."

"You failed to mention how many there were."

"You didn't ask. Plus, I don't like to talk about them, especially now that all of the work was for nothing."

"It wasn't for nothing. Not only were you a candidate, but you possess every quality a partner should have and then some. Changing your mind about wanting the partnership is not the same as failing to achieve it." I may have stunned her silent.

A few solid minutes pass before she whispers, "Thank you."

I press my lips to her cheek before moving a chair around the desk. She sits at my desk and thumbs through the images. She pulls her lower lip between her teeth again. Holy hell! *Focus!* Chief Walker's men were thorough. There is an image of the front and back of each award.

"Does anything look off?"

"No," she replies as she flips through the stack. "Honestly, I left the awards ceremony, set the plaque in the drawer, and went home. I never studied them in any detail. I may have earned these with my work, but I didn't work to earn these. Does that make sense?"

"Yes." *More than you know.* I didn't risk my life to bring those men home for accolades. I did it because I expect them to do it for me. No award will bring them back to their families. No award made me take that risk, one never could.

"This is the one from two years ago," she says after making it halfway through the stack. "All the plaques for billings and revenue have looked the same since I started at Quinn Sterling. There is nothing unique about this one. Each is laser engraved with the company logo, recipient's name, and the year on the front. The back is just a bar code from the award company and the slot to hang it on the wall."

"Let's compare the first one you ever received to the one from last year."

Setting the photos in a grid, we compare them. The front of the plaques are identical except for the year. The back is the same except the bar codes differ. I jot down the year and the bar code. Systematically, I make a list of the bar codes for each award.

"Only the bar code from two years ago is different," I note. "Does the number mean anything to you?"

"No, it could be an access code to a file, but I have no idea which one. Each employee has a twelve-digit access code. Each file requires permission and the employee's access code as well as the twelve-digit file number. That isn't the access code for the Moretti Brand."

"What are these awards for?" I ask, indicating the acrylic awards with a swirl on top.

"Those are for customer confidence. They're voted on by clients."

"Is there one for the Moretti Brand?"

"No." That makes sense considering she has only had the file for seven months. "Did Blaine get a copy of the check?"

"Yes, but he said it was odd."

"Why?"

"There were two checks deposited into the scholarship fund three days after the award ceremony. Do you always donate all of the bonus?"

"Yes, I donate the entire amount each year. I do the work for the clients, not the bonuses or awards. Creating the scholarship put the money to the best use I could think of."

"It's an amazing plan, babe."

"As far as the two checks, I recall that but didn't think anything of it at the time. I figured Mr. Sterling wanted to keep the amount of each check less than ten thousand dollars."

I hand her the copies of the two checks. "The total is fourteen thousand. Two checks make sense, but didn't the message say something about the prize being relevant?"

"Yes." I see her brain working, and it's sexy as hell.

"The first is for $6,983.86 and the second is for $7,016.14 for a total of $14,000.00. If put together, it would be a twelve-digit number, but I don't know what it means or which file it corresponds to."

"Okay, you'll figure it out. You have all the pieces now, right?"

"I think so. I have the image of the award, the amount of the prize, and the entire Moretti file."

"We'll come back to it tomorrow. You and I need some sleep."

She doesn't argue with me, taking my outstretched hand as I lead her to the bedroom. After stripping out of my clothes, I climb into bed. Norah walks around the room and rifles through the bag before pulling out something to sleep in. While I'm enjoying the view, her shapely legs and ass on display, it dawns on me. Throwing back the covers, I grab her hand, her bag, and lead her to a door to the left of the bathroom.

"Why don't you put your clothes in here?" When I refurbished this house, I turned a powder room for the office into a closet and joined it with the master closet. The master closet is huge. I barely use a third of it.

"Are you sure?" A shred of doubt creeps into her voice, causing it to crack.

"Norah, I love you. I want you to stay. Move your clothes into the closet and the empty dresser." I take her mouth and kiss her until her knees weaken.

When she regains her footing, she demands, "Say it again."

"I love you, Norah."

"I love you." She kisses me softly before speaking again. "You realize I will fill this when I have all my shoes, right?"

"I'll build you a closet just for your sexy shoes if you want one." Something flickers in her eyes, but I don't acknowledge it. Norah doesn't have a large amount of clothes here right now. I hang her clothes while she puts her lingerie and other clothes in the empty dresser beside mine.

"Ready to get some sleep now?"

She nods, sliding her fingers between mine. As we climb into bed, I haul her against me.

"Good night, Norah."

"Good night, Jacob." A content sigh passes her lips when I kiss the nape of her neck. Mere minutes later, she's sound asleep in my arms, exactly where she should be.

NORAH

Part of me is grateful that Stan gave me the Moretti file all those months ago, the rest of me, not so much. My integrity brought me here, indirectly anyway. My integrity necessitated my need for personal security. He's the best I know. Now, I just need to get rid of the Morettis. To do that, I need to solve the puzzle sprawled out on the floor in Jacob's office. The drawback is I need to leave the warmth of his arms to do it. I suppose a better way to look at it is, he asked me to stay. I can step into his arms whenever I need to.

I try to slip out of bed, but Jacob's arms tighten around me.

"Stay with me," he murmurs against my skin, sending tingles down my spine.

"You aren't a very good influence on my work ethic, Mr. Blackthorne."

"Maybe so, but you're very good for my work-life balance."

"Am I now?"

"Absolutely. If you were my client but not my...."

"Still not a fan of girlfriend, huh?"

"No."

I would love to know what would be enough. Truthfully, I'm fine without a label if we are on the same page. Even more so if I wake up and fall asleep with him.

"If you were just a client, I wouldn't be with you. I would have passed the day-to-day security off to Nolan or Christoph so I could focus on finding the answers to remove the bounty."

"Fair enough, but you wouldn't be able to decipher the Quinn Sterling files or the clues."

"True."

"You need me."

"I do, but I would prefer it for only me, not dealing with the Morettis."

I lean closer, pulling his lower lip between my teeth. He growls softly.

"What was that for?" he asks.

"You're making progress with words. You deserve a reward."

"Well, if you are going to kiss me thoroughly every time I use words, we won't get anything done, especially if you kiss me like that."

"I'll just have to save them up for one long series of kisses each evening."

"Deal. We need to get up, so we don't get caught in bed when the team arrives."

I pout but move to the bathroom anyway.

Over the course of the next few days, after the morning meeting with the team, we hunker down in Jacob's office. He works on Blackthorne business while I study and pick apart the Moretti file, looking for something that works with the prize code. I've haven't found anything of use so far. Sadly, I won't be able to go home for Thanksgiving, but Jacob is having his family over again, so at least I'll be able to have some pumpkin pie. However, they refuse to let me cook this time.

I know both of us are doing our best to find the answers for the ledger. I'm also sure I won't complete the task by Friday's deadline. There's nothing more I can do. I have been systematically combing through thousands of pages of numbers since I got them. Mr. Sterling certainly didn't make the ledger easy to find. Although I'm sure that was his intention.

I hear Jacob on the phone but tune him out, continuing through Rosita's last vendor file, Mancini Textiles, that she has in common with Sergio. I shift my eyes back and forth between the two, everything seems to match up until three years ago. That was when Rosita turned thirty. From the outset, she was siphoning money away from the family with Sergio's help. Where did that money go?

"Hey, I think I have another angle," I say out loud before I remember he's still on the phone. "Sorry," I whisper.

He smiles over at me. Finishing his call, he moves onto the couch next to me. "I have news too."

"Go ahead."

"Blaine was able to figure out the sides. It appears that Stan was working with Sergio and Rosita to oust Gustavo as CEO and president.

Stan and Sergio have been working together since Rosita received her own company."

"Damn!"

"What?"

"Remember the SEC filings I reviewed, that was creating Rosita's company."

"Everything was accurate and legal, right?"

"Yes, my review was thorough and accurate. However, there's no telling what Stan did after I returned it to him."

"When Gustavo learned about their subterfuge last year, he reached out to Robert Quinn. Blaine has the phone records and emails to prove that Robert is on the right side of this."

"We can trust Robert?"

"I believe so. I want to give Blaine a bit more time to solidify his opinion and find more concrete evidence that Robert is clean before we reach out to him. What angle did you find?" he asks.

"We need to follow the money."

"Meaning?"

"Let's assume that Sergio and Rosita weren't happy with Gustavo's plan to go legit, as it would diminish their lifestyle. With Stan's help, they started siphoning money away from the conglomerate when Rosita attained age thirty. If Rosita's company is hiding money, where is it? We need to find it. Would Blaine be able to safely determine accounts that

Rosita and Sergio have? If I can match the deposits and balances to the discrepancies in their companies, I won't need the ledger."

"You're brilliant!" He kisses me hard and moves back to his desk, calling someone immediately, presumably Blaine. After relaying what I just shared, he hangs up. "Blaine will get you whatever he can by Friday afternoon. Starting now, we're done until then."

"What do you say we order some pizza, grab some wine, and watch a movie?"

"Sounds perfect."

We settle downstairs on the plush couch with our dinner. Now we have a true test of our relationship. Who gets to pick the movie? Jacob hands me the remote. He says nothing as I scroll through the available titles. Jacob is either wise beyond what his relationship experience would suggest, or he truly doesn't care what we watch. I opt for *Casablanca* before settling back against him.

"Nice."

"You approve?"

"It would seem we have similar taste in movies as well as wine."

"I wonder what else we agree on."

"We have plenty of time to learn," he replies.

If he only knew how his words affected me before he was able to share his feelings. I lean up to kiss him.

"What was that for?"

"Words, Jacob. Words."

"Is that all for the day?"

"Not even close, but you earned a teaser."

After the movie, we curl up by the fireplace and watch the light snow fall.

JACOB

Early on Thanksgiving morning, I slink out of bed and into my office to verify some details for later today. After confirming, I pad to the kitchen to make coffee and feed Tank. Two hot cups in hand, I make my way back to the bedroom. Her long hair is spilled all over my pillow, her skin looks flawless against the white sheets clutched in her fists. I almost don't want to wake her, but I need to keep her busy in the house until at least eleven. That isn't going to be an easy feat.

Setting the cups on the night table, I slide back into bed.

"Jacob."

"Morning, gorgeous."

"You're a god."

I chuckle. "What kind of god am I?"

"A coffee god."

"That's it?"

"Definitely not, but I'm not properly caffeinated to discuss further."

"Well, sit up and you can have this cup."

Instead of immediately sitting up, she kisses a path up my side, circling my nipple with her tongue before making her way to my mouth. "Hi."

"How badly do you want that coffee?"

"I can survive a while without it. Have something else in mind?" she asks, arching her eyebrow. I spend the next few hours showing her what else is on my mind—her under me, over me, engulfing me, tasting me while I do the same to her.

After catching my breath, I turn to face her. "I'll make more coffee while you shower. The parade starts in less than an hour. Plus, I have a surprise for you."

"What kind of surprise?" she asks as I stand, pulling on some shorts.

"You're just going to have to wait a bit longer to find out. Go."

Reluctantly, she stands. I almost make it out of the room, but her naked body just begs to be caressed with my tongue. I wrap my arms around her waist, pulling her pink nipple between my teeth.

"Jacob," she moans, "you can't expect me to be ready on time if you keep—"

I cut off her words with my tongue. We truly don't have time for another round of body-bending sex. Placing her feet back on the floor, I kiss her lips once more and walk out of the room.

I purposely take my time making the coffee. If I'm lucky, she'll be out of the shower and partially dressed. Thankfully I stall long enough and I find her drying off. I hand her a fresh cup, kiss her softly, and step into the shower.

"No time for gawking, beautiful."

"No fair!" She smiles and walks out of the bathroom.

Right on time, we start watching the Macy's Thanksgiving Day Parade. It's a tradition that I normally share with Jill and Cam. Well, we did when we were kids. I have been watching alone for the past six years. Oddly, I don't feel sad. Having Norah here to share this with me makes me happy. Colorful, fanciful balloons cross the screen. High school bands from across the country stop and play in front of the flagship store.

"Did you watch with Mara?"

"Sort of. Jill, Cam, and I watched every year. Mara joined us when she could. Why?"

"I always watched with Kelly, but Joseph wanted nothing to do with it."

"You miss them?" I ask quietly.

"Yes and no. I don't see them very often, but we talk at least weekly. It's weird not having updates about James and Jackson, or the latest goings on at the shop or Nicholas's latest role and milestone updates for baby Nick. I miss chatting with Kelsey too. She's my closet shrink." I chuckle at that.

"You don't need a shrink. You just need a bestie to dish or gripe about me to. What was her advice to you when you called her at the Michelsons'?"

"Thank you for knowing I needed to talk to someone. She told me to own my feelings, suck it up, and prepare myself to walk away brokenhearted or tell you I broke my promise."

"And now?"

"I'm fairly certain we're side by side on the same page."

I glance at my phone. "We are." Sliding my hands around her face, I show her how I feel with my mouth. Her lips are so soft, it's almost unfair. "Come on. Surprise time."

"Really?"

I take her hand and lead her into my office, guiding her into my leather chair. I log into Zoom. Shortly thereafter, Kelly and Joseph appear on the screen.

"Hi, guys!"

"Hi! How are you?" Kelly asks, trying to make sure she and Joseph cover the entire screen.

"You are already together? It's early," Norah asks.

"We wanted to say hi before you had dinner with Jacob and his family."

"That's nice. I'm hanging in there. I crave order, so this is difficult for me."

"We know," they reply in unison.

"Is Kelsey there too?" Norah asks.

Kelly and Joseph step to the side as Kelsey moves closer to the camera.

"What are you doing there so early?" Norah asks Kelsey.

"I came to drop off goodies before going to Mari and Zoe's for dinner." Mari and Zoe are her sisters-in-law. They have been married for almost three years. They have been working on adopting a child for almost a year now.

"Connor, where do you want...?" Christoph asks him. His voice coming through the computer.

Norah turns to look at me. "They're here? All of them?"

I smile and nod as she jumps into my arms, kissing me hard.

Pulling back slightly, she exclaims, "Thank you doesn't begin to cover how grateful I am. I love you so much!"

"I love you. Go, I'll be right over."

She takes two steps away but turns back, her face emanating genuine happiness. It's a look I see more often as I allow her to burrow deeper into my soul. Eliminating the threat to her and ensuring her happiness vacillate between the first and second items for me each day. I shut off the computer and step into the bedroom to grab a hoodie for her. Chances are she slipped on my slides and ran over.

When I make it to the barn, she's animatedly talking with Kelsey, Kelly, and Genevieve while their other halves and James talk nearby. I lean against the door, watching her. Her youngest nephew, Nick, on her hip. He grabs a fistful of her soft hair. She gently pulls it away before rubbing her nose to his to distract him. Norah with a child in her arms is a vision. Imagining her holding our child hits me deep in my chest. I never considered having a family until Norah asked. I want it with her. Norah's life may be in danger, but at least today, she appears to be free from worry.

"Well done, Jake."

"Thanks for your help, C. It's the best I can do right now."

"It appears to be enough given the circumstances. Where do you want me to put their luggage?"

"Put Kelly's and Kelsey's to the left and Genevieve, Joseph, and the boys' luggage to the right. That guest suite is big enough for the four of them."

"Will do. What time is our family arriving?"

"In about an hour."

Connor nods and pulls the luggage behind him. I walk over toward the ladies when Norah's nephew James approaches me.

"Hi, I'm James." Tank circles around him. James laughs while bending down to pet my dog.

"Hi, James. His name is Tank."

"He's great! His fur is super soft."

"It's nice to meet you in person. Norah has told me a lot about you."

"Really? Like what?"

"You're super smart, love math but not English, and are great with dogs, especially Kelsey's dog, Knox. You love Lego and have built almost all the city sets. There are still three that you haven't built yet."

"Wow, Auntie was thorough. She hasn't mentioned you though."

Straightforward is apparently a Cavallaro trait.

"Well, that's a bit complicated."

"Nothing's complicated if you love her."

I'm dumbstruck by his statement.

"Do you?" he asks.

"How old are you, James?"

"Almost ten."

"That was a very mature statement."

James shrugs.

"Yes, I love her." More than anything, more than I thought possible.

"Good, she looks happy here."

I smile, and he scampers back to the group of men with Tank on his heel. He's astute for a young kid. An old soul some might label him. I approach Norah from behind, setting the hoodie on her shoulders and kissing her cheek.

"Thanks."

I look down at her feet. Just as I suspected, her polished toes are peeking out of my slides that are three sizes too big. "I'm going to chat with the guys."

"Okay," she replies before placing a chaste kiss on my lips. Her eyes however scream that if we didn't have an audience, the loft would be used again.

NORAH

No words. I have no words. He brought my family to me. I hurry to the barn to find my entire family ready to hug me. Jacob is working on using words, but he certainly understands a grand gesture. Before I reach them, James is beside me.

"I can't believe you're here! Thank you for coming!" After I hug everyone, the guys move away. Nick reaches for me. He's nearly eight months old now. With him perched on my hip, Kelly and Kelsey start digging for details. Genevieve is quietly looking around the barn.

"How are you?" Kelly asks.

"Are you two together?" Kelsey wonders aloud.

"This place is majestic!" Kelly admits.

They inquire rapid-fire.

"Slow down. I'm overjoyed right now. I can't believe you're here. Where's Dad?" I ask.

"He's with Mabel in Colorado," Kelly answers. I'm sure this surprise came together in the last few days.

"Overall, I'm okay. Arguably, I can't leave here. It's beautiful, and you have only seen maybe a third of it."

"What label did you pick?" Kelsey asks, glancing over at William. Kelsey and William are expecting early next year. Pregnancy looks fabulous on her. Her bump now noticeable but barely. Her skin is glowing. He keeps looking this way as if she needs extra protection because she's carrying his child. William has always been overprotective of Kelsey from the moment they met.

"We didn't really pick a label, but he and I are together." I don't plan to share that Jacob isn't a fan of the term girlfriend, although nothing else really applies right now.

"Are you coming home when you can?" Kelly asks softly.

"I don't know."

"I wouldn't leave here," Genevieve interjects. Truthfully, Gen and I are acquaintances. We were friendly as kids, but mostly she spent time with Joseph not Kelly and me. I would rather talk to my brother. My youngest nephew is cooing and babbling in my arms.

"It's peaceful here like Aspen. I see the appeal," Kelly says, looking directly at me.

Her husband, Nicholas, is originally from Colorado. He has a home in Aspen as well as in Maine. They spend most of their time in Maine. Their wedding was in Aspen, and it was epic. *So was my night with Jacob.* That night in Aspen was almost as hot as our first night together. I push the memory away as fast as it comes because now isn't the time to be blushing.

"Where did your mind just go?" Kelsey asks.

Caught! "I don't know what you're talking about."

Kelsey is the only person here who might have an idea, but she won't say anything.

"Those rosy cheeks say otherwise."

As if he could hear the girls ribbing me, Jacob slides his hand across my back, resting it on my hip.

"My family and Connor's will be here in a little less than an hour. Do you want your family to get settled inside before dinner?"

They're staying here. This man is too much.

"Sure."

He takes my hand and moves to the barn door. Everyone dutifully follows us into the house. Jacob shows everyone to their rooms and me into the master.

Thankfully, there's a lock on the door. Walking back until his legs hit the mattress, I push him down onto the bed, landing on top of him with a bit more force than necessary. I take this time we're alone to kiss him thoroughly. Between kisses, thanking him profusely. "Thank you for bringing them here. How did you pull it off? I have been beside you almost 24/7."

His smile is so wide, tempting me. I would strip him naked if I thought I had enough time. Naked time with Jacob is never quick. "I actually started with William because calling him wasn't suspicious. He conferenced in Joseph and Kelly."

"When?"

"After the second video. I knew you wouldn't be able to leave. I also know that, despite your acquiescence, you miss them. I brought them to you."

"Thank you doesn't even begin to express how grateful I am."

"I can think of a few ways you can express your grat—"

"Why am I not surprised?"

He smirks up at me.

"Is there anything I can do to help with the food?" I ask.

"Not really. Joyce and my mom are bringing the main meal items, and Jill handled the appetizers. Kelsey brought dessert."

Just thinking about Kelsey's yummy desserts makes my mouth water.

"Ready? My family will be here soon."

"Absolutely." I grab some socks and shoes before following Jacob into the kitchen.

We were in the bedroom a bit too long. Joyce, Connie, and Kelsey are chatting away, moving dishes into the oven to keep them warm or into the fridge.

Both Joyce and Connie hug Jacob and then me. "How can I help?" I ask after greeting the women. Jacob disappears out the front door with Connor and Christoph who just brought in Kelsey's desserts. Kelsey immediately hands me a cheesecake to put in the fridge. Kelly soon joins us in the kitchen while Nicholas, holding his son, looks out the French doors toward the backyard.

"This is my sister, Kelly. Kelly, this is Joyce, Connor's mom and Connie, Jacob's mom." Pleasantries extended and the moms put Kelly to work. We bring the dishes into the barn, which now boasts two large tables set to accommodate this gathering. Jill runs over to hug me after I set the cornbread stuffing on the table.

"It's so good to see you again," she remarks, pulling me in for a tight hug.

"You too. Thank you so much for the food for our date. It was amazing."

"You're welcome. My brother is finally happy again, and that's because of you."

"I don't know what to say, Jill. He's something else."

"He's special, Norah, and so are you." She hugs me again and walks away as Jacob approaches.

"What was that about?" he asks.

"You."

JACOB

"Me? What did I do wrong this time?" I ask, feeling a bit exasperated that Jill always finds something I did wrong.

"Nothing. Absolutely, nothing. She was thanking me actually."

"For?"

"For making you happy."

"She's right. You do, more than I thought was possible. I feel different with you." I press my lips to hers.

The volume of the barn immediately plummets. The only thing I hear is Nick's babbling. I feel everyone's eyes on us. When I pull back, her eyes are reciprocating my feelings.

"Are you playing later?" I ask Norah.

"Playing what?"

"Football."

"Hell yes!"

I slide my fingers into hers and continue to introduce the rest of our guests until everyone has at least met one another. Mom, Joyce, and Jill have outdone themselves with this meal. Along with the normal Thanksgiving staples like turkey, stuffing, and cranberry sauce, Jill added a ham, mashed sweet potatoes, glazed carrots, and some other root vegetable.

Normally, each adult would share something they're grateful for. This year we are taking a moment to reflect before dinner. I'm grateful for Norah. Her patience with me and understanding about Mara is more than I deserve. I never thought I would ever find someone to love me as I am, nor did I think I could ever let go of the guilt I've carried for the last six years. She gives that to me.

The dishes start rounding the table, and everyone partakes in this amazing meal. Joseph and Nicholas are chatting behind their wives while the women laugh and eat. Most notably, Norah has a huge smile plastered on her face. I had one goal for this surprise. Dare I say, I've accomplished helping her forget the bounty on her head and the danger outside the fence. Hopefully, for the next day or so, Norah will feel normal again. The moment she figures out where the ledger is, our lives will move forward—together.

"Jake, is it time yet?" my brother, Cameron, asks.

Norah raises an eyebrow, and I shake my head.

"Soon, Cam, soon."

Our family starts laughing.

Leaning closer, Norah whispers, "What is he asking about?" I'm sure she isn't intentionally setting off my nerve endings, especially with our families here.

"Football," I reply quietly.

She nods and continues her conversation with Kelsey. Unfortunately, Genevieve looks uncomfortable now that she and Kelly aren't chatting anymore.

Leaning back toward her, I ask, "Norah, should we do something about Genevieve?"

"There isn't anything we can do. She's always like that. I'm sure Joseph dragged her here."

I nod and kiss her cheek before pulling away. Soon after Cam's request, we start to clear the dishes. My team and siblings carry the dishes into the kitchen while Norah and I set half in the dishwasher and handwash the rest. Generally, there's nothing fun about washing dishes, but nothing with Norah is ever boring. We laugh, joke, and kiss until the last dish is dried.

Cam and Connor have taken control of setting up the game. Two-hand touch football. Connor marked off with cones for the out of bounds and a line for the end zone in my backyard. Normally, the game is small, but more guests means larger teams. The teams are set. My team has James as an extra player because he's ten and there's an odd number of players. Connor is crafty. He purposefully separated the couples. Norah is on his team instead of mine.

Genevieve, Maia, Joyce, Connie, Jill, and Jackson are sitting along the sidelines. When I leave the huddle with my team, I glance over and see Nick curled up in my mom's lap. The sheer glee of holding a baby is impossible to miss. Gen has a more relaxed look on her face. I don't know her well, but something is up. I'll make a point to ask Norah later.

We line up. Connor is defending Christoph off to my right. Kelsey and Norah have James, and the dads are matched up. Nicholas and Kelly are jockeying for position. William and Cam are still sizing each other up. Joseph lines up in front of me.

"Are you any good, Jacob?" Joseph asks.

Hearing Norah giggle, I smirk. "I can hold my own," I reply, dropping back.

Christoph takes off down the sideline, and so does James. James slants to the right, but Norah has him well covered. James doesn't care. He has a huge grin on his face. I release the ball, and Christoph hauls it in with minimal effort. He scampers backward and hops over the line for a touchdown. After the play, Kelsey swaps out with Maia. After verifying Kelsey's fine, William rejoins us in the huddle.

In previous years, I played quarterback for both teams. Apparently, Nicholas has some experience playing a quarterback for a movie role, so he is doing the honors for Connor's team. After a few series, the score is tied at two points for each team. We take a quick drink break before lining up again. We continue playing for another half hour before Kelsey indicates dessert is ready.

In the huddle, I explain the last play to Joseph and James.

"Mr. Jacob, Auntie is all over me. There's no way I'm going to be open."

Joseph laughs. Norah has been keeping James close the entire game.

"She is, but I'll take care of her. Just be ready to catch the ball."

"I'll do my best," James states empathically before lining up with Norah.

I nod to James and Joseph. I take one step back, pitching the ball to Joseph. James is running toward the endzone with Norah stride for stride. I make a beeline straight for Norah. Joseph is uncovered waiting to throw the ball. When I get close to James, I shout, "Cut left."

James goes right, which was set up in the huddle. I cut left, following Norah. I grip her hips with my hands, hauling her against me. I curl around her, landing on my back in the remaining snowbank near the gate. James is celebrating in the endzone when I'm able to look over.

"You set me up," Norah pushes out in shallow breaths. Her breasts flush against my chest.

Tugging her closer, I admit, "It was the only way I could get my hands on you appropriately with this audience. Even this is barely enough."

"You're sneaky, Mr. Blackthorne. Very sneaky."

"Admit it. You love it."

"I do, I truly do." A huge grin stretches across her face.

"Come on, lovebirds, dessert is waiting," Jill shouts from the sideline.

Norah buries her face in my neck. I'm sure her face is bright red.

"Norah, it's just us," I murmur.

Before lifting her head, she kisses along my jaw to my mouth, but she doesn't stop there. She continues along the other side of my jaw before drawing her tongue along the shell of my ear.

"Woman, I need you to stop! I won't be able to go inside for a while if you don't."

Norah nips my earlobe before whispering, "Fine, but I need some alone time later. Deal?"

"I'll give you all the time you want later." Every second for the rest of my life.

Norah plants her lips on mine, kissing me deeply. I growl because I truly don't want her to stop, but I know our guests are waiting.

"Ready? Kelsey's desserts are waiting."

"As ready as I'll ever be." I roll over, caging her beneath me before I move to my feet. Extending my hand, I pull her up from the ground and lead her back into the barn. We share dessert with our guests before cleaning up and retiring to the house.

NORAH

Yesterday was a whirlwind. I should be exhausted, especially considering Jacob and I didn't sleep much last night. He gave me his time and numerous quiet orgasms last night. Stifling my pleasured screams with pillows or burying my face into the comforter was necessary with our houseguests. It's near ten and we're heading out for a hike around Jacob's property. As expected, Genevieve and Joseph decide to stay at the house. They even offer to watch Nick so Kelly can join us.

Kelly and Kelsey are dying to talk more about Jacob and me, but there really isn't much more that I'm willing to share. He makes me feel like we could have it all, now that I believe he feels that way too.

Jacob takes a different path than we have followed before, but I know where we'll end up. We meander down the path toward Jacob's favorite spot. The guys are just walking and talking occasionally. This is mostly for me. I needed to get out of the house for a bit today. Luckily, some of my girls are here to trudge along with me.

"You weren't lying, Nor. This is serene and peaceful like Aspen," Kelly pushes out as we crest the hill.

"If I were you, I would stay in Aspen, but I get it, the shop is in Maine," Kelsey adds.

"It truly is amazing here. There are so many more stars visible here than in Maine at night. It's gorgeous," I add.

Jacob pulls out the blanket, laying it on the platform, and the ladies take a seat. He curls around me, his lips against my neck. I sigh inwardly and lean into him. I feel his phone vibrate in his pocket. At first he doesn't move to check it. Then a loud alarm starts blaring, and he tenses around me.

"What the hell is that?" I ask, craning my neck to look into his eyes. Fear, I see fear.

"It's a perimeter alarm." Jacob whistles for Tank, who wandered off a bit when we arrived.

Moments later, he's dutifully sitting at Jacob's side. Jacob rises and tugs me to my feet. "Norah, take Tank and go back to the house. Kelly and Kelsey will go with you. Nicholas, you can stay with us or go, your choice. Go inside and engage the alarm. Do you remember the commands for Tank?" he asks me.

I nod. He kisses me hard, fearful and possessive, at the same time Nicholas and William kiss their wives. I draw back slightly, my Jacob, fun, playful, amazing-in-bed Jacob is gone. He mouths "I love you" and turns away.

I've seen this Jacob before and know to just listen. His protector mode just flipped on. Fierce, decisive, unflinching, moving toward unknown danger.

After releasing me, he starts talking to William. I hear him ask, "Are you armed?" Fear slices through me. I grab Kelly and Kelsey's hands and start back for the house.

"How are you so calm right now?" Kelly asks as we walk away from our men. Kelsey just nods. Maybe William's protective armor comes out less now that they're married, but she understands.

"This isn't the first time protector Jacob has come out since I left Maine. I'll tell you more later. Kels, you good?" I slow my pace a bit to make sure Kelsey is okay.

"Yup, I'm fine. Still working out daily, even with the little bean. Doc says I have a few more months until I need to slow down a bit."

We're about halfway back to the house when we spot Christoph running toward us.

"Keep going. Maia will be at the house. Where were you?" he says when he stops before me.

Tank sits by my heel, waiting for me to move again.

"At Jacob's spot. Nicholas and William stayed with him."

"Thanks." He turns and continues running toward Jacob.

When we reach the gate, Maia is watching from the back porch. Maia in work mode is intimidating despite her stature.

"Is everyone okay?" she asks once we are in earshot.

"Yes, where is my brother?" I ask Maia.

"Your brother and nephews were in the family room when I got here. I asked them to stay inside."

"Thanks." I move to the front door, engage the alarm, and give Tank the commands Jacob taught me, even though it probably isn't necessary considering Maia is here and armed.

"Start spilling, Norah," Kelly states after falling onto the couch with a thud.

"I'll share with you, Kel, but it's worse than this. Are you sure you want to know?"

"You have been protecting us this whole time?" she asks quietly.

"Yes. There are some seriously bad people after me for something. Until recently, I didn't have the pieces of the puzzle to locate it. I have been working with the data for the last week or so. I'll find what they want, but I won't turn it over unless my name is clear. I won't go down for something I didn't do just because Mr. Sterling felt it necessary to loop me in."

Kelly turns to face me. "Okay, I won't push you. Though I will admit, Jacob is hot. Protector Jacob beats everyday Jacob by a mile."

Both are intoxicating. I simply smile and nod. I don't trust my words right now.

There's a small knock on the door. Maia disengages the alarm and admits Nolan into the house. She's whispering to him as the alarm reengages. Just as I get comfortable, Joseph, Gen, and the boys come upstairs. Jackson is perched on Gen's hip, and James is between them. Kelly takes Nick from Joseph and retreats to the couch near Kelsey.

"What is going on?" Joseph asks.

Rising from my seat, I walk over to them. "A perimeter alarm sounded. Jacob sent us back here so he could check it out with William. Nicholas opted to stay. Christoph raced past us, and Maia came here." I keep my voice level and calm so as to not alarm them. I don't know if there is anything to be alarmed about.

"How dare you?" Gen questions in a tone I don't like at all. Jackson buries his head into her shoulder.

"Excuse me?" If she's fixing for an argument, she can have one.

"How dare you put my family at risk bringing us here?" Gen shouts, narrowing her eyes at me. Joseph sets his hand on her shoulder, but she shakes him off.

Thanks, big brother, but I can handle your wife. "I didn't bring you here. Jacob invited you here. As I'm sure my brother dragged you here kicking and screaming, you didn't have to come. For once, Gen, this is about me. Not you. Jacob knew it would be difficult for me to miss celebrating with all of you, so he surprised me."

At this moment, I notice Kelly and Kelsey standing near the couch. Neither is moving to avoid taking a side. I don't expect them to. Maia and Nolan are near the front door side by side. Tank is sitting straight up and alert at my side.

"I—"

I cut her off and continue. "I'm not done. He would never jeopardize my safety by inviting you here. If he didn't think it was safe, not only for me but for you, you wouldn't be here. You have no idea what I have been handling since the attack in my townhouse. Clearly, my *brother*—your *husband* thought it was safe to share the holiday here. Next time, don't bother." I take a step back and move around my brother and his family down the hall. Poor James looks stunned. I don't think I have ever raised my voice in front of him.

"Norah, I—" Gen starts to say, turning in my direction.

"Gen, let her go. If you've learned anything since childhood, you know to let her walk away for a bit," Joseph says.

Kudos to my brother for standing up for me. I plod down the hall and slam the door to the master bedroom before curling up with Tank on the bed. It isn't long before Kelsey knocks on the door. Kelly drew the short straw to placate Gen.

JACOB

This can't be happening. The moment the alarm sounds, my protectiveness increases one thousandfold. I fail to hide my concern too. She felt me tense up. I would never risk her safety. I'm unarmed like at the Michelsons'. There is no reason to arm myself every day at my home. My security system has never failed before. Someone who doesn't belong is on my property. Sending her to the house alone nearly gutted me. She will do as I asked. I know she will. Not once has Norah ever questioned me or my team regarding her safety and security.

I purposely avoid watching her walk away with Kelly and Kelsey. Instead, I immediately start to plan with William. Nicholas, who surprisingly opted to stay, is listening intently. The perimeter alarm along the western edge of my property was set off. I can pinpoint on my phone where the alarm tripped. Once we have a plan and begin to move, Christoph comes running toward us.

"Where is everyone else?"

"I saw Norah, Kelly, and Kelsey about halfway here." Good, her pace was steady. "Maia is meeting them at the house. Nolan will likely be there as well. He was otherwise engaged."

I nod, the knot in my stomach loosening, but only marginally. Christoph falls in step with us as we move toward the breach.

This edge of my property abuts a state forest. Rarely does anyone cross onto my property, especially there. I believe there have only been two other instances. One was Connor when he heard a woman in distress in the park, and the second was an injured kayaker. The closest marked hiking trail is almost a half mile away from the line. There are private property signs posted at equal intervals along the property line. My alarm is set up about two hundred yards onto my land.

As we near the area, I hear the roar of motors, two, probably three. Once I meet the edge of my land, I note three young people on ATVs riding recklessly along the outer boundary of the park and my land. The fear in my heart diminishes exponentially. The heaviness lessens considerably. Norah is safe. There's no threat to her or her family. Well, no threat to her here at least. The Morettis are another larger, more complex matter. I call the ranger station and the local police before texting Maia.

> Me: *There's no threat to Norah. Some kids riding ATVs in the park crossed the perimeter.*
>
> Maia: *Okay. Everyone is in the house. Tension is high.*
>
> Me: *It'll be a bit before we get back. Waiting on ranger and CBPD.*
>
> Maia: *Okay. Nolan and I will stay here.*
>
> Me: *Thank you. I appreciate it.*
>
> Maia: *You're welcome.*

"What's the plan?" Christoph asks.

"I called the ranger station and Crescent Bay PD. I need to wait for them. If you prefer to head back, I can handle this."

"It won't take that long," Christoph replies. William and Nicholas reply in kind.

"I assume you told Maia that everything is clear," William asks.

"I did. Everyone is in the house. I got the impression something went down, but I'm not sure who."

"I would put money on Gen and Norah," Nicholas supplies, looking over at the three riders who are buzzing by us completely oblivious to our presence. William laughs.

"Why do you say that?" I ask. Norah is levelheaded and analytical. She doesn't become extremely angry. Pissed at Stan and Agent Morse, sure, but she's entitled. In fact, I've never seen her argue with anyone.

"Gen's world revolves around Gen. She has a plan for everyone in her family. If you deviate from that plan, she gets upset. Apparently, you were not in her plans for Norah," Nicholas states as if it's a known fact.

I don't know Gen at all other than she's Norah's sister-in-law and they have known one another since childhood.

"She doesn't truly know me." Hell, the list of people who truly know me is short, extremely short.

"That doesn't matter. Gen pulled this with Kelsey as well. She freaked out that Kelsey was going to buy the Perk to be near me. They had a falling out for a fair amount of time. Kelly was the one who pulled Gen back to reality. She's likely trying to talk some sense into Gen as we speak. Kelly doesn't like strife among her family and friends," William adds.

"Definitely true." Nicholas nods in agreement.

As I ponder their take on the situation, I see the ranger and CBPD approaching from the park land. It isn't until they are close enough to contain the riders do they put on their sirens. If William and Nicholas are correct, Norah is curled up on our bed waiting while everyone else hangs out in the house. *Our bed has a nice ring to it.* I smile inwardly.

"Mr. Blackthorne, thank you for the call," Ranger DeLeo states, approaching us. "How did you know about the riders?"

"I have a perimeter alarm on my property. When I came to check it out, I found those three speeding around in circles." He doesn't need to know that my heart was in my throat when the alert sounded or the panic coursing through me for Norah.

"Thank you. Either I or Captain Greenfield will send you a statement for signature early next week."

"You're welcome."

As he walks away, Captain Greenfield approaches the three of us. He's an older man, likely in his mid-fifties. Due to my work with Nicholas and other celebrities, I know the look of recognition. Greenfield tries to mask it but fails.

"Good evening, Mr. Blackthorne. Thank you for the call."

"You're welcome. Captain William Ramirez from York Beach PD and Nicholas Barnett, this is Captain Greenfield. They are visiting for the holiday."

"Pleasure to meet you, gentlemen. I'll forward a statement to you."

"Thank you. Have a good night."

"Would you like a ride back?"

I would prefer to walk, but the sooner I tuck Norah against me, the better. "Thank you. That would be appreciated."

The ride back to the farm is largely silent. At the gate to the private road, we hop out and thank the deputy for the ride. After closing the gate, we take a golf cart up to the house.

When we enter the house, it's eerily quiet. It's impossible to believe that nine people are in my house. Nolan and Maia are sitting on the couch talking. The television has a kid's show on. Presumably, James or Jackson was watching, and they didn't change the channel.

"Where is everyone?" I ask.

Nolan shuts off the show while Maia responds. William and Nicholas anxiously waiting for her reply.

"The Cavallaro family went back downstairs. Kelly is in the guest room, and Kelsey is with Norah and Tank in the master bedroom."

Nicholas excuses himself to find Kelly.

"Thank you for coming over. I appreciate it on your day off. Maia, please be prepared to return to Maine tomorrow with Nicholas and Kelly."

"I'll be ready, Jacob."

As Maia and Nolan leave through the front door, I don't miss his hand on her lower back as he guides her through the door first. I'll deal with that when a mission requires everyone. William follows me to the master bedroom. Slowly, I open the door. Tank is sitting just inside.

"Your training skills rival Bear's from the navy." Bear is William's former K-9 partner from the navy. He and Kelsey also have a new addition named Knox who is making progress in his training.

"Thanks. I'm considering getting another for Norah. Tank normally comes to the office with me."

"She isn't staying?" William sees my feelings too.

Clearly, I was wrong when I thought I was being discreet. "I asked her to stay."

William nods, and the conversation ends when Kelsey slides away from Norah curled on the bed. She slips out the half-open door right next to William. His hand grips her hip possessively. He has a protector mode too. I suppose all servicemen have it, whether military or police. I wonder if it increases during pregnancy. I expect it does.

"She nodded off about twenty minutes ago. On top of everything else, fighting with Gen really got to her."

"Thanks, Kelsey."

"You're welcome. I'll start dinner in an hour or so."

"Thank you." I release Tank and lock the door. Just the sight of her soothes my soul. I lower myself onto the bed and curve my body around hers.

NORAH

As I snuggle deeper into his arms, he murmurs against my hair, "Tell me, gorgeous." I have never been the girl to swoon over nicknames, but sweet mercy, his get to me like no one else.

"Nothing to tell. It isn't new that Gen only cares about herself. I just hoped that Kelsey's reaction to her plans would have made Gen pause before accusing me of risking their lives."

"I'm sorry."

"No, this isn't your fault. You brought them here for me, and I know you wouldn't have if you had any single shred of concern for me or them, even if it meant I couldn't see them. This is Gen's fault."

"Will it help if I talk to her?"

"I won't stop you from trying, but presumably you're part of the problem. I don't care about Gen's opinion." I turn in his arms, sliding my lips across his. "I love you. That's all that matters."

"I love you." He kisses me softly again. "Are you sure? I could try to smooth things over."

"I appreciate it, but she's not easily persuaded. It took Kelsey over a month to get an apology from Gen, and they're besties for life."

"I'll leave it alone."

"Thank you. What time is it?"

"Near four. Why?"

"I should get started on dinner," I reply, attempting to move from the bed.

"Kelsey said she would do it. Give me a few more minutes, and we will both go help," he implores, tugging me closer.

I nod against his chest. I may not know what my professional life holds, but I'm staying here with him. I don't need to find a job right away. We need to talk about how that would work. I sigh.

"Want to share what that deep sigh is about?"

"It isn't bad. We don't have time to talk about it now."

He kisses my hair before lowering his lips to mine. "What is the topic?"

"Where I want to live and what to do about work," I mumble.

"Where do you want to live?" he asks tentatively as if anywhere but here is an actual option.

"With you."

Faster than I can blink, Jacob has me pinned beneath his delicious body and his lips on mine. "That makes me very happy," he says against my mouth.

"I hope so, you asked, and you gave me space in the closet. Can we keep that between us for now? It's already tense; I don't want to make it worse right now."

"Of course." He pushes up to his forearms.

"We should go help."

He nods, sinking back to his heels. "I want to talk about that more. Maybe Connor is free on Sunday so you can see Crescent Bay."

Smiling, I follow him to the kitchen.

Jacob and William chat at the island while I assist Kelsey with dinner.

"You good?" she asks while we have our backs to our men.

"I am. Gen's opinion will not impact my choices. I know what I want."

"Jacob," Kelsey whispers, nudging me.

"More than anything."

"I remember the day I knew Will was it for me." A smile spreads across her face.

"So do I." I inhale. "Jacob not William." Taking into consideration all the sweet things he has done over the past few years without a second thought, the clincher was my necklace.

Kelsey giggles. "I know what you meant."

"Do you know what the bean is yet?" I don't know if it's a secret or if they decided not to find out.

"We decided to find out on his or her birthday," Kelsey replies.

"Would you prefer yellow or green?"

"Either is fine. We're going with a wood-tone crib, and we'll decorate after he or she is born. You aren't coming home, are you?" Kelsey asks quietly.

"No, but I haven't told anyone but Jacob yet."

Kelsey nods and turns back toward the island. William and Jacob are staring at us in silence.

"What were you two chatting about?" William asks suspiciously.

"You two, of course," Kelsey replies before rounding the island to kiss him.

Jacob leans across the island to meet my lips.

"Ewwwww, gross!"

I pull away from Jacob as Kelsey and William separate to see who is disgusted by our displays of affection.

"Do all adults kiss one another?" James asks.

"At least ones who are married or dating, yes," I reply. We did for two plus years before making a commitment, but I decide not to divulge that part to James.

"I vaguely recall having this conversation before, James," William says.

"We did, but then it was just you, Miss Kelsey, and my parents. Now it's you plus Auntie Kelly and Mr. Nicholas, and Auntie Norah and Mr. Jacob. That doesn't even include the family that isn't here, like Auntie Maggie with Uncle Grant, and Uncle Peter and Aunt Billie. The list of people who are single is much shorter. The only single family member is Uncle Scott, but I think he has someone in mind."

"Really? Who, James?" Kelly asks as she joins the group, her interest clearly piqued.

"He didn't tell me her name, just that he liked someone."

I wonder who Scott is interested in.

A hush falls over the group as Gen steps into the kitchen. I busy myself in the corner of the kitchen to avoid her. I barely have enough time to settle myself before Jacob's hands slide over my hips, clasping around me. I lean back slightly.

"I've got you."

I drop my head in acknowledgment.

Kelsey announces dinner is in less than thirty minutes, prompting the chatter to resume in small groups. I hear Joseph guide Gen to their room with Jackson babbling, but James stays out with everyone else.

Dinner passes without an issue. Gen doesn't attempt to seek me out nor talk to me, which suits me fine. I don't plan to address her statements any more than I already have. Immediately after dinner, Gen takes Jackson into their room to put him down to sleep.

"Norah, could I have a word?" Joseph asks.

Jacob asks without asking if I want him to join me. I indicate no. Kelsey is setting out dessert with Kelly's help. I'm sure there are some leftovers, but she made something new today as well. It doesn't matter what she bakes, every single dish is delectable.

"Sure." I lead my brother into the office. Jacob's office is comfortable but professional with the wall-to-wall shelves and comfy leather couch.

"I know better than to apologize for Gen. It needs to come from her. You were correct; I did force her to come here, so for that I apologize. I gather the safety concerns are more dire than you have led us to believe."

"Thank you. I didn't sugarcoat the danger I'm in. I won't share any more details with you or anyone. I won't risk it. I hope to be out of this mess soon."

"Are you going back to work?"

"All I know for sure is it won't be at Quinn Sterling. I don't trust anyone there."

"Fair enough. How long have you been dating Jacob? I feel as if I missed a ton of signs."

"You didn't miss any signs. There weren't any. Jacob and I have been seeing each other for over two years, but we weren't dating until very recently."

Joseph sits back in the chair and considers my statement. If anyone understands not wanting to commit, it's my brother. After choosing his trust fund over Gen, he allowed our father to steer appropriate women his way until he met Stacia, James's mother. After that, he opted to ignore our father's warnings regarding his trust fund and took Gen back.

"For what it's worth, I'm sorry for my part in ruining our visit."

"Thanks."

He leaves me in the office, presumably to find Gen. My excitement for this visit was genuine. Now Gen's sharp tongue and blame placing spoiled Jacob's incredible gesture.

JACOB

On one hand, I know bringing her family for the holiday made her happy. Circumstances out of our control turned the visit into an uncomfortable family event. Early this morning, her family and friends leave to return home. Not only is she relieved, but sad as well. Her goodbye with Kelsey and Kelly lasts longer than anyone else.

Armed with a cup of coffee and surrounded by the Moretti files, Norah tucks her feet underneath her and focuses on work. Watching her work is mesmerizing, even without her lower lip pulled between her teeth.

"Any progress?" I ask a few hours later.

"Not really. I mean, I know what the numbers aren't. I missed the deadline, but did Blaine have any luck getting access to Sergio and Rosita's accounts?"

"I have a suspicion that deadline wasn't firm, considering those were Stan's words. Either whoever had him didn't like him giving you another week or Stan was making a last-ditch plea to save Delores. He failed. Plus, we didn't get another video."

She nods.

"I haven't heard back from Blaine about that."

"How trustworthy do you think Robert is?"

"What are you thinking?" I ask, settling next to her on the cozy leather couch in my office. I'm willing to hear her out. Her observations are more on point than any other client Blackthorne has ever had. She isn't just a client, but either way I appreciate her insight.

"I'm fairly confident those two numbers will open a file. The bar code is likely Stan's access ID. The numbers from the bonus check is the admin access to a file. I already had the Moretti file number."

"Okay. Connor and I are working on a file to make sure there are no holes. It'll be handled properly."

"I understand."

"What else, gorgeous?"

"Nothing."

"Norah." Reaching out with my hand, I turn her gaze toward mine. "Whatever it is, we can handle it."

"I'm ready to move on from this. I know it isn't over, but I feel stuck. That sounds horrible. We have made decisions, but we can't act on them yet. It sucks. That's all. I'll be fine."

I draw her into my arms, holding her snuggly against my chest. "What else do you need to do with those files?"

"I've examined them again like I did before Stan took it from me. There isn't anything else for me to do unless or until Blaine comes through." She sighs. "I found all there is to find."

"Let's assume you could do anything you want, what would you do?"

"I appreciate what you're trying to do, but I won't let you, Connor, or Christoph take any extra risks for me."

"Why did you say only Christoph and Connor?"

"They are the only ones local at the moment, right?"

"Your analytical skills are off the charts. Yes, they're the only ones not on assignment right now. Please tell me anyway."

"I would go for a horseback ride on a white sand beach. Salty breeze, warm water, no other people."

"Not even me?" I feign dejection.

"Only you, always you."

Bringing my lips to hers, I lock her request into my memory. I can't make that happen right now, but I can once she's safe.

After clearing up the files, we sit at my desk and order some groceries, and Norah orders more clothes, boots, lingerie, and shampoo. Her shampoo is not available in the grocery store here.

We rummage through the fridge and decide on cheeseburgers and fries for dinner. I watch her cut the sweet potatoes into thick slices and bake them. While I handle the burgers, she makes a small salad as well. After eating, we start a fire and sit on large chairs in the backyard. Hours later, we turn in.

Ideally, Blaine will come through soon. I would prefer to have every angle buttoned up before approaching the authorities with what we have uncovered. It took Blaine over a week to access the bank accounts. That isn't a complaint. I'm sure he was acting as quickly as possible within the parameters he can work with. Since then, Norah has been poring through them for hours each day. While she works tirelessly with that, Connor and I are assembling the presentation for the authorities. We have been working on it here in my home office for the last few weeks.

"When do you think we should involve Robert?" I ask Connor who is pacing behind me.

"If we can get someone above Agents Brown and Morse who is willing to hear us out, I think we get everyone to one place and present the evidence. Giving Robert Quinn and Gustavo Moretti time with this information without the authorities present isn't the best plan."

"I want stacks and stacks of evidence to prove everything that has happened was at Sergio or Rosita's request. That Norah wasn't aware of Stan helping Sergio. Proof that Sid and Carlo confronted Norah in the parking garage. Evidence Morse was at her townhouse. Proof that Sergio or Rosita hired Iris to abduct Norah but instead took Maia. I don't want to tip off Robert too early. If he knows where the ledger is, presumably so does Gustavo. We might lose our leverage against Sergio or he might bolt, especially if his father gets a hold of him."

"Perhaps William could be of assistance there."

I place a call to William, leaving a detailed voice mail. Connor and I go over the timeline and supporting evidence incident by incident. We're only missing a precise accounting of the monies that Sergio and Rosita have funneled away from the Moretti Family Brands. Norah is working on it. I know better than to ask how long it will take. She's ready to move forward with her life, and I don't blame her. I also know that she worked for six months to find the discrepancies that brought her here in the first place. It has only been a week. She'll sort the data and find the money.

The three of us take a dinner break; afterward, Connor leaves for the day. Norah and I watch another classic movie before turning in for the night. I spent six years feeling guilty. That isn't true. I spent four years completely alone, wallowing in guilt. Then I met Norah. At the beginning, I took the easy route, no strings attached. Now it's time for me to have it all, with her. First, I need to clear her name.

NORAH

Blaine came through with the bank records for Sergio and Rosita. There are seven accounts in total. I have been poring over them for the last week. I don't think Stan realized he was assisting me when he scanned my work onto the server. The pattern that Stan used to siphon the money also guides me to how they moved the money.

There are seven different accounts at several banks in the Cayman Islands. Either Sergio or Rosita owns each account with one other family member. I assume the other family members are unsuspecting. It's smart. Never say criminals aren't crafty and clever. They likely plan to use the accounts as leverage against the family members who decide to come clean or plan to turn them in. Somehow Jacob saw this wrinkle coming or at least something like it.

I have two more companies to go through. I have accounted for almost thirty-six million dollars. Missing dollars here and there is one thing when you are accounting for a multibillion-dollar conglomerate. Millions and millions are something else. Millions means malfeasance. I glance out the window as my stomach rumbles.

"Hey, gorgeous, could you come here?" Jacob calls from the kitchen.

"Everything okay?" I ask, entering the kitchen.

He's leaning against the island, a water in hand and his forearm tight.

"Yes, everything is perfect. I have a surprise for you. Could you get dressed to go outside?"

"Is it people?" I attempt to mask my sadness. Surely, I failed. It isn't Jacob's fault things went sideways during the holiday.

"No, it's not people."

"What are you up to?"

"Just go, beautiful. The sooner you add some layers, the sooner you will find out."

The nicknames, seriously. They make me all mushy, but never with any other man. I rise on my toes and kiss him before hurrying down the hall. Less than five minutes later, I return to the kitchen. Jacob is standing by the island with a huge grin on his face. Taking my hand, he brings it to his lips before leading me out the front door into the barn. When I step inside, I'm floored. There are two gorgeous horses, one black and one brown. I reach up, setting my hand on the muzzle of the black one while Jacob pets the brown.

"How did you…? What am I going to do with you?" I cover my mouth with my hand to contain all my emotions. If I sat down and wrote all the qualities I would want in my forever, Jacob surpasses the list by miles. Everything from the sweet notes, morning coffee, and coming when I need him. That doesn't even begin to cover all the things I have learned since this started, like his ability to refurbish a house, his love of exemplary wine, and the vulnerable Jacob just beneath the soldier exterior that only I see.

Surrounding me with his strong arms, he says, "I don't have white sand here, but I will take to you some as soon as I can. Will you ride to lunch with me?"

"I'll go anywhere with you." I kiss him tenderly.

He threads his fingers together, I slip my left foot in, set my hands on his shoulders, and push up to the saddle, grabbing the horn. "What's his name?"

"His name is Midnight, and his partner here is Sedona." Jacob mounts his horse next to me.

I lean over to kiss him again. "You don't have to do all this for me."

"I know. That's exactly why I do and I want to."

"Lead the way."

I'm itching to feel the wind whipping around my face and the sound of Midnight's hooves crunching the snowy ground. Jacob kicks Sedona who moves forward out of the barn. Turning left, he heads down the driveway a bit before turning right toward the shore. Once there is some space on either side of us, I kick Midnight, urging him faster. I'm just feeling him out, gauging his comfort zone. He moves up to a trot, and we pass Jacob and Sedona easily.

"Did you fail to tell me you're an experienced rider?" Jacob shouts from behind me.

"Not a ringer, but I know my way around a horse. I rode a lot when I was younger. One of my middle school friends was uber rich, and she had a few horses. I took care of them when she went away. I always wanted one of my own."

"You should get one. We have plenty of room. You might need a fenced area though."

We, he said we. "Are you sure you don't mind?"

He pulls back on Sedona's reins, stopping. I walk back to him, searching for any sign of wavering.

"You can do whatever you want inside or outside of the house."

"I'll consider it. There's one thing we should do right away."

If he is concerned, he hides it well. Not a flicker, a grimace, nothing to indicate his feelings. *Note to self, don't play poker with Jacob.*

"We need bigger towels."

"We don't need bigger towels. I'm a fan of you using the small towels." He smirks. "Truly, that's all?"

"Jacob, you created a gorgeous, comfortable home with plenty of room. It doesn't need anything except maybe some shelves for my shoes."

"I'll make that happen."

I smile, turn Midnight, and trot away. After a few hundred yards, I increase up to a gallop toward Jacob's favorite spot. He and Sedona are close behind me. We tie the horses to a tree and eat our lunch on the platform.

"Thank you. This is perfect."

"You're welcome."

After eating, we ride side by side to the edge of the property where the alarm went off before racing back to the barn. Both horses are fast. Sedona is a bit faster, so Jacob wins this race. It doesn't matter; I'll get the next one. No one is keeping score.

After a wonderfully long lunch, I tackle another Moretti company and find an additional fourteen million dollars over the last eight years. I consider tackling the last one, knowing I'll finish tomorrow but decide against it. Armed with that knowledge, I seek out Jacob.

Connor and Jacob are painstakingly going through a stack of papers.

"Hey, Connor."

"Hi, Norah."

I round the desk as Jacob pushes his chair back to kiss me.

"Did you finish?" he asks.

"Almost. I found fifty million, but I still have one more company to go through. So far the deposits in the Caymans match up."

"Perfect. We're pretty well set here too," Jacob replies. A satisfied smile graces both of their faces.

After another brief kiss, I leave them in the office to start dinner. A wonderful dinner and conversation end with Connor leaving for the day. As much as I want this to be over, I'm nervous about how we work when I don't need his professional services anymore. Truthfully, it doesn't matter. I want to build a life with him.

JACOB

Our plan is set, and we have prepared more than ever before. Every team member except Callen heads to Maine this morning. After a bit of wrangling and the promise of criminal activity by one of his agents, Special Agent in Charge Alex Bishop agreed to meet us in York Beach. We asked him to keep those in the know small.

"Morning, Cash," I greet our pilot as I enter the plane.

"Hi, Jacob. Good to see you again. Hi, Norah."

"Hi, Cash. How is Noelle?"

"Great. I'll tell her you said hello."

Norah refuses to release my hand. Her grip is extraordinarily tight this morning. We settle into our seats for the flight to Portsmouth. Only once during the flight does Norah let go of my hand. From there we'll separate into two teams. Maia and Norah are both dressed the same and wearing blonde wigs this time. It's simply an extra layer of security. I don't think we'll need it this time. William will have everything under control on his end.

Upon landing, Cash taxis to his private hangar. Once we deplane, I walk Norah to the SUV for a private moment, as private as we can get right now.

"If Bishop needs to talk to you personally, I'll see you at the precinct. If not, I'll meet you at your townhouse. I mentioned it before, but please prepare yourself, your home is trashed. I had the food cleaned and the doors replaced, but nothing else was touched."

Norah nods.

"This is almost over. I'm sure you feel strange not being at the farm, it's normal." I slide my hand along her jaw, my fingers grazing the back of her neck. I draw my thumb across her lips before kissing her softly. "I love you, Norah. I'll be back beside you as soon as I can."

"I love you. I'll be fine with Christoph and Nolan."

I hesitate just a moment more as Nolan and Christoph walk toward us. Steeling myself, I walk to the sedan where Connor and Maia are waiting.

"Jake, you have prepared everything in excruciating detail. Let's go clear her name, lock up Sergio, Rosita, and Morse," Connor states.

I nod and start the car.

A short ride later, we enter the rear gate of the precinct and escort Maia inside as if she's Norah. Intel from Blaine indicates that the Morettis and Agent Morse are aware of the meeting with Agent Bishop. I'm fairly confident that our carefully placed misinformation will allow me to present this evidence before they react.

"Captain. Good to see you again."

"Jacob, good to see you as well. Connor, Norah, right this way." William is aware of our entire plan. He knows its Maia but is playing along. "Sgt Washington will be joining us."

If I recall correctly, he's Gen's brother-in-law.

"Special Agent Bishop, this is Jacob Blackthorne, Connor Michelson, and Maia Park of Blackthorne Security." We exchange handshakes and take a seat.

"Thank you, Captain," I begin while Connor distributes a summary of our findings as well as a timeline of events. "Agent Bishop, I have compiled evidence pertaining to the Moretti Family Brands with the assistance of Norah Cavallaro. She uncovered a scheme to siphon money into offshore accounts. When she brought this information to her superior, Stan Sterling of Quinn Sterling, he immediately removed her from the file. Since then, Miss Cavallaro has been threatened, intimidated, assaulted, and chased by members of the Moretti family. I want to be clear, there are two factions of the family. The first, led by Gustavo Moretti, is working with Robert Quinn, attempting to root out his family members embezzling money. We have determined that Sergio and Rosita Moretti are the culprits." I take a moment and gaze over at Agent Bishop. He appears to be listening intently.

"In that file, you'll find a complete forensic accounting tracing the monies from the Moretti Family Brands to seven offshore accounts in the Cayman Islands. Miss Cavallaro determined that either Sergio or Rosita and one additional unsuspecting family member hold the accounts."

"Mr. Blackthorne, I appreciate your presentation. I have no doubt the Morettis, at least some of them, are dirty. A small task force has been looking into their businesses for the last two years. Mr. Quinn has been working with us for the last sixth months, give or take. We are fully aware that Miss Cavallaro was not involved in the scheme to hide the money for the Morettis." I nod as he continues. "I'm more interested in evidence that points to my agents assaulting Miss Cavallaro."

I exhale slowly, moving on to the assault portion of the presentation. "If you flip to tab four. Miss Cavallaro was drugged in her townhouse the day after she told Mr. Sterling of her findings. At her interview in your office, she recognized tattoos and the voice of Agent Morse as her assailant."

"I understand. Where is Miss Cavallaro?"

"She is nearby. Her findings speak for themselves, and her last meeting with your office didn't go well. At the behest of the Morettis, Miss Park was abducted because she was mistaken for Miss Cavallaro. She's rightfully concerned about attending another meeting unless absolutely necessary."

Bishop nods. "I'll review all of this information immediately and place Agent Morse on desk duty until such review is complete. At some point in the future, I insist on a meeting with Miss Cavallaro. It need not be in person."

I release a breath as discreetly as possible. "She'll be available upon your request." Almost immediately, my phone, Connor's, and Maia's buzz in concert.

Christoph: Townhouse compromised. Told client to follow Plan K.

"Christoph, talk to me," I bark into my phone.

"It's me," Norah replies in a shaky but not yet panicked voice.

"Norah," I breathe.

NORAH

Leaving the hangar wasn't as difficult this time. I'm confident in Jacob's ability to clearly set forth everything that has occurred since my meeting with Stan.

Christoph, Nolan, and I head directly to my townhouse. Jacob attempted to prepare me for the condition of my home. Honestly, after the initial shock, I know I'll be fine. I'm not staying. I just want to pack my clothes, decide what to keep or toss, and settle in at the farm.

"Nolan will go clear your house, and then will we follow," Christoph indicates as we park along the curb. It's just past the morning rush. The complex is quiet at this time.

"Okay."

We sit in the SUV and wait for Nolan to report all clear. After a solid ten minutes pass, I note Christoph getting anxious.

"Norah, something is wrong." I nod. Fear courses through me knowing Nolan went inside for me, instead of me. "I'm setting this timer for five minutes. If I don't come out to get you before it expires, you send this text and drive to your sister's. Do you understand?"

"Yes."

When Christoph escorted me back from Boston, we were going toward safety. Now, he's walking away from it, into unknown danger.

His work mode is equal to Jacob's. It's comforting both for me and his safety.

"Do *not* under any circumstances come inside. Do you understand?"

"Yes."

He sets the timer and takes off into my townhouse. The seconds tick by like molasses. My concern level increases the closer the timer gets to zero. Nolan could be injured. What if I could help? *No. Do not go inside. They are doing their jobs. Risking their lives for me. Do what Christoph said.*

Wrapped in the thoughts in my head, I jump when the timer blares. Inhaling sharply, I send the text with Christoph's phone and start the SUV.

Immediately the phone rings.

"Christoph, talk to me," Jacob shouts when I answer.

"It's me," I reply.

"Norah, what happened?" His voice cracks as he speaks. I relay the circumstances, including that Christoph sent me to Kelly's. "How long ago did you leave?"

"I'm leaving my complex." My nerves are still steady at this point, although the crack in his armor doesn't help.

"Tell me the route you'll take to Kelly's."

About a half mile into the drive, an SUV cuts in front of me. Fear of crashing into someone who wants to harm me makes my throat constrict. I slam on the brakes, barely avoiding a collision.

"Noooo!"

"Norah!"

"I'm fine. An SUV pulled out in front of me and is crawling. It isn't a coincidence. The vehicle is a rental. I can't see the driver though."

"Can you give me the plate?" he asks, I assume to relay it to William.

"PR340, but it isn't Maine. It's Rhode Island."

"I'm sure you know the roads better than whoever is in the SUV. Is there somewhere with a large, accessible area without a lot of people?" he asks, and I hear talking in the background.

"I would say the high school, but school is in session. The golf course would be closed at this point."

"Hold on, let me talk to William for a moment. He's driving." Minutes pass as I move along the route to Kelly's.

"Okay, I need you to take as many backroads as you can to get to the golf course. Once you turn away from that SUV, they will follow. Drive safely but as fast as you can. I'll be at the golf course."

"Don't hang up!" I can't handle this alone. He's keeping me calm as I wind through these backroads.

"I won't. I just need to update William. I'll be here the entire way. Read out the streets as you turn. That way we can estimate when you'll get here." I exhale and hear talking over the line but not his actual words. "Norah?"

"I'm here." I call out the next street name. Just three more turns and I will be at the golf course. Almost every member of Jacob's team has been injured to protect me. It's a lot to process.

"Any change?" His voice is calm. The crack allowing vulnerable Jacob through from before was a momentary lapse in his demeanor. Protector Jacob is fully in charge right now.

"Now there are two SUVs behind me." A list of potential drivers filters through my mind. It could be... I have no clue who it could be other than Morse. I highly doubt that Sid and Carlo would drive all this way.

"You're almost here, gorgeous. You've got this." His confidence in me is unwavering. I'm terrified. My hands are turning white from clutching the steering wheel. I'm vibrating with fear. I have no idea how this will turn out. I keep reminding myself that Jacob and William have a plan.

"Norah, when you get here, speed up, drive to the right of the row of cars, continue around, turning left, and drive straight behind them parallel to the clubhouse," Jacob calmly relays through the speaker.

"I will." I channel my training and breathe in and out in regular intervals.

I take the last turn and slow for the speed bump before speeding up to the next bump. I don't see them yet because of the curvy driveway, but I'm sure the vehicles are there. As I round the bend in the road, I see a row of police cars in front of the clubhouse. There's approximately a full car length between each one, ten vehicles long. As I turn right toward the end of the row, additional units pull between me and the two SUVs. I continue driving as instructed to the end of the row of cars. As I move past the cars, I hear crunching, breaking glass, sirens, and shouting.

"Norah, you can stop driving, but stay in the truck." Jacob's voice breaks my cold stare out the windshield.

"Uh-huh." I glance out my window and see the two SUVs at a halt, the second one crashed into the first, likely due to the spike strips running along the ground. Red and blue lights are flashing, and there are at least fifteen officers in various uniforms, mostly YBPD, surround the two SUVs.

"Breathe, beautiful. It's almost over."

I let out a shaky breath.

"Again, sweetheart."

I exhale again.

"I'm coming over to you. I'll approach on the passenger side of the truck."

I lower my head to the steering wheel, regulating my breathing even further.

The door flies open, and I slide across the seat into his strong arms. The only place I want to be every single day.

"Are Nolan and Christoph all right?" I rasp against his lips.

"They're being checked out at York Memorial. Just let me... please."

I melt into his embrace. His arms wind around me so tightly his fingers grazing my rib cage from behind, my feet barely touch the ground. Feeling his heartbeat against my chest solidifies that my Jacob, vulnerable Jacob is resurfacing as he holds me close. Honestly, I'm surprised he isn't running his hands over the length of my body to make sure I'm uninjured.

"Is it over?"

He lowers me to the ground, interlaces his fingers with mine, and leads me around the line of police vehicles. We're just in time to see Agent Morse, Agent Brown, and another woman shoved into the rear of police cruisers. "Damn! I was really hoping to be able to knock him out."

Jacob laughs, loud and genuine. "I would have liked a front row seat." We stand off to the side watching the scene. A few minutes later, a tall man wearing an FBI jacket and William approach us.

"Well done, Norah."

"Thanks, William." I'm still shaking a bit, but my nerves are calming.

"Miss Cavallaro, I'm Special Agent in Charge Bishop." He extends his hand to me. "I appreciate your assistance with Agents Morse and Brown. I apologize on behalf of the Bureau for their actions. I will levy whatever charges are appropriate. When I can review the extensive documentation provided by Blackthorne, I may reach out with questions."

"You're welcome. I just want to clear my name."

Bishop nods and turns to Jacob. "Mr. Blackthorne, I look forward to reviewing your documentation and working with you in the future to complete this case."

"As do I, Agent Bishop."

He walks away.

"Can we go to the hospital now?" I implore.

"You don't need to go. They'll be fine," Jacob replies.

"I want to. We have no way to get there." I sigh.

"You will in a few minutes. I had Officer Smithson escort Kelsey from home to your townhouse to get your car. She should be arriving any minute. Officer Cappelli went to York Hospital with Christoph and Nolan." Just as he finishes speaking, Kelsey pulls into a parking spot to our right.

After parking she walks over to us and kisses William softly.

"Hey there, sweets. How are you holding up?" she asks, turning to me.

"I'm better now." This nightmare is ending. I'll be able to make choices for my life, both personally and professionally.

"Good. Your car is insane. If it weren't for this little person," she says, rubbing her belly, "I would consider getting one for myself."

I laugh, taking my keys. William slides his arm protectively around her.

"Do you need anything else from me, William?" I ask.

"Not now. I'll need you to review your statement and sign it, but nothing else. We can do that over email if you prefer."

"That works." I hug Kelsey. "Maybe I'll see you in the morning, Kels."

"Sounds perfect. A Maine Christmas might be in order too?"

"I don't know about that. We'll talk more soon. Love you, Kels."

"Love you too, sweets."

William and Jacob finish their conversation, and we leave for the hospital. As we approach the passenger door, I hand Jacob my keys.

JACOB

"You're going to let me drive?" Surprise doesn't begin to cover how this moment feels.

"Why wouldn't I?"

"Um, you love this car."

"I love you more. Let's go."

I wait for Norah to settle into the seat and close the door. Rounding the car, I adjust everything and head toward the hospital. Nurse Reynolds greets us as we enter the emergency department.

"Mr. Blackthorne, Miss Cavallaro. Right this way." She leads us through two sets of double doors. Officer Cappelli is standing guard outside the door. I feel Norah shudder.

Leaning over, I whisper, "I've talked to both Nolan and Christoph. It's just a precaution."

"Okay," she whispers.

As we approach, I note a shift in Officer Cappelli's stance. He softens as Willa nears him. He's interested in her. Can't say I blame him. She's beautiful. Long, dark hair, big blue eyes, and those scrubs don't mask her curves at all. As we step inside the room, she pauses to talk to him. I only overhear a small portion.

"Hi, Willa. Nice to see you again."

"You too. Glad your arm healed well."

The door closes slowly, and I focus my attention to my team. Connor starts to speak immediately.

"Hi, Jake. Norah."

Norah steps to the side of Christoph and takes his hand. The anguish on her face is difficult for me to see. She blames herself for his injuries. He has a large shiner near his left eye, and his arm is in a sling. However, she doesn't understand it's his job. Maybe she does understand that portion, but seeing it makes it all too real.

"I'm fine, Norah. Don't blame yourself. Thank you for listening."

"You're welcome. I will admit, I considered going after you, but then both of us would be answering to Jacob."

Christoph smiles at her admission. "You're right."

It appears Nolan sustained more injuries. He's either sedated or sleeping. His left leg is resting on a few pillows, his knee wrapped. He has a bandage on his arm. Maia is pacing the length of the bed. Worry mars her face. I no longer believe nothing is going on between them. Her expression screams something more. If there isn't, they both want something to happen.

"Nurse Reynolds indicated they would be free to leave this evening, but they can't fly until tomorrow," Connor explains.

"I'll book some rooms, have some food delivered, and contact Cash. Then take Norah to her townhouse. Hopefully, we can accomplish what needs to be done before this evening," I inform everyone.

Maia nods but doesn't slow her pacing. "That works. Let me know if you need anything from me while I wait here."

Retaking Norah's hand, I lead her back to the parking lot. I hand her back her keys while opening the driver door.

"You can keep driving; it's fine with me."

"Thanks, but if you drive, I can make all the arrangements on the way." Entirely lost in my phone and making things happen, I fail to notice that Norah didn't drive directly to her townhouse. She parks in front of a small building. There are picnic tables scattered on the green lawn.

"Where are we?" I'm not even angry. Right now, she feels safe and free. Considering Morse is in custody, I don't blame her. I'll make certain she feels this way everyday going forward.

"This is Dunne's Ice Cream. It's heavenly even in the winter. They have tons of amazing flavors." She reaches across the center console and into the glove box. After rifling around a bit, she pulls out some cash. "Come on." She's prepared, I have to give her that.

I round the car and open her door, offering her my hand. As she takes it, I close her door and allow her to lead me to the window. She wasn't kidding. The flavor list is large. We take our ice cream to the farthest table. She slides the spoon into her mouth and literally moans. She chose the Maine blueberry and black raspberry while I opt for cookies and cream and java crunch.

"You *cannot* make those sounds in public."

Laughing, she replies, "Don't you worry, these are different than the ones you draw from me."

I feel my skin turning bright red. *Holy hell!*

We enjoy the scenery and our scoops despite the chilly temperature.

"Ready?" I ask. "We have some shoes to pack." I polish off my ice cream. She's right, it's some of the best I've ever had.

"Yes, I'm ready. Want to drive?" she asks, dangling her keys in front of me.

"Hell yes! Your car is insane." I pull her against me, kissing her soft lips. She tastes fruity from her ice cream.

Smiling, she puts her address into the GPS before taking my hand in hers.

"Is this normal, Norah?"

"What do you mean?" she asks with a hesitance in her voice.

"When we started seeing each other, I saw you maybe twice a month. I didn't really know you as a person." I left the details about what I did know alone. "Since your text, I've learned so much more about you, but you weren't completely yourself. You were with me because of the Morettis. Is this happy, mostly carefree person you?"

She leans over, kissing my cheek.

"What was that for?"

"Words, Jacob, words. It's pretty close. I still need to grasp not vying for the partnership and deciding what I want to do with my professional life. The only reason I felt comfortable enough to drive here is because you're with me and Morse is in custody. Plus, it'll be a while before I come back here again."

I consider everything she just said but decide to leave her last comment alone. It's just two weeks before the holiday, and Gen still hasn't apologized for her behavior. I gather that means she doesn't want to travel back here for Christmas.

"What do you want to do professionally?"

"I don't want to work at Quinn Sterling. I need to resign. Beyond that, I have no idea. I could open my own practice, open my dream store, even do nothing. Still working that out in my head."

I want to tell her she doesn't need to work, but I don't know how well that will go over. Aside from her nest egg, I have one myself, although mine is a bit larger.

"Do you want to keep your townhouse?"

"I don't need it if you're still willing to put up with me indefinitely."

I pull into her garage and throw the car in Park. "Norah, I love you. Will you move in with me?"

She smirks. "I love you. Yes, I'll move in with you." I tug her closer, kissing her again. "As far as my townhouse, it's paid for. The monthly carrying costs are minimal. Would it be beneficial to keep it for you or your team to use?"

"Maybe. We would have to look at the numbers."

"That works. I don't need to decide right now."

I follow her inside. She stops short one full step into her home. I didn't mince words when I said it was trashed. "You weren't kidding."

"No, I wasn't." I slide my arms around her from behind, burying my nose in her hair. She is back to her shampoo. The scent drives me crazy.

She shakes off the condition of her home, stating, "Let's get started." She pulls a hair tie off her wrist before twisting her hair on top of her head. I follow her into the office. After pulling out some totes, we move into her bedroom and start packing. I line the totes with her shoes while she goes through the hanging clothes in the closet. Expertly, she sorts them: damaged or keep. She pauses when she reaches a suit that isn't damaged. Placing it in the keep pile, she moves on. When she pulls her black silk dress out, it appears damaged.

"That's too bad. I love that dress."

"You may have mentioned that before." She winks at me. "I'll have Kelly make me a new one."

Making a third pile, she finishes the closet and moves onto the dresser. Most of the clothes in the dresser appear untouched. After packing them into a tote, she moves on to the top of her dresser. Norah doesn't have knickknacks or other décor in her bedroom. There's a jewelry box, perfume, a photo of James and Jackson, one of Nick, and one of a striking woman near her bed. She draws her fingertips down the glass before setting it in the box.

"Your mom?"

Norah nods.

"I see where you got it from."

She sighs and wraps her arms around me. Kissing her forehead, I ask where to go next. After getting me started in the bathroom, she finishes her night table before moving into her linen closet. We tackle her office together and finish packing her personal items. Lastly, we determine which furniture needs to be removed.

"I can have Scott come in, remove the damaged furniture and fix the kitchen and office cabinetry," she suggests.

"Remind me, who is Scott?"

"James's uncle. He works in construction. He did the build out for Kelly's expansion at So Elegant."

I checked him when Kelly hired him to expand. No need to do it again. "Makes sense." My phone buzzes in my pocket.

Connor: We're leaving for the hotel. Do you need assistance?

Me: No, we're almost done. We'll be there within the hour.

Connor: Roger.

We arrive at the Union Bluff just before seven. After checking on my team, we order room service and turn in for the night. Curling around her soft curves is even more perfect now that she's safe.

NORAH

The winter sun is crawling along the sand, casting shades of red, orange, and yellow. I wrap myself in Jacob's jacket and slip onto the balcony of our room. It's crazy early. I didn't want to wake him. The cold, salty breeze is just as soothing as a warm one. Ideally I want to start researching some options for the store. I'm leaning in that direction. I suppose I could still take some private clients as well.

"Morning, gorgeous." Just the sound of his voice makes my heart skip.

"Morning."

He takes my hand, pulls me to standing, takes my seat, and pulls me into his arms. "You okay?"

Here wrapped up in you. Absolutely. "Yup. How are Nolan and Christoph?"

I'm sure that was the first thing he did this morning.

"They're both up and around. Nolan is hobbling along. Christoph is sore. Both will be fine in a few days."

"Good. What time are we leaving?"

"Either nine or ten. Cash is checking the weight of your car, personal items, and the passengers. We may need to wait for a different plane based on his determination."

We stop at the Perk and fill up on lots of Kelsey's goodies for the trip as well as the next few days at home. Unfortunately, Kelsey isn't at the bakery this morning.

Several hours later, Jacob drives slowly through a small town that looks eerily like York Beach and nearby Ogunquit melded together. There are cute little boutiques and souvenir shops as well as a few restaurants. No amusement park though. I did see a sign for a beach about a half mile back.

"Where are we exactly?"

"Crescent Bay, Maryland."

"It's super cute. Just like Maine." There are groups of people milling around. Across the street from Jacob's office is a general store, a hardware store, and a chocolate shop.

"The towns are remarkably similar. Although I think the locals spend more time in town here than in York Beach."

He parks in front of a storefront. The door is etched with Blackthorne Security, Inc. After guiding me inside his office, he grabs a pile of mail and a set of keys before relocking the door.

"Good afternoon, Jacob," an elderly woman says as he closes the outer door to his office. She's tiny with perfectly coifed hair. She must have just left her weekly salon appointment.

"Hello, Mrs. Dwyer. How are you today?"

"I'm well. Aren't you lovely?" she says, taking my hand.

"Thank you. I'm Norah."

"About time, Jacob. I hope to see you around, Norah. Have a great afternoon."

A smile graces Jacob's gorgeous face. The small-town vibe is strong here too. Everyone knows everyone's business.

"How serious are you about opening your store?"

I raise an eyebrow. It would be a dream come true. Deep down, I don't want to work seventy or eighty hours a week as an accountant. I'll send my resignation tonight.

"I'm leaning that way, why?"

He unlocks the door to the left of his office. I step inside before him to an empty storefront. The space is a blank slate, no fixtures or anything denotes what the previous tenant used it for.

"This space is empty and has been for the last year. If you want it, it's yours. There isn't a bookstore within thirty miles of here, and it certainly isn't one like your dream." He researched for me. This man is perfection.

"Are you serious?" I turn to face him.

He slides his arm around me, pulling me close. "Definitely. I own the building. It's perfect for you."

"I don't know what to say." Everything seems to be falling into place. It's incredible and terrifying all at once.

"You don't have to say anything right now. I know moving is a substantial change, as is making professional choices. Think about it and let me know."

"This is huge, Jacob. I have dreamed about my own store since I was young." Is it possible that everything I ever wanted is here? With him. "I may have conditions if I decide to do this." There's no way I'll just use the space. I need to do it as an actual business despite the fact my boyfriend—I agree, it doesn't work—is my landlord.

"I would expect nothing less." He brushes his lips across mine before teasing me with his tongue. "Ready to go home?"

"Yes, so much!"

Jacob stops at the gate to his private road to input the code. As we park in front of the house, Gemma and Mr. Blackthorne greet us.

"Great timing. Nice ride," he says, hugging both of us.

"Thanks."

"She let you drive?"

Jacob laughs. "She did."

We chat for a bit with Mr. B before bringing my totes into the house. Surprisingly, Jacob lets me help. While I unpack my clothes, Jacob answers a few work calls. On a return trip to the bedroom, Jacob waves me into his office.

"Of course, Agent Bishop. She's right here." I hand Norah the phone.

"Hello."

"Miss Cavallaro?"

"Norah, please call me Norah."

"I have a proposal for you. Your work with the Moretti file was exemplary. I would like to offer you a forensic accounting consulting position with the FBI."

"Thank you."

"I'll send the details to you and you can get back to me when you're ready."

"Thank you again, Agent Bishop." Once I end the call, Jacob rises from his chair to tug me into his lap on the couch.

"I just moved all my clothes into the closet. I don't want to move, Jacob. I want to stay here."

"That makes me extremely happy. You won't have to move."

"Really?"

"Yes, really. Look it over, and we can talk about it more."

"Can we talk now, or do you have more work to do?" I ask.

"We can talk while we do one thing together."

"What do we need to do?"

He takes my hand and leads me straight into the master bedroom. After guiding me into the chair, he rushes away.

"How are you winded?" I ask with a chuckle when he returns with a tape measure.

He shrugs. "How many pairs of shoes do you have?"

"Overall?"

"Yes, overall."

"More than thirty. Why?"

He leads me into the closet. "If I remove this mirror, I can build shelves here from floor to ceiling for your shoes."

An elated look crosses my face before I jump into his arms, peppering his face with kisses.

After finishing the measurements, we curl up and discuss all the options for my professional life.

"What are you thinking about work, gorgeous?"

"I want to take the offer."

"Which one?"

"Both." I should be able to pull both off at once. It isn't as if the consulting will be a full-time job, just when the cases require my expertise.

"What are your conditions for the bookstore?" he asks, knowing I would never just take the keys and use the space.

"I need to do this myself. Do you know a local attorney who I can call to start my business?" He nods. "I want an actual lease at a fair rent."

"I'll give you whatever you want. Anything else?"

"In the spring, I want to build a fenced area for our horses."

"Our?"

"Yes, you need one too. I need to win a race or two." I lower myself on top of him.

He kisses the top of my head, clasping his hands at the small of my back. "Anything you want, beautiful. Also, William couldn't give me your phone back, so I ordered you a new one and transferred all your data. You can call and text to your heart's content."

Oddly, I'm not jumping at the chance to text people. Being away from them really gave me a bit more perspective on how they see me, especially Gen.

"Thanks. I have been meaning to ask you. When we were skating, you turned on the music from your phone. What service was it?"

"I created the playlist. Why?"

"You specifically chose all those songs?" A single tear streaks down my cheek.

He kisses it away. "Yes. I have been compiling that playlist since you got here. I used the songs to say the words I couldn't."

"You did though, that night."

"I did, but I tried so many times before that; I still wasn't sure I could say the words."

Sliding his hands along my jaw, he sets his forehead to mine. "Norah, I love you. I'm ecstatic you're here to stay."

"Me too. I love you."

JACOB

Christmas is rapidly approaching. Norah plans to stay home for the holiday. We'll spend the holiday at my parents' with the Michelsons. With her help, our home looks festive. I haven't had a tree in years. No reason to have one for just me. Now we have a large tree nestled to the left of the fireplace in the living room. Lighted garland hangs from the mantle along with two new embroidered stockings.

Norah is at a meeting with her attorney to finalize the paperwork to open her store. She plans to have a grand opening in early March. She's been working in the store every day while I work at my office next door. It's good for both of us to get out of the house. Working from home was necessary while she needed round-the-clock security, but now home is just for us.

There's a knock on my office door. Tank lifts his head and resettles once he notes it's someone he knows.

"Come in." The door opens, and Callen walks in. "Hey, Callen, good to see you."

He just finished a long-term job for a client. Miss Goldberg's father raved about Callen's job performance on set. Thankfully, it turned out better than I anticipated.

"Morning, Jacob. I wanted to wish you a Merry Christmas before I leave for my vacation."

"Thank you. Have a wonderful time. I'll see you in a few weeks."

As Callen leaves, Gemma appears in my doorway, stating, "There's a delivery that you need to sign for personally."

"Thanks, Gemma. I'll be right out."

I sign for the package and retreat to my office. I resist the urge to open the box, because I have no idea when Norah will return. I'm sure it's perfect.

Connor drops into the chair in my office. "What time do you need me to bring your surprise to the farm?"

"Can you do it by four? Everything is ready in the barn."

"Sure. I'll see you in a few days at Mom's." I love that Connor calls my mother "Mom" too. "I'll handle the calls if there are any. You deserve everything you want, Jake."

"Thanks, C." I'm grateful for him. A lesser man could have shut me out after Mara's death.

Connor retreats to his office before heading home to complete my delivery. I'm not nervous about her. I'm nervous about me. As if I called her, my gorgeous woman appears at the threshold of my office.

"Hey, babe. Are you ready to go home or do you need more time?"

"I need about an hour or so. I would prefer to finish here and not have to work at home."

"Okay, I'll be next door planning. I want to rearrange the floor plan to add some more intimate reading spaces." She steps around my desk and kisses me softly.

"I'll come over when I finish." I consider adding a reminder to lock the doors, but she will. She's still cautious even here.

I rebury my nose in the pile on my desk. A few days off with my woman alone before the holiday sounds perfect.

"I'm heading out. Merry Christmas, Jacob."

"Bye, Gemma. Safe travels home. Please say hello to your father for me."

"Will do." She grabs hers tote and walks out the door.

Turning back to my files, I hear something crash to the floor next door. Tank's ears perk up, but he doesn't alert. My brain races through the layout of the store and what could have possibly fallen. Coming up empty, I decide to walk over. Locking the Blackthorne office, I use my key to unlock the door to Norah's store.

A loud noise vibrates from the back room. I hurry to the back of the store. A wave of fear rushes over me when I see Norah fighting someone. The build would lead me to believe it's a man, but her assailant is wearing a mask. Her kick hits the person across the face. Immediately, they crumple to the ground with a thud.

"Norah."

She rushes over to me and collapses against me.

"Are you hurt?"

"No, I'm fine."

Securing Norah behind me, I take a few steps backward before pulling out my phone, my right arm curled behind me holding her close.

"Captain Greenfield, this is Jacob Blackthorne. Miss Cavallaro was just assaulted at her store."

"I'm on my way."

Whoever entered the store hasn't moved. Surprisingly, she isn't shaking like I would expect. She's unmistakably calm.

"Tell me what happened."

"I came back here for the measuring tape. When I bent down to pull out the toolbox, whoever that is, wrapped their arm around my waist and pulled me away from the counter. I stomped on their toes and struck my elbow into their abdomen and scurried away. When they came at me again, I kicked them."

Sirens increase in volume, and flashing lights paint the walls.

"Mr. Blackthorne. CBPD."

"Back here."

Captain Greenfield and a few officers flooded the room. Moments later, EMTs enter the space, which now feels immensely smaller.

"Miss Cavallaro, are you hurt?" he inquires.

"No, I'm fine."

Greenfield has Norah explain what happened. As she speaks, the EMTs work on her assailant who still hasn't moved. She gasps when they remove the mask.

Morse.

I snap a photo with my phone and immediately dial Bishop.

"Jacob, what can I do for you?" he answers on the first ring.

"I just sent you a photo. How did he get here? Why weren't we informed of his release?"

I hear tapping on a keyboard.

"According to our records, he's still in custody in Massachusetts. Let me talk to the commanding officer on scene please." I hand my phone to Greenfield and draw Norah closer to me.

"I understand, Agent Bishop. I'll secure him at the hospital until your team arrives," I overhear Greenfield say to Bishop. The EMTs wheel Morse by us toward the ambulance. He's stirring on the stretcher, but he's restrained with handcuffs.

"Are there functioning security cameras in this area of the store, Mr. Blackthorne?"

"Yes, we can review the feed in my office if you would like."

"Thank you. The sooner the better." Greenfield orders his officers to secure the store as we leave.

Norah sits in my desk chair and moves to the side. The video feed depicts exactly what Norah described. It also shows how Morse entered the store through the basement. Greenfield reviews the footage back about two weeks before he's satisfied that he knows all the details he needs.

"Please send a copy of that to my office and to Special Agent Bishop for the last two weeks. Miss Cavallaro, I need you to come to the station to sign your statement in the next few days."

"I will. Thank you, Captain."

I escort him to the door and assure him the video will arrive today.

Returning to my office, I see Norah hasn't moved. I step in front of her, raising my hand for her to take. I tug her up into my arms. Her head rests against my chest, her hands flat on my back.

"Watching the playback is almost as good as watching you kick his ass in person."

She laughs against my chest.

"Are you okay?"

"Frankly, I just reacted. Defending myself today was subconscious. When I first started training, it was simply because the other sports my mother suggested didn't work for me. Tennis—bleh. Swimming—boring. Karate was the best option she offered me. Now, it likely saved my life. I didn't know it was Morse until they removed the mask. I'm angry that he is out, but I can't live in fear of him. Bishop will find the truth."

"He will. Ready to go home?"

"Yes."

I smile inwardly. I would prefer not to put off my evening plans.

JACOB

The ride to our home is largely quiet. I love that. *Our.* Tank's head is resting on the center console of Norah's car. Honestly, I'm shocked she lets him in her car. After parking in the garage, we set our work bags in the office.

"Are you up for a walk?"

"Definitely."

I raise an eyebrow.

"Truly, babe, I'm fine. This isn't me just saying I'm fine so you'll stop asking. He didn't hurt me this time. Plus, the crunch of his face against my foot was gratifying, especially learning it was Morse."

I smile.

Pocketing some flashlights, I take her hand before leading her to the barn. Connor already delivered the first surprise of the evening. I hear a small whimper from the back of the barn.

"What was that?" she asks.

"Go look." I smile, following her a few strides behind.

"You got me a puppy?"

"I did. After today, I feel a tad more justified. You were able to defend yourself. I'm grateful to your mother, but some backup is never a terrible thing."

She leans forward, offering me a sinful view of her curves, to open the crate. Scooping up the furry bundle, she turns toward me.

"Is it a boy or girl?"

"A boy."

"Does he have a name?"

"No, you can name him."

"I'm sure we can choose one. Did you bring a leash?" she asks.

After I attach the leash to his collar, I lead them across the back lawn and out the gate. We walk hand in hand with our new puppy hustling to keep up.

My heart is racing. Never did I ever think I would be in this position again. The last time, I planned each detail down to timing the sunset. Now I know that isn't the important part. It's the everyday. It's knowing how she takes her coffee, her favorite cologne, even knowing all my hoodies will smell like her.

The closer we get to my spot, the more nervous I become to the point where I release her hand. She'll suspect something is wrong if she feels my hand shaking again, which it is, more than in the hay loft.

As we crest the hill, I stop to grab the blanket in the box. Norah keeps walking a bit further, gazing toward the horizon, our new addition sitting at her feet. After spreading it out, I wrap my arms around her from behind, and her curves melt into my body.

She turns her head, pressing her lips to my cheek. "You're shaking again," she says against my skin.

"I am. I made you a playlist so I could express my love for you in case I couldn't say the words. For the past month, I have been working on the right words to say to you."

She turns in my arms and is facing me. I have seen the look before, precisely three times. She knew even then I was in love with her. She knew her soul speaks to mine, even before I told her about Mara.

"I never thought I would be here again. I gave my whole heart away a long time ago. A few wise people reminded me that what I can give isn't measurable. The depth is up to me. The walls around my heart were high and thick. For almost three years, you have been removing each brick carefully and with precision. I didn't even realize it until your text. I knew from that moment, I wouldn't be able to let you go."

I take a step back, taking her hands in mine and dropping to one knee. She gazes down at me with the deepest love in her hazel eyes. I pull the pavé set, cushion cut diamond out of the box.

"Norah, you're everything I need and some things I didn't know I needed. Girlfriend doesn't work for me. When you agreed, I knew it would never be enough. Fiancée will work for a brief time. Will you be my once in a lifetime?"

"Yes." Her response falls from her lips in a whisper.

I slide my ring onto her finger before standing to kiss her slowly. Every shred of concern I had for saying the right words, gone. This amazing woman is my forever love.

"I love you, Norah."

"I love you."

"Can we keep this to ourselves for a few days?" I plan to enjoy it before we tell the world.

"Absolutely."

She bends down, lifts our unnamed puppy, and sets him in my arms. "Last one naked makes breakfast." She throws a wink over her shoulder and takes off for the house.

My sly woman has a decent head start because of the furball.

I lose the race to the house, but I'm not complaining. After crating the puppy, I find my fiancée wearing nothing but her engagement ring.

True to our agreement, we don't share our news for a few days. Once we do, our phones are flooded with well wishes.

Christmas is my favorite holiday. Bright and early, I take Tank and Sabre out for a quick walk, attempting some basic training skills for Sabre. He's making great progress. I'm sure it has something to do with Tank following my commands as well.

When we amble back into the house, Norah's in the kitchen with her back to me. Her hair is piled on top of her head, and her silky robe is tied at her waist. Sliding my arms around her, I nip the curve of her neck.

"Merry Christmas, gorgeous."

"Merry Christmas."

I take the cup from her hand, setting it on the counter before I untie the sash of her robe. Guiding it to her elbows, I kiss a path over her exposed skin.

"Jacob, we should—"

A few hours later, after twisting our sheets into a tangled mess, we head to my parents' for dinner. I should have anticipated our reception when we arrive. After seemingly short hugs, Mom, Jill, and even Joyce are gushing over Norah's ring.

"Did you help?" Jill asks.

As Norah is shaking her head, Mom jumps in, "Jake, this is gorgeous."

"We're so happy for the two of you," Joyce adds before hugging me again. "She's perfect, Jake," she whispers.

"She is," I reply in a hushed tone.

After the ladies finish swooning, the questions about the wedding start almost immediately. I lean over, kiss Norah's temple, and move to the group of men. Connor hands me a drink.

"We're happy for you, Jake. To Jake and Norah." My family raises a glass, and we celebrate again.

After a delicious meal and some shouting at the television during the football game, Norah and I return home. Our first engaged holiday in the books, and it's only the beginning.

EPILOGUE

NORAH

TWO MONTHS LATER

"Babe, are you ready to go?"

He's taking his time this morning. Normally, that wouldn't concern me, but we need to run a few errands before our guests start arriving.

"I'm ready. Let's go."

"Hey, aren't you forgetting something?"

He stops and turns, drawing me against him before taking my mouth. This man seriously knows how to make my knees weak. Soon, it'll be official.

"Better?" he asks.

"Much. Now we can go."

We spend a few hours readying last-minute details and picking up fresh ingredients that Kelsey requested. Kelsey, William, Nicholas, and Kelly will be arriving later today. The rest of the guests will arrive tomorrow morning. Kelly will bring my gown and dresses for Joyce and Connie. She also has my rehearsal dress—a replacement for my damaged dress but in ivory. Kelsey will be using our kitchen to finish our cake.

Our friends arrive just before dinner.

"I'm so happy you're here!" I greet my friends when they arrive.

"I want to see." Kelly, whose ring is equally impressive, lifts my hand for inspection. "The picture didn't do that justice. It's gorgeous."

"Thanks. Hey, Kels. How are you feeling?"

"I feel great! I have a few more weeks before the little bean joins our crazy family." Pregnancy looks fantastic on her.

"Thank you for enduring the car ride here. I'm sorry you couldn't fly."

"It's no problem. My husband is more protective than he was before."

The girls and I chat while we stash their luggage. The guys are talking on the back porch.

"I don't intend to bring you down, but is Gen coming?" Kelly asks cautiously.

"No. It's her choice, Kelly. She made a half-hearted apology just before Christmas. When I didn't travel to Maine at her request, she got salty again. I just hope that Joseph and the boys come anyway." What that choice might do to their marriage is on her, not me.

The girls and I spend the evening chatting and drinking. Nicholas walks by with Nick in his arms, his gaze cast downward. He puts his son to bed in the guest suite and drops the monitor off near us when he rejoins the guys.

"I can't wait to see that," Kelsey says softly.

"What?" I ask.

"My husband with his eyes cast down on our child." Kelsey sets her hands on her belly and glances out the French doors toward William. He catches her eye and smiles.

"Me too." I add.

"It's amazing to see them change when a baby is born," Kelly adds. Due to the long day of travel, the ladies turn in. I pad to our bedroom and curl up, gazing out the window. Not long after, the guys turn in as well.

Despite her upcoming due date, Kelsey is up with the birds, buzzing around the kitchen. It's mesmerizing watching her work. In the last few hours, she has constructed our cake and will decorate it later today.

Our rehearsal dinner starts soon. Everyone has arrived except Joseph and the boys. If put in his situation, I don't know what I would do. That isn't true. I would choose Jacob, hands down. I sit in the chair to pull on my sparkly shoes.

"You look stunning, almost Mrs. Blackthorne." Jacob's words pull me out of my thoughts.

"Thank you. You look hot yourself."

Tonight, he's wearing a new tailored suit. Tomorrow, a tux. I have seen Jacob dressed in a tux precisely once at the Ramirez wedding. Everything about us circles back to that day. That was the beginning of us. It took us some time to get here, but the wait was absolutely worth it. I set one hand on his chest and the other on his cheek. He leans forward, brushing his lips across mine.

Someone clears their throat, but Jacob refuses to look away from me.

"Sorry, but you need to get outside before the rain starts," Connor states before walking away.

Our rehearsal is short and sweet. Everyone finds their places and we move on to a low-key dinner. Hand in hand, Jacob and I move around the house chatting and greeting everyone.

"Mr. Cavallaro, it's a pleasure see you in person. Mabel, it's nice to see you again."

My father shifts on his feet. He seemed genuinely happy when I told him about Jacob.

Mabel replies for both. "Congratulations, Jacob. Samuel and I are overjoyed for both of you."

My father takes Jacob's extended hand. Mabel draws him into a hug.

"Thank you, Mabel. Sir."

Jacob's hand is shaking in mine.

"Breathe, babe. Everything is fine. I'm not going anywhere."

After speeches from Connor, Cam, and Kelly, our guests start dispersing, and Kelly and I finish cleaning the kitchen.

"Kel, did Dad freak out when you married Nicholas?"

"Yeah, he gave us the cold shoulder until just before he walked me down the aisle."

"This is normal for Dad?"

Kelly shrugs and leaves the room. Hopefully, all will be well in the morning.

"Let's go, Jake. You need to leave before midnight," I hear Connor say from the doorway.

Jacob nods at Connor. "Okay, I just need to talk to Norah for a moment."

Connor doesn't move.

"Alone, C."

He takes my hand, leading me to our bedroom.

"Connor's right, you know."

Jacob nods. "I know, but I have a gift for you." He hands me a small box.

When I open the box, tears well up in my eyes. "How did you…?" I pull my mother's wedding band out.

"Kelly. She carried it, so I thought you could too." He kisses the tear that slides down my cheek. "I'll see you tomorrow morning. I'll be waiting to marry you."

"I'll be the one wearing white." I kiss him softly before gently pushing him out the door. I slip out of my dress and into bed. Tank and Sabre dutifully fill Jacob's side of our bed.

The dark morning sky isn't lifting as the time approaches for me to step outside to marry my forever. Wind whips across the yard, angling the ribbons and tearing apart the flowers we placed out there. A loud crack of thunder makes me shudder. I'm pacing, holding the train of my dress up as I go. Kelly's design is flawless and perfectly me. The French lace forms the straps and an elegant keyhole back. The fitted skirt has covered buttons down to a V-shaped, lace train. Kelly and Kelsey just left to check on some details with the catering.

There's a soft knock on the door. "Oh, Norah. You're stunning," Connie says as she steps into the bedroom.

I hug her tight. "Thank you." A pang of anguish pushes into my heart. I knew this day would be hard without my mom, but I didn't realize how hard. Connie and Joyce have been nothing short of incredible.

"Jacob sent me to see if you want to wait for the storm to pass or move inside."

I draw in a breath and settle myself. I know she's looking down at me. I'm blissfully happy. A little rainstorm isn't going to stop me.

"I don't want to wait. I want to marry your son."

Connie takes my hand. "I'm grateful he found you and pulled himself together instead of pushing you away."

"Me too." I hug her tight, pondering what to do. "Could you move everyone into the barn? If the guys could move the arbor and the runner, that should be fine. There won't be room for the chairs because it's set up for the reception."

"Give me fifteen minutes."

I smile at her. As Connie leaves, Kelly returns with our dad, so he and I can have a few private moments.

"You look beautiful, Norah."

"Thanks, Daddy. Are you okay? You haven't been very polite to Jacob."

"I wasn't prepared for this day. Each time your siblings got married, I knew there was still one more. Now that isn't the case. Jacob suits you. You complement one another's strengths and weaknesses. I'm overjoyed for you, but I'm sad that your mother isn't here. Even though I'm happy with Mabel, I miss her every day."

"I miss her too. She's with us in here." I set my hand on my dad's chest.

Kelly knocks on the door. "It's time." Arm in arm with my father, and my train in the other, I walk to the barn under a huge black umbrella. As we reach the door, I draw in a deep breath and let it out slowly.

The moment I look up at Jacob, my heart explodes. His eyes are filled with tears, his hand over his mouth. Redness creeping into his cheeks. I lock my gaze with his as Connor sets his hand on Jacob's shoulder. It feels like we're walking to him in slow motion. Our officiant's words sound muffled as I long to wipe those tears from his cheeks.

As my father sets my hand into Jacob's, I intertwine my fingers into his shaking hand. Drawing him close, I kiss the tears from his cheek.

"You are the most beautiful bride I have ever seen," he murmurs in my ear. "I still can't believe you're mine."

"I love you, Jacob. How about we pledge our lives to one another right now?"

"Yes." He takes a few moments to compose himself before the officiant starts our vows. The closer we get to those magic words, the less his hands are shaking in mine. As he slides the matching eternity band on my finger, his hands are steady.

"It's my pleasure to introduce for the first time, Mr. and Mrs. Jacob Blackthorne. You may kiss your bride."

Despite our discussions to the contrary, Jacob seizes my lips with a sultry, sensuous kiss that leaves no question how he feels about me.

We walk down the runner and back into the house as our family and close friends cheer and clap. I have never been happier than I am with him. After a brief time alone, we return to the barn and dance the afternoon away with our family and friends.

As early evening rolls around, we slip away to change for our flight. I have been looking forward to this trip since we planned it. Two weeks on a private island with my husband. After that, a lifetime together.

COMING SOON

Two new stories are coming soon!

MORGAN BROTHERS NOVELS
Until I Kissed You (Samson and Savannah)

YORK BEACH SERIES

THE CAPPELLIS
Chasing Forever (Luca and Willa)

MY BOOKS

YORK BEACH SERIES:
A New Beginning with You (Genevieve and Joseph)
Taking A Chance on Me (Kelsey and William)
Just One More (Maggie and Grant)
Kiss You Like You're Mine (Billie and Peter)
Only with Him (Kelly and Nicholas)

MORGAN BROTHERS NOVELS:
One Unforgettable Favor (Cassius and Noelle)

Did you love *My Once in a Lifetime?*

Thank you for taking the time to read it. I hope you loved it!
If you liked this book or another one of my books, please leave a review.

A short line or two will be perfect!
I appreciate your support and feedback.